The new principal took | She had creamy skin, golden-br[own?] and eyes that shone like sapphires. She was small and slender but had curves he couldn't miss. She was almost the exact opposite of Gracie, who had been both model slim and tall. Emmit knew he was staring, but he wasn't the only one.

"Pops, what's the matter witcha?" Fletcher wanted to know, jumping out of Casey's lap and moving toward him, sizing him up. "You's ain't sick, are yah?"

Emmit shook his head to clear it. He glanced back at Principal Walker as she, too, became aware of the girls once again. He tweaked Fletcher's nose.

"Nah, kiddo, I'm fine, just fine," he said as the principal held out her hand.

"Mr. McKay, I presume, I'm Savan…um, Principal Walker. Sorry you had to come out here," she said and after one brief shake, dropped his hand.

"Ma'am. Well, you being the new principal and all, we were bound to meet sooner or later." He almost smiled, then motioned to his girls. "Who wants to explain to me what happened this time?" He looked from one guilty face to another. Feet shuffled and hands clasped.

"Daddy, it was all a big misunderstanding. Things were said, and then one thing led to another, and well, here we are," Alexandra explained in the wispy voice he knew she'd been practicing in the mirror.

Let the Dead Lie

by

W. L. Brooks

The McKay Series, Book One

Let the Dead Lie

Cover Art by *RJ Morris*

The Wild Rose Press, Inc.
PO Box 708
Adams Basin, NY 14410-0708
Visit us at www.thewildrosepress.com

Publishing History
First Crimson Rose Edition, 2017
Print ISBN 978-1-5092-1651-2
Digital ISBN 978-1-5092-1652-9

The McKay Series, Book One
Published in the United States of America

Dedication

This one is for my mom.
Thanks for lending me that romantic suspense novel...
it kind of changed my life!

Chapter One

Emmit drove through Blue Creek on autopilot, only becoming aware when gravel crunched under his tires as the SUV pulled into the winding drive of his childhood home. It would be theirs now. A week after Gracie's funeral, he had put their house in town on the market. It sold within a month, and he was relieved he would no longer have to live with the memories, or the ghosts.

The McKay home was a picture. The property itself was a total of twenty breathtaking acres, half of which was still untouched forest. His great-grandfather had built the house more than a hundred years ago. The foundation had been repaired and the main house had additions, but the general structure was the same. From the swing his grandfather built for the wraparound porch to the screen door that always creaked a little, this place was a part of Emmit's very soul.

Putting the SUV in park, he glanced in the rearview mirror at his three daughters. His chest tightened with the knowledge that he, despite recent events, blessed.

There was Casey, ten years old, her blue-black hair braided in pigtails, and her violet eyes luminous behind wire-rimmed glasses. She was a prideful little thing with a major superiority complex. Then, there was eight-year-old Alex or, as she requested he call her,

Alexandra. Her eyes were a deep blue, and her mass of hair reminded him of cherry oak. She was his "girly girl," extremely prissy with an attitude. Finally, his youngest daughter, Fletcher, was seven. Her given name was Jamie, but she had demanded he change it to Fletcher J. McKay. Most people called her a tomboy, even though her brown hair was long enough for her to sit on. Her eyes were a mischievous blue-green that changed with her mood.

They made him laugh, pissed him off, and controlled his life. He didn't mind. They were his world.

"You know, Daddy, staring is an atrocious habit. And it's making me self-conscious," Alexandra said, gingerly patting the bun on top of her head.

"Oh, give me a break," Casey said, then snickered as she mimicked, "It's an atrocious habit."

"Yeah! You's such a prissy pants, Alex," Fletcher added.

Emmit, hiding his grin, held up his hands in mock surrender. "All right, I'm sorry to have made you uncomfortable, Alexandra. I was thinking how lucky I am to have three unique little girls."

The comment was met with three different responses.

"I'm not little!"

"That's more like it."

"Don't unique mean weird?"

"It's *doesn't* it, not *don't* it, you pea brain," Casey said, rolling her eyes at Fletcher.

Emmit laughed.

"I's ain't no pea brain. You's are!" Fletcher said, then jumped out of the back seat, only turning back to

2

stick her tongue out at Casey, who then made chase.

Emmit opened the back door for Alexandra and followed her onto the porch. The side door, leading to the kitchen, was opened by an older woman with dark silver hair, which she wore loose so it touched her shoulders.

"Good heavens, I could hear those two over the TV," said Sadie Madison, Emmit's longtime friend and neighbor. She put her hands on her apron-clad hips and narrowed her chocolate-brown eyes toward the two girls chasing each other. "Both up to no good, as usual, I suppose. Well, come in. I've prepared a nice stew for supper, and I put the coffee on for us," she drawled, then winked at Emmit.

"That's awful nice of you, Sadie. We thank you for going to all this trouble, don't we, girls?" Emmit glanced toward the two girls, who came panting to a stop beside him. While both Casey and Fletcher shrugged, Alexandra nodded with enthusiasm; she'd told Emmit many times that there was no finer lady in Blue Creek than the Widow Madison.

"Good, good, now wash up, girls," Sadie said.

"Are you joining us, Sadie?" Emmit asked.

"Yes, I'm going to finish making the iced tea for the girls." She unknotted her apron and hung it on the pantry door.

When everyone was seated around the table, Sadie asked the girls who was going to say grace.

"Oh, it's my turn, Widow!" Alexandra exclaimed, raising her hand, which made Casey roll her eyes and Fletcher snicker.

Emmit sighed. Many years ago Sadie had given herself the title of the Widow Madison, and the name had stuck. Emmit was one of the few people who still addressed her as Sadie—Alexandra nudged him. He looked at her for a moment, then realized he hadn't yet bowed his head.

"Sorry," Emmit mumbled and did as he was supposed to.

Alexandra let out a pained sigh and began. "Dear Lord, we thank you for the food we are about to thoroughly enjoy. We thank you for our many gifts and our family. We also thank you for bringing the Widow Madison back from her long, long trip. She will no doubt educate us in the finer qualities of womanhood. Amen."

"That was very nice, Alex. Thank you," Emmit said, wincing when a small foot kicked his shin under the table. He glanced to Fletcher, the owner of the foot, with a raised brow. She not so subtly motioned to Alexandra, who was staring at him. He cleared his throat, realizing his mistake. "That was very nice. Thank you, Alexandra."

Alexandra gave him her thousand-watt smile, while both Fletcher and Casey dramatically wiped their brows. Sadie dabbed at her mouth trying to hide her grin.

After supper, the girls washed dishes, and then went to their rooms on the second floor. "What are you going to do now?" Sadie asked after refreshing her coffee and taking a seat next to Emmit.

"Do with what?" Emmit asked as he fiddled with the handle of his mug.

"You know what I'm asking, young man. What are you planning for the future? Moving in here was a good first step, but what about other things? For instance, who's going to watch the girls while you're working? Who's going to cook, clean, and do laundry, for goodness sake?"

Emmit stroked his stubbled jaw and regarded Sadie with a slight smile. He knew she meant well, and it was nice to know she cared. "We all do our part here, Sadie. We're a team; everyone pitches in." He chuckled. "Well, Alexandra doesn't cook, says it's not in her blood. As for watching them, they do go to school, Sadie, and I'm usually home right after the bus drops them off, so they won't have time to get into trouble."

Sadie widened her eyes.

"Not much anyway."

"I wouldn't mind watching the girls after school sometimes, Emmit. I have more free time than I know what to do with. The girls keep me young." She paused, her eyes twinkling. "Besides, they might teach an old dog new tricks."

He wasn't about to comment on the latter. He knew women had a thing about age. "That's awful nice of you, Sadie, but not necessary. We'll try a few weeks on our own and see how it goes." The twinkle faded from her eyes, and he rushed on to add, "You're welcome here anytime, Sadie. The girls adore you. You know that." He let out a relieved breath when she smiled.

Both Sadie and Emmit jumped when the screen door slammed open and Judge J. T. Vaughn stumbled in surrounded by a cloud of fetid cologne, which failed to mask the whiskey.

"Where are you, you lousy son of a bitch?" the Judge spat, his deep voice thundering across the kitchen.

Sadie gasped. Emmit, on the other hand, wasn't

shocked. He was annoyed. The Judge, also his father-in-law, had been pointing the gavel at him since Gracie's first bout with cancer. During Gracie's remission, it seemed the Judge had stopped blaming Emmit, but that wasn't the case. Later, if Gracie had a headache or a cold, Emmit was in some way responsible. And the Judge had all but accused him of murder after the wreck that took Gracie's life. Emmit could almost accept it. He knew fate was blind, but regret was like rust, slowly eroding a man's soul.

Chapter Two

"Oh my, Granddaddy's here carrying on again," Alexandra announced from her position near the top of the stairs. Fletcher's bedroom was next to hers, and Casey's was across the hall. She contemplated chewing her nails, but that was gross, so she chewed on her lower lip instead.

Two heads popped out of their doorways and peeked toward the staircase.

"You thinking what I'm thinking?" Casey asked Fletcher.

Fletcher nodded. "Gonna be blood."

"There will be no fighting. Daddy is a gentleman," Alexandra said. "So is Granddaddy."

"The Judge isn't my granddaddy if he treats Pops that way," Casey said. "No sir, he can go straight to hell for all I care."

Alexandra gave a dramatic gasp, but it failed to stop her big sister from heading down the stairs. Fletcher grinned at her, then followed Casey. Alexandra chewed her lower lip harder, then sat down taking her place in line. She whispered, "It's not ladylike to eavesdrop."

"Then carry your lady's ass back upstairs or shut up," Casey hissed over her shoulder.

"It's okay, Alexandra." Fletcher patted Alexandra's knee. "It ain't eavesdropping. Is it our fault they're talking loud?"

"Good point," Alexandra said.

The three girls focused their attention at the kitchen door below.

****

"How about you calm down, J. T., and have a cup of coffee?" Emmit asked trying to smooth things over. He had been expecting a reaction from J. T. today; the people who bought their house in town had moved in, and Emmit knew, for the Judge, it was one more reminder that Gracie was no longer with them.

"I don't want no damnable coffee, McKay!" The Judge slammed his fist down on the kitchen table. "You don't even care Gracie's gone!"

Sadie made herself busy with the coffeemaker, and Emmit sighed. He knew her late husband had been good friends with J. T., and Sadie still regarded him as such. It was hard for Emmit to take these verbal assaults from his father-in-law, but he straightened his spine and tried to keep his anger in check.

"Do you honestly think I wanted this, J. T.? Did it not cross your mind we're suffering here too? God, how can you not know that?" Emmit said as calmly as he could.

"You don't know a damn thing! You're as worthless as you were as a teenager." He let out a bitter laugh. "Hell, you're still working the same damn job. My Gracie needed a strong man, not a damn pussy," the Judge shouted, sending saliva down his stubbled chin. He was normally a distinguished man with sharp blue eyes and silver hair. But the whiskey made him haggard and his big frame frail. Though Emmit knew this, J. T.'s words cut to the bone.

Sadie had dropped her coffee cup, and Emmit jumped up to help, but she shook her head. He turned away, but he'd seen the sorrow that glazed her eyes.

"J. T., I think you should leave, before you go any further than you already have," Emmit said, his tone cold.

"Son, I haven't even begun to tell you what I think of you," J. T. slurred as he stumbled around the kitchen table pointing at Emmit. "My daughter was devoted to you, and you didn't care about her feelings. You went and adopted the kids and then what? You left her here with the constant reminder that she couldn't have children of her own. I'm starting to wonder if you even wanted those girls, or if you were just punishing Gracie—*oomph*..."

Emmit had J. T. by the collar of his tweed jacket and pulled him toward the door. The older man kicked back against Emmit's leg making him loosen his hold.

The kitchen door hit the wall as Fletcher stormed in with Casey right behind her. Alexandra came in last trying to control her tears.

"That ain't true, is it, Pops?" Fletcher said. "What the Judge is saying is a lie, right?"

Casey added, "It isn't true, right, Pops? The Judge doesn't know nothing."

Emmit turned to his daughters. His heart caught in his throat, and his eyes stung at the hurt they couldn't hide and the small sobs Alexandra tried to muffle. He came toward them, bending down on one knee and gathering them close. He glanced over his shoulder to where J. T. stood frozen in place, then turned back to his daughters.

"No, girls, it's not true. And I know *you* know it's

not true. The Judge is hurt, and he doesn't realize what he's saying," Emmit said, keeping his voice low. He had never disliked anyone as much as he did J. T. at this moment. He rubbed Alexandra's hair between his thick callused fingers and looked each girl in the eye. "I promise."

Emmit was relieved when they nodded. Three pairs of accusing eyes peered toward the man they had come to know as Grandfather. J. T. struggled with his words. Emmit was almost positive the girls' tears had cut through the whiskey-induced fog that had been controlling his father-in-law.

"Girls," J. T. whispered.

"You don't want us? Fine!" Casey decreed. "You don't like Pops? Peachy! But as of right this minute, you're nothing to us." Her sisters nodded in agreement.

"Granddaddy, I mean, Judge, I'm sorry you don't love us anymore," Alexandra said and ran out of the room with Casey on her heels.

"Here's it to you's straight, Judge." Fletcher crossed her arms over her chest and rocked back. "We's may be orphans, or were, but we's people too. Our blood bleeds red just like yours." Fletcher sneered, then walked over to the Judge and spat on his shoe before stomping out of the kitchen.

J. T. stared after her, tears in his old blue eyes. "Emmit," he said as his Adam's apple quivered, "I didn't know they were there. I swear I...I didn't know." He bowed his head and walked out the screen door.

Emmit stared after him a moment, then remembered J. T. was intoxicated. Before he could follow, Sadie placed her hand on his arm. "I'll drive him home. You go talk to your girls," she said, nodding toward the hall and the staircase. When Emmit met her eyes, she reminded him, "Those girls are fiercely protective of each other, and there's nothing wrong with that. Now go on." She gave him a weak smile, then left with her purse in hand.

The girls weren't in their rooms. He had a moment of panic before he remembered the attic. Emmit took his time massaging his temples as he went. He tried to think of what to say, replaying the entire scene in his head. Emmit didn't have any words of wisdom—hell, he couldn't even give himself advice—but he needed answers to give his daughters and quick.

Emmit wasn't used to his girls being upset. Sure, he had been playing the role of mother and father since...well, for a long time, but how do you fix something like this? How do you explain to three young girls who haven't had easy lives that someone who truly loves them can be so cruel? There wasn't a doubt in Emmit's mind that J. T. loved his granddaughters and they loved him back. But how could he show them forgiveness was crucial in a situation like this? Especially when he was mad as hell himself. He sighed and took the steps to the attic.

"What did you say to the Judge, Fletcher? You gotta tell us!" Casey asked Fletcher as he stopped at the top of the landing unnoticed.

Alexandra was sitting in an old rocking chair and blowing her nose into her pink hankie. She asked, "Please, what did you say? Was it awful?"

"It's what he had coming, saying all those things to Pops. Then talking about us like that. Pops should've kicked him in the ass!" Fletcher narrowed her eyes at Casey, who was now lying on her back on the floor.

11

"What I's want to know is why you's didn't do nothing? Answer that for me, Casey, cause I's just don't understand it." Fletcher scowled at her.

Casey sat up swiftly. "You know what, Fletcher?"

Emmit cleared his throat to intervene. "Girls, we need to talk." Casey and Alexandra glared at Fletcher, who fiddled with her braids.

"Daddy, are you mad at us?" Alexandra asked when Emmit came into the room and stood with his arms crossed over his chest, feet apart.

Okay, show time! "No, I'm not mad at you, any of you, not really. In fact, I'm sorry you had to hear what was said. But I *am* disappointed you eavesdropped." That sounded like a good place to start.

"It isn't eavesdropping if it's about you, and it was about me and them," Casey pointed out, looking toward her sisters, who both nodded.

Emmit tried not to smile and succeeded. "That may well be, Casey, but the point is it was an adult conversation that, A, you shouldn't have been listening to, and, B, you never should have involved yourselves in." He squatted so he was eye level with Casey and Fletcher. He glanced at Alexandra. "If you overhear things from an adult that upset you, talk to me about it, and we can try to work things out together. Your grandfather is grieving, and people don't always act like themselves when they're hurting like this."

"Not to mention he's drunk as a skunk. Don't forget that, Pops," Casey said with a smirk.

Emmit sighed. Didn't they miss anything? "Yes, the Judge had too much to drink and wasn't thinking clearly. I know he loves you all very much." He waited, hoping that sank in. "Now, since you all participated in an adult discussion, you will have to participate in very big, very adult behavior." They eyed him, and Fletcher scooted in closer. "Each of you needs to forgive the Judge for the things he said, and you all need to apologize for the things you said. Okay?" I'm good, damned good.

"Now wait just a dang minute, Pops," Casey said. "I understand we should forgive him. Yep, I got that. But saying I'm sorry isn't happening anytime soon."

"That goes double for me," Fletcher said pointing to herself.

"I didn't say anything hateful," Alexandra reminded him rocking back harder in the chair and pursing her lips.

"Yeah, besides we were hurt and angry, and people say things they don't mean when they're hurt and angry. Isn't that what you told us, Pops?" Casey asked, her violet eyes flashing.

Emmit glanced around the room. Surely they hadn't just used his own words against him, had they? The smirks on his girls' faces gave him his answer. Well, damn. He cleared his throat and stood up. "Yes, but you have to forgive him and apologize anyway. And that's that." He would not say "because I said so." He held his breath until they all nodded in agreement, then he released it in a gush. Sure, both Casey and Fletcher had mumbled something under their breaths, but they *had* agreed.

"Good. Now that that's done, it's time for bed." He checked his watch; it was indeed past their usual bedtime. "Are you sleeping in your beds or up here tonight?" They sometimes liked sleeping in the attic—some kind of a sleepover deal. Girls. Emmit shrugged.

He didn't understand their rituals, but what the hell. They all agreed in unison that they would be sleeping in the attic. He gave them each a good-night kiss and headed downstairs. He needed some sleep too. He only hoped his memories would allow him.

Chapter Three

The letter he'd been waiting for came a week later but not as he'd expected. Before Gracie's accident, they'd been introduced to another orphan and had petitioned to adopt her. The girl's name was Charlie, and she was eight. After Gracie's death, Emmit struggled with what he should do. In their letters to Charlie, they had promised her a home and a family. All that was left was going to court and making it official. But this letter said Social Services wasn't keen on the idea of Emmit, a single father, adopting another child. How was he going to care for another little girl? He might have too much trouble with the ones he already had, and Social Services would be checking into that situation as well.

Emmit fixed himself a cup of coffee and glanced out the window before he took a seat at the kitchen table. He didn't hear Casey come in. No one ever heard Casey or Fletcher coming, unless they wanted you to hear them. Emmit had learned how to walk quietly when he was young, and he'd taught his girls. They all had it down but Alexandra. She insisted on wearing dresses, which wouldn't be a problem if she didn't also insist on wearing dress shoes with tiny heels that clicked and clacked with every step. That, at least, made him smile.

"Hey, Pops, what's up?" Casey asked.

"That's fresh from Mabel," Emmit said, gesturing to the milk she pulled out of the fridge.

"No wonder the Widow's cow won so many blue ribbons," she said as she poured herself a glass. She gave Emmit a thumbs-up and gulped down the milk.

"I got it from Sadie today when I installed the tub she ordered."

Emmit ran the only hardware store in Blue Creek. The shop kept him sane for the most part, and his taking over the family business gave his parents the excuse they'd needed to move to Florida. He enjoyed the work; he had a knack for fixing things and had always loved the store. It was in the middle of town, next to Ida Mae's diner, and hard to miss.

"I just don't get it," Casey said with a furrowed brow and milk mustache.

"What don't you get, Casey?" he asked, looking up from his stack of mail.

"Why anyone would get so bent outta shape over a stupid old tub. I mean, jeez, all a body's gotta do is wash and go about their day." She shook her head and wiped her mouth on her sleeve.

Emmit laughed. "Yeah, well, it makes Sadie happy, so…" He shrugged, winking at her.

Fletcher and Alexandra came traipsing through the kitchen throwing down plastic lunchboxes and backpacks as they went. Emmit leaned down for Alexandra's customary kiss on the cheek and tugged on one of Fletcher's braids.

"How was your day?" he asked. Casey and Fletcher grumbled.

"Those two got into a fight with Marylou Thomas on the bus again today," Alexandra told him as she pointed to her sisters. "But the bus driver didn't see them. My day"—she touched her chest—"however, was very good. I got an A on my spelling test."

"Tattletale," Fletcher hissed.

"Showoff," Casey mumbled.

"That's wonderful, Alexandra," he said, then turned to Casey and Fletcher. "You both know what the punishment is for fighting."

They nodded. No TV for the rest of the week was the usual punishment. He would probably have to change that soon. Casey and Fletcher rarely watched TV anymore because they were always fighting with someone about something. And the fact that Casey and Fletcher both shrugged only proved his point.

"Sooo, once again, Pops, what's up?" Casey asked.

From what happened next, Emmit knew his oldest sensed something was wrong. Casey nudged Fletcher, who in turn elbowed Alexandra. Maybe a little too roughly because Alexandra rubbed her arm and glared at her sister.

"I got a letter today about Charlie. It seems they don't think a single, widowed father is what she needs."

"You mean they don't think we're good enough to keep her?" Alexandra asked, her big blue eyes narrowed.

Emmit tucked a loose tendril of her dark red hair behind her ear. "Not you, sweetheart, me."

"They want a fight?" asked Casey, nodding her head. "Is that it, Pops? We gotta fight for what's ours?"

"Seems that way. If that's what we all agree on." He looked at each of his daughters. Casey and Alexandra nodded. Fletcher peered up at him and grinned. It was the mischievous grin that made him want to swallow.

"We's ain't no sissies. They want a fight, we's'll fight!" Fletcher whooped.

Chapter Four

"Where in the hell is my damn tie?" Emmit roared, tearing through his closet. He hated ties. The last time he wore one was five months ago at Gracie's funeral. His heart clenched at the thought. It wasn't as painful now, and he was healing, thanks to his girls. Sadie was also a great help, always keeping an eye out for him and his little heathens. Well, Casey and Fletcher anyway; Alexandra was determined to be a real southern belle like the Widow Madison.

He glanced at his watch. They couldn't be late! Today, a judge would decide whether they could adopt Charlie or not, and he couldn't even find his blasted tie.

"Damn it," he repeated, slamming a drawer shut.

Alexandra walked in, wide-eyed. "Daddy? Why, whatever's the matter?" she asked in the prissiest tone he'd ever heard. That made him smile, then frown when he noticed what was in her hand. His tie!

"Thank you, sweetheart. You're a lifesaver."

Alexandra beamed and, though somewhat reluctant, handed it over.

Emmit eyed his daughter in the mirror as he knotted his tie. She had an odd smile playing at her little mouth. "You look real nice in your new dress. Is that the one you and Sadie bought in the city last week?"

"Yes!" Alexandra held out the sides of the skirt and

spun around. "It's peach, not pink," she said. "And these white daisies were embroidered by hand." She then pointed to the bun on top of her head. "The Widow Madison came by earlier and fixed my hair too. It's just like the ballerinas wear."

"It's lovely, sweetheart," he said, picking up his jacket from the bed and slipping into it.

"Thank you, Daddy! Oh, Uncle Evan called while you were in the shower," she told him while he searched for his keys.

"What did he say?" His good buddy, and one of the girls' honorary uncles, Evan Jessup, was manning the store for the next few days so Emmit could take care of things.

"He said he liked the new shelves you put in," she said while he checked to see if his keys had fallen behind the dresser.

Emmit grunted. If not for the break-in two months ago, he wouldn't have had to replace anything. For the first time in the history of the hardware store, someone broke in, stole the money from the register, and trashed the place. Neither he nor the sheriff had any leads. It was bad enough it happened, but the fact no one saw anything really bothered—

"Are you looking for your keys?" Alexandra asked. "Because I'm pretty sure they're in the kitchen."

"Thanks!" he said, standing. He straightened his jacket and checked his watch again. "Where are your sisters? We need to get going."

No answer.

He turned around to look at her. She was staring at her shoes. He walked up to her and leaned down. "Alexandra," he said firmly.

No answer.

He lifted her chin and looked her in the eye. "Where are your sisters?" She bit her lip, her gaze darting from side to side. He stood, hands on hips, and narrowed his eyes. This pose meant that he meant business, and they both knew it. He started tapping his foot. Alexandra clasped her hands and twisted her fingers. Oh yeah, she knew something.

"They're out on their bikes," she blurted, then quickly covered her mouth with her hands.

"Hell and damnation," he growled, running both hands through his thick hair. "Why of all the days?" He peered up to the ceiling for a response. None came.

"Daddy! You messed your hair up." With a grin, she held out a comb. "They did wear their helmets."

He stared at her as if she sprouted wings but took the comb anyway. He fixed his hair until she nodded her approval and snatched the comb back.

"Where did they go, Alexandra?"

She shrugged one shoulder. Exasperated, he turned her around and marched her toward the kitchen.

The room was spotless as it had been for the past five months, everyone making an extra effort to impress the social workers. He found his keys on the counter and pocketed them. Alexandra sat at the kitchen table swinging her legs, her head following him as he paced. He glanced at his watch and swore under his breath. If they didn't leave in ten minutes, they ran the risk of being late.

"Damn it," he muttered.

"If you continue to speak that way, what will the judge think?"

He muttered an apology and began pacing faster.

"I hear them!" Alexandra said.

"THANK YOU, GOD! Come on, Alex, let's go," he almost growled, but she didn't budge. "Sorry, *Alexandra*, it's time to go now."

She grinned and hopped up. The clatter of running feet on the porch got his attention as he locked the door. Two pairs of eyes darted from him to Alexandra.

"I won't even ask where you were until later. We're late." He stopped, turned, and inspected the two of them. Casey had her hair in a ponytail, and Fletcher had braided pigtails. Casey had on a khaki skirt and a blue polo shirt. Her glasses had fogged up from the ride. He looked toward Fletcher.

"What?" she asked, squirming under his scrutiny.

"What?" he mimicked. She had on dark-green overall shorts and a white T-shirt. "I thought we agreed on a dress."

"I's ain't got a dress! And possession's nine-tenths of the law," she said, crossing her arms over her chest.

He shook his head. At least they had managed to stay clean.

A half hour later, they arrived at the courthouse, where Kyle Ruthie, their attorney and a good friend of Emmit's, was waiting. He was well liked by the ladies for his blond hair, brown eyes, and handsome smile. Emmit not only trusted him but also admired his integrity. Besides, he was the girls' other honorary uncle, and that said more than enough.

"Hey, folks, don't you all look sharp," Kyle said as he ushered them into the courthouse, going over what was going to happen. The judge, Judge Mason, wanted to talk to the girls alone.

"Wait a dang minute. I didn't know I had to talk to

no judge," Casey seethed. She was five when Emmit adopted her and, having been in the system her entire life, had a sincere aversion to authority.

Emmit squatted down. "Casey, they just want to talk to you; that's all, honey. This will help us." He searched her eyes. "Nobody's going to push you around, I promise."

She thought about it for a moment, then sighed. "Okay."

Emmit cupped her cheek and smiled. They both knew he'd never broken a promise. Standing up straight, he looked at Kyle, who was hunched down listening intently to the whispers of his other two daughters. Emmit raised one dark brow, and Kyle winked as he rose.

"What was that about?" Emmit asked.

"Can't say; lawyer-client privilege." Kyle chuckled, making a production of pocketing his five dollar retainer.

****

The girls spent at least forty-five minutes behind chamber doors. Emmit would have been concerned, but Judge Mason was Judge Rebecca Mason, and the girls, mainly Casey, didn't feel threatened by women.

"I can handle any prissy-pants woman judge. No sweat," Casey informed him.

Of course that would have worried him if Alexandra hadn't said, "Casey, she's a lady and a judge, which means she's very smart."

And then Fletcher said, "Smart, yep, and tough too. A judge's gotta be real tough. Nope, Case, she ain't no prissy pants." For some reason that, more than anything, had absolved his worry.

Now Emmit tensed as the court discussed his finances openly. His bank account was his business, not that of the people in this room, though thankfully there were only a few. He understood they had to make sure he could be a good provider, but it made him as uncomfortable as hell. And the state's attorney's questions sounded like accusations.

"Mr. McKay owns a hardware store and has money invested, but is that enough for raising three girls, let alone four, Your Honor?" he challenged.

Kyle stood with a rebuttal. "Your Honor, the hardware store alone provides quite well. But the money my client has invested makes a yearly profit that's more than sufficient. Here is a copy of his brokerage statement, Your Honor." Kyle handed the document to her after she told him to approach the bench. She looked it over, then had the bailiff hand the papers to the state's attorney.

Judge Mason glanced at Kyle, who had returned to his seat, then at the state's attorney. "Well, as you can plainly see, Mr. McKay is more than capable of financially providing for a houseful of children. Next time, I would suggest your research be more thorough, before you put your foot in your mouth. If there is nothing else…"

Emmit wanted to loosen the tie that was choking him but stopped himself. He made an honest living, but he wasn't a millionaire by any means. Most of his family's wealth, if you could call it that, had been wiped out in the Great Depression. His grandfather and father had both worked most of their lives to regain what they had lost. He, himself, never needed much, but he enjoyed the idea of being able to afford college for each of his girls and maybe pay for big weddings one day. He was smiling when Kyle announced that there was someone who would like to speak on Mr. McKay's behalf.

Emmit glanced at Kyle, who winked at him, then toward the howls of giggles being muffled by small hands. He looked at his daughters, who then stopped laughing and covered their faces so only their big eyes showed. He gave them a questioning smile as Judge J. T. Vaughn walked in the door. Emmit hadn't seen J. T. since that night in his kitchen. He didn't know what to expect.

"Your Honor, Judge J. T. Vaughn," Kyle said.

Judge Mason nodded. "Yes, we're acquainted. J. T., long time."

"Good to see you too, Your Honor. I hope you don't mind my coming here today. But I thought I might add my input."

"Of course, J. T." Judge Mason motioned for him to take a seat after the State agreed to accept his testimony.

"Judge Vaughn, what is your relationship to Mr. McKay?" Kyle asked after J. T. had been sworn in.

"Emmit McKay was married to my daughter Gracie until her death."

J. T. told Judge Mason about his daughter's marriage to Emmit and her ovarian cancer. He shifted in his seat. "It didn't matter to Emmit that she couldn't have babies. He told her they'd adopt a bunch of kids and be happy. They adopted those three there." J. T. motioned to where the girls sat behind Emmit. "And I'll tell you they're a handful." He cleared his throat and continued.

Emmit was torn between being uncomfortable with what J. T. was saying and being grateful. He was taken aback as J. T. confessed about the confrontation they'd had. It surprised Emmit that his father-in-law would lay himself bare like that.

"It was a wake-up call for me, so to speak. That night, as I mentioned, I said some awful things, but Emmit vouched for me. He reminded the girls that, sometimes when people are grieving, they—"

"You was drunk as a skunk," Casey hollered from her seat. Emmit winced, while the rest of the courtroom laughed. Judge Mason called for order and for J. T. to continue.

"Yes, quite right, Casey. Emmit told my granddaughters people needed to be forgiven. About two weeks after that night, Alexandra had Mrs. Sadie Madison bring her to my home to tell me she forgave me and still loved her granddaddy." His eyes were misty, but he blinked the moisture away.

"This morning Casey and Fletcher showed up at my door apologizing for what they said and forgiving me. They asked me to come here today because they want Charlie to be their sister. Emmit is a dedicated father, and any child would be hard pressed to find better. And that's all I have to say about that."

J. T. was dismissed after the State declined to ask questions. Judge Mason called a brief recess, and Emmit went over to J. T. as soon as she had left the room.

"J. T., I can't thank you enough for coming out here," Emmit said, shaking his hand.

"No thanks necessary, not on your part anyway. I was under oath, after all—my testimony was sincere."

He shrugged and stepped back. "I figure it could only help you to have a retired judge on your side willing to throw himself under the bus to show what kind of man you are. I owe you that much." J. T. cleared his throat. "The child deserves a loving family. I'm going to kiss and hug my granddaughters. Hopefully, I'll be introduced to another one soon."

"No question, J. T. Besides, with my parents in Florida, the girls need all the family they can get."

J. T. nodded and proceeded toward his granddaughters.

Emmit shook his head. He couldn't believe J. T. would to go to such extremes for him. He stood aside while his daughters hugged their grandfather. And in that moment, there was no doubt in Emmit's mind who J. T. had done this for.

Emmit waited a couple of minutes after J. T. left before going back to where his girls were sitting. "Well…" Emmit looked at them intently. "…you went to the Judge's house this morning." He gestured to both Casey and Fletcher, then nodded to Alexandra. "And you knew where they'd gone." They all nodded and smiled. "At least you admit it, because you're all grounded for a week."

"But, Pops, we did a good thing here," Casey argued, sitting forward in her seat.

"Yes, what you did was good, but A, you left without telling me. B, you rode your bikes alone through the woods, which you know is against the rules."

"But Daddy," Alexandra cried and pointed to herself. "I didn't go anywhere."

"Ah, and that brings us to C, accessory before the

fact. And that accessory, Alexandra, my dear, is you." Their faces were priceless. Furious! These were the times when he wanted to say, "Ha! Outsmarted you this time!" But grownups didn't do such things, at least not in court. Just as he took his seat, Judge Mason came back in. They all rose, then sat down again. It hadn't even been fifteen minutes. Was that good or bad?

"This court has heard an abundance of things today," Judge Mason began. "We looked at you through a microscope, Mr. McKay, and I must say it was all rather impressive." She stopped and glanced down at her papers, her face unreadable when she looked up again. Emmit tried to relax as he glanced over his shoulder to where the girls were holding hands.

"I must admit the conversation I had with your daughters had the most influence on my decision. They came into my chambers and demanded I give up Charlie." Emmit groaned, and Judge Mason smiled. "Casey, who is the spokeswoman of the group, said, and I quote, 'We aren't leaving without our sister, and that, Miss Judge, ma'am, is that.' " Judge Mason cleared her throat. "After what we've learned here today and in speaking with your girls, Mr. McKay, the court feels there is no place Charlie would belong but with you and your family. And that *is* that. Adoption approved! This court is adjourned. Congratulations."

Everyone clapped. Emmit hugged his daughters and shook hands with Kyle.

"We won!" Alexandra exclaimed.

"Did you think we wouldn't?" Casey asked shaking her head.

"Yes, girls, we won, but so has Charlie," Emmit reminded them, grinning.

****

Around eight that night, Kyle Ruthie pulled into the McKays' driveway. Three pairs of eyes watched him closely from the kitchen window as Kyle got out of the car and opened the door to the backseat and a young girl stepped out.

"She's chubby," Casey announced.

"So are you, Casey. Be nice," Alexandra said.

Fletcher snickered.

"I can still kick your scrawny tail, Alex," Casey reminded her getting into a boxer's stance.

"You girls aren't arguing, now, are you?"

"No, Pops!"

"No, Daddy!"

"Good! Here she comes." Emmit stood in front of his daughters who were in their pajamas. He shook his finger. "No scaring her, or fighting, don't tell her any tall stories, and don't try to intimidate her." He looked from daughter to daughter. "Is that clear?" They all nodded. "Good."

"Hey, hey, hey, the gang's all here," Kyle said as he walked in the door. "Ladies, gentlemen, and Fletcher, may I present the newest member of your family, Charlie McKay."

"Tah dah!" Charlie shouted throwing out her arms and bowing. Blonde curls were tumbling out of two pigtails on either side of her head. She peeked around with big doe eyes and grinned.

Emmit, embarrassed to be choked up, cleared his throat while squatting down to be eye to eye with Charlie. "Welcome home, Charlie."

"Wow," she whispered, "you're bigger than I remember. Huge, like Daddy Warbucks in *Annie*!

Which is my favorite movie, just so you know." She took a breath and grinned. "What do I call you?"

Charmed and somewhat awkward, Emmit said, "You can call me Emmit or Pops or Dad, whichever one you want. And I'll call you Charlie." Emmit stood up.

"Hokey dokey. Pops it is." She gave two thumbs up.

"I'm Casey. This is Fletcher, and that's Alex," Casey told her, pointing everyone out. Emmit could tell his oldest was sizing up the new girl.

"Alexandra," Alexandra corrected, making both Casey and Fletcher roll their eyes.

"What are you supposta be?" Charlie asked Alexandra.

"What do you mean by 'be'?" Alexandra asked and crossed her arms.

"You know...never mind, I get it. You're the princess, and these two are the evil stepsisters," Charlie said with an open-mouthed smile.

"You ain't seen evil yet." Casey jumped in and was restrained by Pops.

"Now, girls, I think Charlie was just joking," Kyle said.

"Are you guys dense? I was talking about Cinderella, you know." Charlie's eyes darted between the girls. "The Disney movie. You do know what I'm talking about, right?"

The three girls looked at one another, glanced at Emmit, then back at Charlie. Fletcher nodded, stepped forward, and patted Charlie's shoulder. "You're it." And with a shriek, they all ran.

"That seems to have gone well," Kyle said, peering

through the door the girls had run through.

"Yeah, well, I'll help you get her stuff," Emmit said, moving toward the screen door. Kyle stopped him.

"This is it," Kyle said, nodding at the old suitcase he'd brought in with him.

"It is?" Emmit asked with a frown. "The people running the orphanage told me she'd collected a bunch of stuff over the years." He had been glad to hear she had been able to keep things; he was still haunted by the memory of the lone—practically empty—trash bag they had handed him when he adopted Casey, Alexandra, and Fletcher.

"Apparently, whatever she did have, she gave to the other children there. She told me she got what she'd always wanted, a family, and that was more than she needed. I swear I almost cried." Kyle shook his head. "I've never met a sweeter girl in my life."

Emmit smiled. Sometimes, life was good. He got a new daughter, his girls got a new sister, Charlie got a family, and Kyle got in touch with his emotions.

"What a day," Emmit said as he walked Kyle outside. "Thanks again for everything." He clapped his friend on the shoulder.

"Hey, no problem." Kyle shrugged. "I like happy endings as much as the next guy." Kyle grinned as he got back in his car and started the engine. Emmit had just turned toward the house when Kyle called him back through the open window.

"Yeah?" Emmit asked, turning around.

"Judge Mason said something to me after the proceedings. It was strange, and I didn't think about it until right now. Just slipped my mind."

"What was that?" Emmit asked walking closer.

"Well, she said it was rather peculiar Social Services would waste the court's time with your case. She said it was obvious what the best decision would be. The entire situation seemed off to her."

"How so?" Emmit's gut clenched.

"She didn't say exactly. I mean, yes, it isn't every day an adoption is sought by a single father. But with your connections and the fact that you've already proven yourself..." Kyle shrugged. "Judge Mason said you should watch your back. She has a reputation for being an eccentric. Maybe that's all it is, but I thought you should know."

"Thanks, Kyle," Emmit said. Waving his old friend off, he started for the house but stopped at the sound of giggles coming from inside. Emmit smiled. He knew raising four girls would be hard but worth it. Well worth it.

Chapter Five

Two years later

The first week on a new job was enough to make anyone anxious. Add moving to a small town where strangers were put under microscopes, and that would sum up Savannah Walker's unease. She had been in Blue Creek for only a month, and every person she passed on the street seemed to know her name.

Where Savannah had lived in Maryland, she was just another face in the crowd. Here, she stood out like a river in the desert. She wasn't used to people she didn't know knowing her. It didn't help, Savannah guessed, that she was renting her apartment from Mrs. Sadie Madison and everyone knew Sadie.

The way people called Sadie "The Widow Madison" was strange. It was like they were saying "The Queen of England" or "The President." Thinking of Sadie made her smile. The older woman was a sweetheart, and Savannah had grown close to Sadie in a short period of time.

Sadie hadn't been kidding when she'd warned Savannah about small town living. Savannah hadn't even finished unpacking when the sheriff knocked on her door wanting to welcome her personally. Sheriff Jasper Hart hadn't fit the picture Savannah had in her mind of a small-town sheriff. No potbellies here. The sheriff's five-foot-eight frame was well toned, and his blue-green eyes were watchful but kind. He seemed to be a nice, honest man who was quite proud of his town. Though she felt he was a bit meddlesome, Savannah had enjoyed meeting him.

As she told the sheriff, she'd moved to Blue Creek because of her new job. She'd heard about the position through an old classmate. Her friend's great aunt's dearest friend, Sadie Madison, had mentioned the town needed a new principal because theirs had retired.

Savannah had a master's degree in education and had taught for four years before becoming a vice principal last year. She assumed those factors made her resume stand out, because she was accepted for the position within two weeks of sending in her application. Now here she sat as the principal of Blue Creek Elementary and Middle School.

Savannah sighed and studied her mother's picture on the corner of her desk. She had come here to get a fresh start. Her mother had passed away last spring, and Savannah couldn't stand the constant reminders of a life she no longer had. Or if she were honest, a life she never wanted in the first place.

A knock at the door brought Savannah back to the here and now. She glanced at her watch; it was after noon.

"Come in!" Savannah called out. Her office was small but comfortable. Bookshelves lined the walls, and she sat behind a Queen Anne desk. Even though she tried to make her office less intimidating to children, she couldn't part with the desk that had been in her family for years.

A short middle-aged woman named Mildred

Lawrence entered the room. She looked like the stereotypical librarian to Savannah, but she'd been the school's secretary for twenty years.

"We've got some trouble, Ms. Walker," Mildred said in her no-nonsense tone.

Savannah raised an eyebrow.

Mildred nodded. "There was a fight in the schoolyard. The culprits are on their way in now."

"A fight? Already? It's only the first week of school." She hadn't even had the school assembly to introduce herself to the students yet.

"That it is—"

"And why are you bringing them here instead of to the vice principal's office?"

"That old grouch refuses to deal with them, even had a clause added to his contract."

"Added to his…" What in the world? Savannah straightened her suit jacket. She could handle this. "Who are they, Mildred?"

"Well, it would be the McKays. You'll find out soon enough they're heathens, the lot of them." Mildred gave a melodramatic shudder.

"The McKays?" That sounded ominous to Savannah. Like some infamous gang from an old western. "How many are there?"

"Four! Trouble comes in two pairs with them. Always in here, those kids, except Alex. Nope, that one usually minds real well." Mildred nodded with a pinch of her lips.

"Alex?" Savannah's brow pinched.

"Yep, that's the…wait, let me think." Mildred began counting off fingers. "The oldest is Casey, attitude on that one. Charlie's the second oldest, goes

35

more with the majority than not. Alex is the third oldest and well-mannered for the most part. The real instigator usually is the youngest, Fletcher, but mind you"—she shook her index finger at Savannah—"Casey's the enforcer." Mildred harrumphed. "No explaining it, though. Pops McKay is a good father, runs the hardware store in town. He can fix anything!"

Great, just what she needed. A pack of overzealous boys running wild. "They're all in trouble?"

"No, Ms. Walker, only three this time. Casey is a grade or two higher. But third and fourth graders are usually out at the same time. So, you're getting Fletcher, Charlie, and Alex," Mildred explained.

Savannah stood and looked out the window pulling her thoughts together for a lecture. Feet shuffled out in the hall, and she turned toward the door. When the children stepped in, she forgot what she'd been about to say.

"You, you're—" Savannah started waving her hands around. "You're girls!" she finally sputtered out. Her eyes darted to Mildred, only to find the door shutting with a distinct click. She looked back to the children.

"Don't I's know it? I's ain't no sissy girl like Alex there," the smallest girl with long braids and mischievous eyes said, jerking her thumb to the girl with red hair.

"Alexandra, you ninny!" the redhead said, then held out her dirty hand across Savannah's desk. "Alexandra McKay. It is nice to make your acquaintance, Principal Walker."

Savannah took the girl's hand still trying to corral her thoughts. She had somehow gotten the impression these "heathens" were boys. Well, maybe the oldest was. What had Mildred said his name was? Savannah couldn't remember, but these three here were positively not boys. Girls in her experience were not physical when they fought. Catty, sure, but a fistfight at this age? She drew back her hand.

"Nice to meet you, Alexandra. Who might these two be?" Savannah motioned to the other girls.

"That Neanderthal"—Alexandra pointed at the one with the pigtails—"is my younger sister, Fletcher, and that one is my slightly older sister Charlie," she said, motioning to the doe-eyed blonde.

"Ma'am," Charlie and Fletcher said in unison.

Savannah sat down and asked for them to sit as well. "All right, girls," she began, then stopped short when they disappeared. Savannah stood and walked around her desk to see the three of them sitting on the hardwood floor.

"What on earth are you doing?"

"You asked us to sit down," Alexandra pointed out.

"We's sitting, ain't we?" Fletcher put in with a nod from Charlie.

"We are sitting, aren't we? *Or* we are sitting, are we not?" Savannah corrected. "And yes, I did, and yes, you are sitting down, but there are four perfectly good chairs right there." Savannah gestured to the chairs.

"Them's real nice chairs, and we's don't wanna gets 'em dirty," Fletcher said.

"What she means is we're filthy and don't want to be getting your stuff messy," Charlie clarified before Savannah could correct Fletcher's grammar.

"Yes, I'm covered in"—Alexandra gagged—"dirt."

Okay, it made some sense, she supposed. Going

around to the other side, she pulled one of the chairs back against her desk, then sat. Savannah was aware of three sets of eyes staring holes into her.

"All right, we may as well get started. I want to know exactly what happened. You can start," Savannah began, pointing at Alexandra.

Alexandra perked up with a wide smile. She took a gulp of air and was about to speak when the office door swung open and another girl with black hair and glasses barreled in. Alexandra rolled her eyes, then stood quickly with her other sisters. The three girls looked wearily at the newcomer.

"What in tarnation do you three think you're doing?" All the girls started talking at once. Savannah wanted to roll her own eyes. She looked at Mildred, who had just come into the room.

"Sorry, Ms. Walker, I tried to stop her. Slippery like a snake, that one," Mildred said putting her hands on her hips and glaring at the child.

"It's all right, Mildred, I can handle it." I think. She smiled at Mildred, who mumbled under her breath and left. Savannah then turned to big violet eyes.

"Do you care to identify yourself?" Savannah asked.

"I'm Casey McKay. What's it to yah?" Casey asked narrowing her eyes. Fletcher snorted, Charlie giggled, and Alexandra sighed.

Trying not to laugh, Savannah introduced herself as the new principal. She should have known the oldest was also a female. What had Mildred said? Ah, yes, the "enforcer."

"New principal?" Casey scoffed. "But you're a girl!"

"I could say the same about you," Savannah said.

"The rumors were true," Charlie whispered, and Casey nodded.

"What are you doing out of class, young lady?" Savannah asked, bringing the room back to the issue at hand. She wouldn't think about what rumors were being spread about her.

"I heard these three got in trouble, and I came to help. I'm their big sister," Casey said.

"But you're not in trouble. So you may go back to your classroom."

"But I'm the *big sister*," Casey said through clenched teeth. Her sisters nodded in agreement and then turned their eyes to Savannah.

"I'm aware of that and thank you for coming down, but you're not in trouble and this has nothing to do with you." Savannah knew she'd made a mistake by the reaction of the other three girls. Charlie winced, Alexandra started biting her lower lip, and she heard Fletcher's "oh shit" quite clearly. "Oh shit" fit the situation.

Before Savannah could respond to the foul language, Casey marched up to her desk, picked up Savannah's empty coffee cup, and threw the mug, her eyes never leaving Savannah's. It shattered in the corner away from everyone. Savannah gasped.

"Oh, man, Casey, whatcha do that for?" Fletcher asked, eyes wide.

"And you call me the drama queen," Alexandra whispered as Charlie covered her eyes with her hands and shook her head.

"Am I in trouble now?" Casey sneered, cocking her head to one side.

"Oh, Miss McKay, you're in trouble up to your eyebrows. You can sit right here." Savannah pointed to the chair she'd leaned against the desk. She would have sent the child into the waiting area, but she had a feeling she would only be making matters worse. Savannah rubbed her forehead and looked at the other three girls, whose eyes were darting back and forth between Casey and herself.

"You three sit down, as well," Savannah instructed and waited for them to do as she asked. Fletcher immediately began squirming in her chair; Savannah figured she was trying to grind as much dirt in as possible.

"All right, you three tell me what happened," Savannah said.

And they did. Apparently, another girl named Marylou Thomas, or "sissy pants" as Fletcher called her, had said mean things about Alexandra's new dress. Because Alexandra was a young lady and wouldn't fight, Fletcher had taken on the job instead. Fletcher, who "won't afraid of no sissy-sniveling-wimpy girl," was going to fight fairly with Marylou, but things got out of hand. Marylou, who sounded like a spoiled brat to Savannah, had two other friends with her, so Charlie had to join the fight to make things even. But it was still three to two, so Alexandra had to jump in. Fair was fair.

"How many times have I told you not to throw the first punch, Fletcher?" Casey interjected. "Tarnation! You're still grounded from the last time!"

"Whatcha want me to do, Case? I's was fighting the good fight," Fletcher said, then leaned forward and whispered, "Sheesh, why you's gotta be embarrassing me?" She sat back, crossing her arms over her chest.

"Why isn't this Marylou in here with you?" Savannah asked. All four girls burst out laughing, then shrugged. Not seeing the humor, she asked again.

Alexandra was about to answer her, when Casey glared at her, and Fletcher kicked her chair. Charlie sat back and pursed her mouth.

"Well, if you're not going to tell me, I can ask the lunch monitor what happened, or I can ask your teachers." Three pairs of accusing eyes flashed at her, and Casey swiveled in her seat to add her glare to the others'.

Charlie cleared her throat, and Casey nodded. Charlie turned to Savannah. "Do you know the story of the boy who cried wolf, Principal Walker?"

"Yes, of course," Savannah answered, rubbing her temples to ward off the headache she was acquiring.

"Our situation is kind of like that, but not quite," Charlie began as her sisters sat back and rolled their eyes. "You see, we don't cry wolf ever, but because we are who we are, people don't believe what we say." Three girls nodded, but Savannah was lost.

"Charlie, I don't think I'm following you exactly."

"Okay, we are like the *boy* who cried wolf without the 'cried' part. The teachers are the townsfolk. 'Crying wolf' is the label the townsfolk put on the boy, but in our case the label is 'trouble.' Marylou is the wolf, which is both trouble and the bad guy, see? She's a wolf in sheep's clothing, and the townsfolk think she can do no wrong. We all know how that wolf story turned out though. Yep, the wolf killed the rest of the sheep and destroyed the town. So you see?"

Savannah tried to muddle through what she'd heard. The child talked in riddles. "Okay, you're telling me the teachers here have labeled you all as troublemakers, and this Marylou can do no wrong. When, in fact, she is the instigator, but because she's in sheep's clothing, so to speak, the teachers don't put the blame on her. Did I get that right?"

"Absolutely!" Charlie beamed.

"Can't pull the wool over you's eyes, now can yah?" Fletcher put in, laughing.

Savannah smiled back.

"Are we going to be sent home, Principal Walker?" Alexandra asked.

"I think I see what happened, and I'll have to call your house and send you home because you're all filthy." And so are my chairs, Savannah thought, but she could get them cleaned. She glanced at the broken mug on the floor, which she hadn't forgotten. Casey winced and wouldn't meet her eyes.

"Okay, girls, I'll call your mother to come get you. We'll discuss your punishment when she gets here," Savannah said, going back around her desk and taking a seat. The silence enveloped her; it was too quiet, eerily so.

"You act real nice, but you're just like the rest of this damn town. New here or not," Casey began with a shake of her head. "Yep, you pretend to be understanding only to stab us in the back, rubbing our noses in it. Nothing's ever gonna change," Casey sneered. She had gotten out of the chair and moved it, so nothing blocked Savannah's view. She had both hands on top of Savannah's desk, her little nails digging into its surface. Her voice had an unchildlike calm.

Charlie went to Casey and pulled her away from the desk. She tangled her fingers with her big sisters, while Alexandra took hold of Casey's other hand.

"She doesn't know, Casey. She doesn't know," Alexandra whispered.

Fletcher swallowed, then jumped to Casey's defense. "Everybody knows everything in Blue Creek, Alex, and that's a fact."

Charlie looked at Savannah, who was gaping at all four of them in total confusion. "You didn't know their mama was passed on, did you, Principal Walker?" Charlie asked.

Understanding dawned. "Oh no! Oh, girls, I had no idea, I'm so sorry. No one told me." Her chest tightened at the hurt in their eyes. She would not cry; she would not. She was a principal, for goodness' sake. Charlie reached across the table and patted Savannah's hand. Savannah swallowed. Hard.

"See, it was all a misunderstanding," Charlie informed the room at large. They all looked at Casey, who took a deep breath and nodded. Then she released her sisters' hands.

Savannah rubbed the spot right above her heart. Fletcher sat in Casey's lap, Alexandra on the floor beside them, and Charlie behind her. Charlie began playing with Alexandra's hair, and Casey rubbed Fletcher's back. They were comforting each other in their own way.

"You can call Pops; he'll come and get us," Charlie told Savannah. Savannah nodded, picking up the extension to have Mildred call Mr. McKay, only to find out Mildred had already done just that.

Chapter Six

Emmit hated principals' offices. Loathed and despised them. But here he was back again. He had heard about the new principal. Who hadn't? Actually, he probably should have heard *more* than he had. He knew she was from Maryland, young, and well educated. She was staying with Sadie and was supposedly shy.

Emmit snorted. Shy? Ha! Shy didn't move to small towns, and shy definitely didn't rent from a woman who called herself the Widow Madison. He frowned; funny how Sadie hadn't said anything to him about her new tenant. The woman didn't forget things like that. He'd say it was old age, but he didn't want lightning to strike him dead.

Emmit had closed early today as he did every Thursday, so it was fate when Mildred called him. He smiled to himself, wondering what his girls had done now. He had been a single parent for almost three years and doing a pretty damn good job of it. His girls kept him on his toes. Hell, sometimes they were so tight-knit *he* felt like an outsider.

Emmit couldn't even remember a time when Charlie hadn't been with them. How he had made it without her? She was his peacekeeper, and for a ten-year-old, her voice of reason was uncanny.

He opened the door to the main office, and his

stomach turned. Man, he hated coming here. Unfortunately, he was here three or four times a month. His girls kept *everyone* on their toes. He was wondering what Ms. Walker thought of his little task force when he spotted Mildred behind her desk. One thing never changed, with her graying bun and old lady shoes, Mildred was a rock.

"Hello, Mildred. How are you?"

"McKay. I'm doing well, unlike Ms. Walker, I imagine."

Uh oh! "Why's that?" he asked, feigning ignorance.

"Well, let me tell you." With a small smile, Mildred told him how she had misled the new principal to believe the McKays were boys. "Got the shock of her life, I'll tell you."

They both laughed.

Mildred's phone beeped. "Already done, Ms. Walker," she said, replacing the receiver, then pointed Emmit toward the door. "They're ready for you."

Emmit waved and, straightening his shoulders, opened the door.

All of his girls were in the office, not three as he'd been told on the phone. Charlie, Fletcher, and even Alexandra were covered in mud. He looked toward the only other adult in the room, and his heart almost stopped.

The new principal took his breath away. She had creamy skin, golden-brown hair, and eyes that shone like sapphires. She was small and slender but had curves he couldn't miss. She was almost the exact opposite of Gracie, who had been both model slim and tall. Emmit knew he was staring, but he wasn't the only one.

"Pops, what's the matter witcha?" Fletcher wanted to know, jumping out of Casey's lap and moving toward him, sizing him up. "You's ain't sick, are yah?"

Emmit shook his head to clear it. He glanced back at Principal Walker as she, too, became aware of the girls once again. He tweaked Fletcher's nose.

"Nah, kiddo, I'm fine, just fine," he said as the principal held out her hand.

"Mr. McKay, I presume, I'm Savan…um, Principal Walker. Sorry you had to come out here," she said and after one brief shake, dropped his hand.

"Ma'am. Well, you being the new principal and all, we were bound to meet sooner or later." He almost smiled, then motioned to his girls. "Who wants to explain to me what happened this time?" He looked from one guilty face to another. Feet shuffled and hands clasped.

"Daddy, it was all a big misunderstanding. Things were said, and then one thing led to another, and well, here we are," Alexandra explained in the wispy voice he knew she'd been practicing in the mirror.

"We's gots in a fight, Pops. No big deal; nobody even bled. Just a little dirty s'all," Fletcher said with a shrug. Charlie gave him her "sorry, Pops" eyes and smiled while biting her lip.

"That's all, you say? Ms. Walker, maybe you can enlighten me." He faced her again, all business.

"For heaven's sakes! Someone tell him all of it," Casey demanded, and Alexandra spoke up, going into detail. When she was finished, Emmit took a cleansing breath, then studied Casey curiously.

"Then what are you doing here?" he asked her.

"Oh—" Ms. Walker interjected. "She's suspended for two days."

"What!" the rest of the room said in unison.

"Yes, two days' suspension for cutting class, not leaving the room when I asked her to, being disrespectful, *and* destroying my personal property." She finished primly, having ticked off each offense on her fingers.

"Casey, you did those things?" Emmit asked in disbelief. His oldest took a deep breath, then nodded. "Answer me!" He had rules about nodding. His girls knew he hated it when they didn't answer him outright on important matters.

"Yes, sir, I did," she replied, straightening her spine.

"Why in the world did you? Hell, Casey, that's not like you to be so disrespectful. Would you have done that to me?" It came out harsher than he intended. Casey flinched, and he cringed. He squatted down to be eye level with her.

"Casey, honey, I'd like an answer."

"She wouldn't let me stay." She pointed to Ms. Walker then to herself. "I'm the big sister! I've gotta protect what's mine," she whispered, pushing the glasses back up her nose. The action couldn't mask the hitch in her voice. Her answer hit him in the gut.

"That's no excuse to behave that way, and you know better," he reminded her, standing now. He caught the sympathetic look that blanketed Ms. Walker's eyes before she could cover it. If she felt bad, that made two of them. His other three daughters were silent as they always were when one of them got into trouble.

"That's a fair punishment, Ms. Walker, and she *will* be getting you a new mug."

"Yes, sir," Casey said, so only he could hear.

"What about the others? What's their punishment?"

"Being that it's Thursday, they'll have out-of-school suspension tomorrow, and detention all next week. Fighting is against the rules." She paused, then added, "Marylou will have the same punishment. Of course." They all stared at her. Ms. Walker cleared her throat. "It's only fair, seeing as she started the fight, don't you girls think so?"

Emmit smiled. That was how to win over his girls. Beautiful and smart, a dangerous combination to a man like him.

"Girls, what do you think?" Emmit took inventory of their faces. "That's fair, isn't it?"

"Hells bells, that's more than fair," Fletcher said, punching her fist into the palm of her other hand. "I's love to see Marylou's snobby face when she hears!"

"That's very fair," Charlie agreed with a smile.

"Good, that's settled. Thank you, Ms. Walker, and sorry for the trouble," Emmit said as he herded his girls out of the office.

****

Savannah sat down slowly and tried to take in all that had happened. Okay, she admitted, she needed to get herself in check. That man made her sweat. She pulled her blouse forward a bit and used it to fan her overheated skin.

"He's a flipping giant," she said to herself. Mr. McKay had towered over her five-foot-three frame by at least a foot, and his shoulders had been two to three times the size of hers. He was big and rough in his jeans and black T-shirt, which appeared to be molded to his muscled frame. His black hair, which had been long enough to curl around the collar of his shirt, was disheveled, and his eyes were a captivating blue-gray.

Oh, Savannah, you act like you've never seen a man before! It had been a couple of years since the last time someone caught her interest. Hormones, was all it was. Savannah Francis Walker did not need a man. She got up from her seat and shook her head to clear it.

"If this is how life as principal is going to be, at least it won't be boring," she mumbled. Those girls were unlike anyone she had ever met and their father, well...There was something different about that family, but she couldn't put her finger on it. She cleaned up what remained of her mug and threw it in the trash. Her thoughts turned again to Mr. McKay, and she realized she didn't even know his first name.

Chapter Seven

Savannah decided to go to the town's diner the following Thursday after work. Unless you wanted fast food or to drive an extra twenty minutes, Ida Mae's on Main Street was the only place where you could sit down to eat in Blue Creek.

The moment she walked through the door, Savannah was hit with the heavy aroma of coffee. She couldn't help but smile at the old jukebox leaning against the wall. The diner was small, only four tables in the center and booths along the wall. The long stainless-steel counter had stools with red vinyl tops and was shiny enough to show her reflection. There was a pick-up window and swinging doors leading to the kitchen.

A few patrons sat at the counter, and teenagers had crowded into two of the booths. Savannah lowered her eyes as she walked across the black and white tiles. Was it her imagination, or was everyone staring at her? Shaking her head, she chose a corner booth at the back. An older woman came to the counter and held up one finger, letting Savannah know it would be a moment. She pulled out a few files from her briefcase and looked them over.

"You're the new principal, am I right?" asked the woman wearing a gray uniform with red trim. She looked like she was in her late sixties with white hair and warm brown eyes. Her fuchsia lips supported her friendly smile.

"Yes, Savannah Walker. Nice to meet you." Savannah held out her hand. The woman shrugged and shook Savannah's hand briskly before reaching in her apron and pulling out a notepad.

"Nice to meet you, Ms. Savannah Walker. I'm Ida Mae; I run this hole in the ground. That's my daughter, Trixy." She pointed to a busty bleached blonde sitting at the end of the counter. "She runs the beauty shop at the end of the square."

"That's nice, her being so close and all."

"Ain't nothing nice about it. Infuriating girl that one is, had to run a beauty shop! As if this place wasn't good enough for the likes of her. I'm never gonna be able to retire and move to Florida." Ida shook her head and took Savannah's order. After she finished writing, she looked Savannah over. "Where you staying, girl?"

"In the apartment above Sadie Madison's garage. It's nice and more than enough for me right now."

"That garage used to be a barn."

"Really?" Savannah's brows pinched.

"Used to house the Widow's prize-winning cow, Mabel, but couple years back, that cow got out, and no one ever saw it again. The Widow couldn't bring herself to replace the blasted animal, so she turned the barn into a garage and built the apartment above it."

Savannah couldn't help but smile. "That's interesting and explains why the garage isn't connected to the main house."

Ida nodded. "Mm-hmm. The Widow does have an awfully big place. Seems strange being that it's been just her for near twenty years." Ida drummed her fingers against her notepad.

What did she expect to hear?

After a moment Ida huffed out, "Be right back with your coffee."

She shook her head once Ida was out of sight, then glanced down at her files. Before she knew it, Ida Mae had plunked down a mug in front of her. As Savannah fixed the coffee to her liking, the front door swung open.

"Ida Mae, love of my life! I'm home. In the name of all that is holy, feed me!"

Savannah peeked up at the speaker. He was a handsome man. His brown hair was streaked with blond, either from the sun or Trixy over there, she suspected. He was lean and reasonably tall and wearing a black suit with a crisp white shirt and gray tie.

"Oh hush, you scalawag!" Ida told the man, playfully slapping his shoulder as he leaned across the counter. Even from where she sat, there was no mistaking the blush on Ida's cheeks.

The man clutched at his heart. "You wound me, Ida, truly." He turned his head, eyes widening when they landed on Savannah. "And what have we here? Why, I do believe it's fresh blood."

Savannah almost jumped when he came over to her table and sat down.

"Mind?" he asked after he'd taken his seat.

"Apparently not," Savannah said, smiling. He flashed her a thousand-watt grin.

"Kyle Ruthie, attorney at law." He inclined his head. "You need a lawyer?" he asked, shrugging out of his jacket.

"Savannah Walker"—she took a sip of coffee—

"and not at the moment."

"Good for you; lawyers are bloodsuckers," Kyle said so seriously that Savannah laughed. "Beautiful...with a sense of humor. Wait, Walker..." His brow furrowed. "Why do I know that name?"

Savannah was flattered, but she didn't react to his compliment. "I'm the new principal at the elementary and middle school."

"Yes!" Kyle snapped his fingers. "That's it." He studied her a moment, then shouted his order to Ida Mae, who grumbled about forked-tongued lawyers, but she brought him his coffee within seconds. "You've probably heard of my goddaughters, but if you know them personally, I'll disown them."

"I wouldn't want you to 'disown' anyone." Maybe she was more exhausted than she thought, because his attitude rubbed her the wrong way.

"Oh, I only disown them for a while; then I reclaim them." He winked as he took a sip of his coffee. "I think I've told them they were without a godfather nine or ten times already. Besides, I'm more like an honorary uncle anyway."

"What do their parents say?" she asked, moving her papers back into her briefcase.

"Parent," he corrected, then added with a mischievous grin, "He's just jealous he can't do the same thing now and again."

"Now I'm curious. Who are you talking about?"

"The McKay girls, of course." Savannah choked on her coffee, and Kyle's eyebrows bunched in sympathy. "I guess I've disowned them again," he said, as if it pleased him to no end.

Savannah laughed. "Yes, well...I wouldn't go that

far. I only met them in person last week."

"Them? All of them? Oh, this I have to hear." He motioned for Savannah to continue, so she told him the entire story. "You told Casey to butt out, huh? I'm surprised only your mug got damaged. Mr. Thompson, your predecessor, did the same thing last year; he found his tires flat, all four of them, the next day." He waved a hand before Savannah could speak. "I'm not saying Casey did it." He shrugged one shoulder. "But people were talking…as they always do in this town."

Ida served their meals, and their conversation steered to different topics. They talked about colleges and books as they finished eating. They were enjoying a second cup of coffee when a man called Kyle's name.

"Hey, Evan, come have a cup of coffee with me and the new principal," Kyle offered as the man approached their table. He was probably in his thirties, and not as handsome as Kyle or as rugged as Mr. McKay. His black hair was military short, and he had a gold hoop earring. His eyes were as dark as his hair. The man, quite simply, was a tank. Blue Creek knew how to grow men!

"New principal, huh?" Evan asked as Kyle got up to let him slide into the booth. "I guess you know the McKay girls by now?"

"Yes, I do." She waited for Kyle to sit back down. "Kyle and I discussed them earlier." Savannah couldn't help but smile when Evan laughed.

"Did yah now? I'm Evan Jessup, by the way." He shook Savannah's hand, grinned, and thanked Ida when she brought him a mug. "My dad and I own the garage in town."

"Nice to meet you. And please call me Savannah."

He nodded and smiled.

"How's business, Evan?" Kyle asked.

"It's the damnedest thing; I'd been complaining how slow we'd been, then all of a sudden business picked up. These last few weeks have been hectic, and Dad's driving me crazy. I even had to plead with McKay to let me tinker in the store this afternoon. Seeing how he closes early on Thursdays, it was nice and quiet."

Kyle checked his watch. "I'm late," he said as he reached into his pocket and pulled out a business card. "Here, Savannah, call me if you have any trouble. Or even if you don't," Kyle told her as he put his jacket back on and excused himself. He paid Ida and gave a dramatic good-bye bow.

"He seems nice," Savannah said to Evan.

"Who, Kyle?" Evan looked behind him to where Kyle had been. "Yeah, he's a good guy. We all grew up here together—him, McKay, and me. We were the three musketeers. Not no more, though," he said, almost mumbling.

"Why not? What happened?" Savannah asked after sorrow crept into his eyes.

"Life, as it always does, happened. We all grew up and got jobs. McKay got married and got kids. Kyle and me are still bachelors." He shrugged his massive shoulders.

"That's sad," she said frowning.

"Don't be sad. We're all happy, I guess. And I love it here; it's my home. Kyle's here once or twice a month…still has his parents' place. And McKay has his girls. We get together when we can. It works out." He patted her hand and glanced out the window. "I need to get going," he said, rising. "Nice to meet you, Savannah."

"You too, Evan." She smiled as he started for the door. Then he stopped and looked back at her.

"Savannah, just a thought to keep in mind…Blue Creek isn't always what it seems." He nodded and left.

Now what was that supposed to mean? Savannah glanced at Ida, who was shaking her head and offering her a refill on her coffee.

"Those boys." Ida motioned toward the door with her head. "Thick as thieves since they were little."

"That's nice to have friends you're so close to," she said, then regretted it after Ida gave her a pitying glance. She had friends, for goodness' sake, just not any with whom she was "thick as thieves."

"That's life in a small town!" Ida parked herself across from Savannah and set down the coffee carafe. "Now…I've got a five-minute break. Tell me all about yourself!" And with that, Savannah was bombarded with a barrage of questions, and Evan's cryptic words were swept from her thoughts.

Chapter Eight

It was mid-October, and the temperature was turning cool. Savannah loved the fall. The leaves changing colors always captivated her, and the air had a crispness to it that she couldn't explain. With the window of her Jeep cracked, she could smell the fresh mountain air.

Approaching the turn-in to Sadie's driveway, she noticed a child walking with his—or her—bike up the road. Savannah knew all her students, but at this distance, she couldn't tell who it was. The baseball cap hid the child's hair, and the T-shirt and overalls weren't unique. It could be anyone.

As she drove closer, the child pulled off the baseball cap to shove it in the overalls' back pocket. The action itself wouldn't have identified the child except two long brown braids fell out. There was only one child at her school who had brown braids that reached her backside. Fletcher McKay. Savannah smiled.

As Mildred had predicted, Savannah had seen this particular McKay often. The girl was always quick to fight. She had a peculiar way of speaking, and Savannah had tried to correct her grammar a multitude of times, but it hadn't stuck. Fletcher's words may not be grammatically correct, but Savannah found them charming, and she often had to catch herself from laughing. Casey spoke that way too sometimes, but she didn't find it nearly as endearing. Savannah shifted in her seat. The oldest McKay child didn't like her, which was normal being that Savannah was the principal, but for some reason it irked her. Casey irked her.

Since her first encounter with the McKay girls, Savannah had been curious about them. She had asked around, but people dodged her inquiries. Savannah found this odd, considering the town talked about anything and everyone else. Even Sadie was tight-lipped on the subject. Kyle was the only person who had talked about them, and he was evasive at best.

Savannah had gone out with Kyle a few times, not on dates but as friends. He came to Blue Creek a couple of weekends a month. They had a lot in common, and she enjoyed his company. The fact that he was handsome and funny didn't hurt. But she didn't get a tingle. Of course, she tried not to think about the man who did make her tingle.

She had seen Mr. McKay almost twice a week this month alone. Either Casey was in her office or Fletcher. Mainly Fletcher. He'd talked to her about his store and his parents, who lived in Florida. He didn't get too personal. She often felt as though he was making idle conversation to ease his own tension.

Savannah recognized the fact Mr. McKay disliked the dreaded principal's office. It must be awful for him, considering he was her most frequent visitor. She had a feeling Casey did more than her fair share of troublemaking, only she didn't get caught as often as Fletcher. This brought Savannah back to the child in front of her. She pulled her Jeep over to the side of the road, stopped, and rolled down the window.

"Hey, Fletcher, need a hand?"

"No, thanks. I's gots two of 'em already." She held up both hands.

Savannah laughed and turned off the engine. "Yes, I can see that. What I meant was…do you need some help?" She stepped out of the Jeep. "With your bike? Do you need help with your bike?"

"You's can fix my bike?" Fletcher asked, staring at Savannah with her head cocked to the side.

"I can take a look," she said as she shut the Jeep's door and walked closer.

"Okay, if you's think yah can."

"If *you* think *you* can," Savannah corrected.

"That's what I's said," Fletcher said, scrunching up her face.

Savannah bit her lip, studied the bike, and saw the problem right away. "The chain's come off the gears. That's easy enough to fix."

Savannah pulled her hair into a quick ponytail and rolled up the sleeves of her dark blue cotton shirt. After a bit of maneuvering, she was able to reset the chain. "Done," she said, noticing that the child's fingers were as greasy as her own. "Wait here." She opened the Jeep and grabbed a container of moist towelettes from the passenger seat. She kept them handy, mainly because she was always making a mess.

"Here we go," she announced smiling as Fletcher inspected her bike. "Let's clean ourselves up a bit, shall we?" Savannah said and wiped her hands. She then took Fletcher's hands and began to clean them as well. Fletcher hissed.

"What's wrong? Did I hurt you?" She looked up.

"Nah. I's scraped my hands when I's fell." Fletcher

shrugged.

Savannah took the girl's hands and carefully cleaned around the cuts. She then went to get her first aid kit out of the glove box, came back, and sat on the ground patting the pavement for Fletcher to do the same.

"You's gonna get dirty," Fletcher said sitting down.

"A little dirt never hurt me. Besides, they're old jeans." She always changed into casual clothes once the students left the building, and today wasn't any different. She smiled at Fletcher and bandaged her up.

"Pops babies our hurts like this too," Fletcher said.

"Does he?"

"Yep...acts like it hurts him when we get hurt." Fletcher shrugged. "You's grownups are weird."

"I guess so." Savannah chuckled. "There, all better?"

"That didn't sting at all!" Fletcher said, studying the Band-Aids. "Thanks, Ms. Walker."

"You can call me Savannah. School's out for the weekend, so…"

Fletcher was looking at her like she was up to no good.

Savannah rolled her eyes. "Ms. Walker's fine too."

"You's know, Savannah's a real sissy name for someone that can fix a bike," Fletcher said, scrunching up her face like she'd tasted something foul.

Savannah laughed. "Yeah? I like it."

"If you's say so, lady. It's you's name."

"It's your name," Savannah corrected, and Fletcher let out a loud sigh.

Savannah smiled and looked up at the setting sun.

"It's getting late. Why don't I take you home?" she said as she helped Fletcher up from the ground.

"What about my bike?"

"We can put it in the back."

They worked together getting the bike in, then headed for the McKay house.

"Do you's like being a principal?"

"Yes, it's fun." Savannah looked over at Fletcher in the opposite seat.

"If you's say so," Fletcher said and crinkled her nose.

"If you—"

Fletcher crossed her arms and huffed. "That's what I's said."

Savannah bit the inside of her cheek and cleared her throat. "Principals get to boss everybody around."

Fletcher grinned at that. "Now we's talking!" She gave Savannah directions, and soon they were pulling into the drive. Savannah was surprised they were neighbors.

The house was Savannah's dream home materialized. The wraparound porch was exactly what she had always wanted. The only thing missing was a porch swing.

"Pops keeps saying he's gonna fix the one Great-Grandpa built, but he gets busy," Fletcher said. Savannah didn't realize she'd been thinking aloud.

Savannah parked, shut off the engine, and helped Fletcher get her bike out of the back.

"You's wanna stay for supper?"

"Your dad wouldn't mind?"

Fletcher snorted.

She should say no. She had things to do, and she

didn't need to get any more entangled with this family. She was about to make an excuse when Casey came outside wearing an outfit identical to Fletcher's, except Casey's shirt was purple.

"Tarnation, Fletcher, you're one lucky little shit. Pops is late too, so he won't know you was late again," Casey said, then looked at Savannah and winced. "Shit isn't a cuss, it's a bodily function." Her eyes dared Savannah to say something different. But Savannah was trying to keep from laughing.

"That it is!" Fletcher said.

"Casey? Fletcher home yet? Did you ask her if she was making prank calls here again?" Charlie asked, coming onto the porch stirring something in a bowl with a wooden spoon.

"I's here, and I's didn't make no prank calls now or ever, dagnabbit!" Fletcher yelled. "But I's did bring company. I's invited Ms. Walker to supper."

"Why?" Casey asked, her eyes darting from Fletcher to Savannah.

"'Cause she gave me a ride," Fletcher said.

"Good evening, Ms. Walker," Alexandra said, inclining her head. "What a wonderful surprise and staying for supper too! How nice."

"Hello, Alexandra, it's nice to see you too. But I can't stay, really."

"Why not? I made tacos tonight with all the fixings. And it's always nice to cook for someone other than my sisters," Charlie told her, still stirring.

"You cooked?" Savannah was shocked. She knew Charlie was only ten.

"We all cook, and Pops does the grillin'. Just don't come on Tuesday. That's Alex's night and, well, Pops don't like when we dig up the yard," Casey said. Fletcher and Charlie snickered.

"Dig up the yard?"

"You's see, you's eat Alex's food, you's die, and we's haffta bury yah. Nope, Pops won't like that none," Fletcher said.

"Won't like what?" a deep voice asked making everyone jump.

"Leaping lizards, Pops! You scared us!" Charlie shouted as she gave him a one-armed hug.

"Sorry about that." Emmit smiled. "Good evening, Ms. Walker."

"Fletcher asked Ms. Walker to supper, Daddy," Alexandra said, then kissed him on the cheek.

"Oh?" He shot his youngest daughter a curious glance. "That was awful nice of you, Fletcher. We'd be happy if you'd join us, Ms. Walker."

She'd never seen him in his own element…relaxed. Savannah had to come to grips with the fact that she lied to herself every time he'd come into her office. It wasn't her imagination. The feelings he brought out in her were real. She should go. She should leave right now. Yes, didn't she teach her students to "just say no"? That's why her head was saying no, but her mouth said, "All right, thanks." Savannah was so surprised she almost missed the high five between Charlie and Alexandra.

Emmit studied the group a moment, then shuffled them all into the house.

"Why did you think I'd be mad for inviting Ms. Walker to supper?" he asked the girls.

"Oh, because they hadn't asked you for permission," Savannah supplied. Charlie and Alexandra smiled, Fletcher snorted, and Casey's lips twitched.

"That's okay then. Why don't you girls show Ms. Walker around while I wash up?"

"It's Savannah, Mr. McKay."

Emmit regarded her a moment, then nodded. "Most people call me Pops or McKay," he said, shrugging.

"Oh, okay," Savannah replied, tearing her eyes away from his powerful shoulders. Her cheeks heated.

"His first name's Emmit, though," Charlie said. "May we call you Savannah too?"

"Yes, of course."

Emmit glared at Charlie and cleared his throat. "Or call me Emmit, if you'd rather." He turned on his heel and left them to stare at his back. Savannah was pretty sure she heard him say "God, save me from females" as he walked away.

"Why do you call your dad 'Pops'?" Savannah asked the girls.

"He is our Pops," Casey said. "It's just like saying dad. Other people call him that 'cause it was his nickname in the FBI." If Savannah didn't know better, and of course she did, she would have described Casey's tone as prissy.

"FBI?"

Fletcher said, "Yep, he was a sharpshooter; you's know the noise of a gun going off makes a kinda pop-pop-pop sound. He was an agent, and then he got shot and almost died, but hey, the FBI—ouch! You's pissant, whatcha hit me for?" Fletcher asked Casey, who snatched Fletcher's hand before she could retaliate. Casey used her free hand to cover her sister's rambling mouth.

"Casey, let your sister go. You're hurting her!"

Savannah demanded. Her brain was going a hundred miles an hour trying to absorb everything Fletcher had said. FBI agent? Shot? It all sounded outlandish. She eyed Casey, who reluctantly let her sister go.

"Did your father tell you those things?"

"You calling my sister a liar?" Casey asked with narrowed eyes.

Savannah shook her head.

"You calling my Pops a liar then?"

"Jeez, Casey, give her a break. She didn't call anyone a liar. You're just overreacting as always," Charlie snapped.

Alexandra sighed dramatically, halting Casey who'd stepped toward Charlie, and said, "The truth can be stranger than fiction. Our father is a private man, Ms. Savannah, and Fletcher is proud of him. Sometimes pride blinds us...or in my sister's case, makes her lips loosen." She smiled at Savannah, who understood what was not being said—mind your own business.

"Exactly!" Charlie said. "Now...Casey, you come help me in the kitchen, Fletcher, you go wash up, and, Alexandra, Pops wanted us to show Savannah around...that means you."

Chapter Nine

Savannah followed Alexandra as she gave her the grand tour. It was obvious she excelled at being her father's little hostess. The angry whispers coming from the kitchen made it difficult for Savannah not to think about the "information slip." She nodded at Alexandra, who was talking a mile a minute, and tried to give the girl her full attention.

The house was comfortable with natural colors. The furniture was wood-framed, with overstuffed cushions making it cozy. There was a study with a multitude of books, and the den held a deluxe-size entertainment center with more films than Savannah had ever seen in one place.

"Charlie's addicted to movies. She can quote from just about any one of them. It's almost scary."

"Your home is lovely, Alexandra." Savannah would have decorated exactly the same way if it was her house. Alexandra beamed.

"Why, thank you, Ms. Savannah. I did most of the color schemes myself, but when we got Charlie, she added a lot of finishing touches. She has an eye for detail."

"When you *got* Charlie?" Savannah asked, but Alexandra closed up on her and narrowed her eyes to little blue slits. The girl crossed her arms but didn't answer. Something was definitely up, but what?

"So...what's at the back of the house?" Savannah asked, changing the subject.

Alexandra relaxed. "That's Daddy's suite. Well, it's his room, but it's quite large," she said, while leading Savannah to the front of the house. Just as they neared the stairs, Fletcher came barreling down.

"Them's our rooms," Fletcher said on a puff of breath as she jumped the last two steps. Her hair had fallen out of one braid; Savannah reached out and touched it. Fletcher froze, and Alexandra's brow knitted.

"You have beautiful hair, Fletcher," Savannah murmured. Fletcher looked as if she had kicked her, so Savannah dropped her hand.

"It's come out of its trap," Fletcher said, pulling back from Savannah. "I's gots to get Charlie to fix it."

"I'll braid it for you, if you'd like," she offered, not paying attention to the bewildered expression on Alexandra's face.

"If you's wanna." Fletcher stood stock still.

Savannah's fingers moved swiftly and then secured the braid with the band Fletcher held.

"I's can't believe my very own principal trapped my hair," Fletcher whispered, making Savannah smile.

"So"—Savannah took a step back—"all your rooms are upstairs?" Her question got Alexandra's attention.

"Yes, there are five bedrooms and two full baths upstairs," she said, steering Savannah into the next room.

"Yep, Pops calls it the lion's den," Fletcher chimed in, studying the end of her braid.

Savannah inhaled the spicy scent of tacos as she

came into the dining room. There were six chairs, and each place was set Miss Manners perfect. The girls were moving around bringing food to the table.

"Wow! This looks wonderful. You two did all of this?" Savannah glanced between Charlie and Casey. Charlie blushed, and Casey actually smiled. Both of them nodded. "What else can you girls do?"

"We can do just about anything," Casey told her. "Charlie here does most of the cooking and can sew. I can fix anything mechanical. Fletcher can too," Casey said, chest puffed out, then glanced at Alexandra and winced. "And Alexandra cleans like a tornado, best hostess this side of the mountain, and she might not cook, but all the adults say she makes the best coffee, bar none."

Alexandra beamed.

"Amazing!" They were more capable than a lot of adults Savannah knew, but they were awfully young to be weighed down with so much responsibility.

"Yep, we's can all shoot a rifle too, and…*oomph*—" Fletcher stopped when Charlie stepped on her foot. She covered her own mouth and ducked her head.

"What? Your father lets you play with rifles?" Savannah asked. The thought horrified her.

"There's no playing about it," Emmit said, his voice gruff as he stepped into the room. He brought Fletcher to his side and gave her a slight squeeze. "You're an outsider, Savannah, so you don't understand the way we do things here. Boys their age in this town all shoot rifles for protection and for hunting. It may seem odd to a lot of folks that I taught my girls the same as I'd teach a boy. But it's my way of thinking that being female is all the more reason to know how to protect yourself." He remembered they weren't alone and softened a bit. "Now...this meal looks delicious, girls."

They all started taking their seats. "Savannah, do you still want to join us?" Emmit asked. It sounded like a dare to Savannah—or a threat.

"Yes, I'll stay." If it was a dare, fine. She would take it. If it was a threat, well, she would deal with that too. She wasn't afraid of anger. Everyone got mad, and she knew Emmit wouldn't hurt her...physically anyway. What she was concerned about was the peculiar sensation she got when he said her name. That, more than anything else, should have had her running for the door. But here she sat, idiot that she was.

"Pops, here's your coffee," Charlie said. "Savannah, would you like a cup? It's decaf."

"Yes, Charlie, thank you." The coffee was good, Savannah thought, after she'd taken a sip. Better than her own actually. Charlie had put cream and sugar in it too, just the way Savannah liked it. "How did you know how I take my coffee?"

"They have their ways," Emmit told her and patted Casey's back when she choked on her milk.

Things went uphill after that. There was a lot of conversation...more of an inquisition really. Savannah had been asked twenty questions. They weren't the ones she would have expected either. The girls asked her what her house looked like inside, how she had it furnished. What she ate for breakfast and whether she filled her gas tank at half a tank or at empty. Emmit hadn't asked her anything though, which peeved her a bit. The man was too quiet. He let his daughters do the talking for him.

After they finished the meal, Alexandra and Fletcher cleaned up the kitchen, declining Savannah's offer of help. Charlie had kept her busy with recipes, while Casey talked to Emmit about some kind of lock.

Once the kitchen was in order, everyone headed out to the porch. There were four chairs and a huge pile of cushions. The adults took the chairs, while all four girls rested on the cushions.

"The Widow Madison said your ma's dead."

"Casey!" Emmit hissed.

"It's all right. Yes, my mother passed away last spring." She gazed into her mug of coffee.

"What about you's Pops?" Fletcher asked from where she sat.

"Your Pops," Savannah and Emmit said in unison. She looked away when he smiled at her. She felt rewarded, and that made her feel foolish.

"That's what I's said!" Fletcher held up both hands, then dropped back on the cushions with a huff.

Savannah took pity on her and answered. "Father died when I was twelve. It was just me and Mom."

"Sorry about your parents, Savannah. Any kind of loss is painful. We know that better than most, don't we, girls?" Emmit asked. Four girls nodded their heads in the darkness of the porch.

"I've never had a mother," Charlie said. Savannah's brow pinched as Emmit leaned over and rubbed Charlie's hair.

"I thought Mrs. McKay died only three years ago," Savannah said before she could stop herself. She glanced around at the shadowed faces, confused.

"Charlie joined our family five months after Gracie

died," Emmit said.

"Oh." That explained a lot to Savannah. Charlie was adopted. She smiled at Charlie. "It's nothing to be ashamed of, Charlie. I was adopted too," Savannah said. She'd never revealed that to anyone else. She'd been in the dark until she was sixteen. She had to have her birth certificate to get a license, and the truth had come out. It was a painful shock and almost destroyed the relationship she'd had with her mother, but in the end it had only strengthened their bond.

"You's was adopted too!" Fletcher shouted, snapping Savannah out of her memories. All eyes were on her, which she wouldn't have minded if Emmit's hadn't been among them. She controlled the need to squirm.

"Yes, I was adopted as a baby. I didn't find out until I was older."

"We's all adopted," Fletcher got out just before Casey rushed her. "What? It's truth. It ain't like I's lying."

"All of you?" The truth was plain on their faces. Savannah knew the reason they had such a bad rap was because they were adopted. And that pissed her off.

"Gracie couldn't have children, so we decided to adopt," Emmit said.

Savannah smiled, noticing how Charlie and Alexandra clasped hands, while Casey allowed Fletcher to sit in her lap. "I think that's wonderful."

"You do?" Casey said. And by her tone, Savannah knew she was surprised.

"Of course, I do. I know how being adopted feels. But I never would have figured it out without you guys telling me." That was true enough. She knew there was something different about them, but being adopted wouldn't have even been on her top-five guess list. How odd that no one had mentioned it, Savannah thought. Not Kyle or Sadie, not even Mildred.

Emmit looked at his watch. "Well, girls, it's been an eventful evening, and you all have an outing tomorrow with the Judge, so it's best to call it a night."

"Yes, it is getting late," Savannah agreed, rising. "Who's the Judge, if you don't mind me asking?"

"Granddaddy," Alexandra told her. Savannah released the breath she hadn't known she'd been holding.

The girls all said goodnight to Savannah. Emmit told them he'd be up in a few minutes.

"I'll take you to your car," he said quietly and started walking.

"So...FBI, huh? That had to have been something."

"Told you about that, did they?" He chuckled.

"Yes, and about getting shot."

He stopped laughing, glanced over his shoulder toward the house, then back at Savannah.

"Don't be angry with them."

"I'm not; it's the truth. Hard to be angry with the truth." He swiped his hand through his hair and shook his head. "I guess I'm surprised. The girls usually don't open up to strangers; in fact, they're unusually secretive about family history."

"Emmit, I think your daughters are wonderful. A tad wild at times," she said laughing, "but remarkable children." As they approached her Jeep, she stared into his eyes, shivering when he glanced at her mouth. She licked her bottom lip and sensed his body tighten. He bent, she rose.

"I's gots it, I's gots it, Ms. Walker!" Fletcher hollered, jumping off the porch as the two adults put more space between them.

Savannah took a deep breath and turned toward the child. "What have you got, Fletcher?" she asked. Was that her voice? It was husky and a bit breathless. Oh, Lord.

"Van!" Fletcher said, using her hands as if presenting a gift.

"Van?" Savannah parroted.

"Yeah, you's name's Van; it ain't sissy like Savannah. So when we's ain't in school, I's gonna call yah Van." Fletcher was beaming. Savannah laughed and tugged on one of the child's braids.

"Sounds great, Fletcher," she called to Fletcher's back as the child ran inside.

"She likes you. She wouldn't have given you a nickname if she didn't," Emmit said, his tone was flat for some reason.

"I like her too. She's a little rough around the edges, but sweet," Savannah said, still not making eye contact. Chicken that she was. "I know you all have a busy day tomorrow with your father, so…I'll head on home."

"The Judge is, or was, Gracie's father, and I don't go with them."

"I'm sorry. Is it hard for you seeing him?"

"No, it's hard for him to see me. But he loves the girls. He takes them fishing, camping, and hunting. Alex doesn't like most of those things, so he takes her to plays and fancy things so she can dress up. Ever the lady, our Alexandra." He gave a curt bow and smiled.

"Hunting?" Savannah asked, and Emmit's smile

turned into a scowl.

"Of course, that's all you heard!" His fists clenched. "I'll remind you that how I raise my daughters is not your concern! Keep your pert little nose out of my business."

"As you like, Mr. McKay," Savannah spat. "If you would be kind enough to move out of my way, I would be happy to relieve you of my presence." He turned and was back on the porch before she even unlocked the door.

She started her Jeep and pulled out. "That man," she hissed, shaking her head. "Pert little nose?" Savannah mimicked with a whine. "Actually, your daughters are my business, Mr. McKay. I'm their principal!" she shouted. "Of all the nerve!" She was fuming; nevertheless, she admitted to herself that she'd still wanted him to kiss her. "Idiot!"

Sighing, Savannah turned up the stereo, only to hear Stevie Nicks sing "sometimes it's a bitch." Indeed it was.

Chapter Ten

Emmit was painting the attic when someone called his name. It had taken him a week—a few minutes here, a few minutes there—but he was almost finished. He would've been done a few days ago had he not put on another coat of paint. Restlessness had kept him up most nights. Savannah hadn't been here in over a week, but he remembered how she looked sitting at his kitchen table and it made him uneasy. Mainly because she looked like she belonged there. "Doesn't matter," he muttered, then someone called his name again.

"Up here!" he shouted down the attic stairs. Whoever it was either heard him or not, he wasn't inclined to care.

"What in the hell?" Kyle said. Evan was right behind him and stopped dead in his tracks. Evan scratched his head.

"Did you go colorblind, my man?" Evan asked peering around the room. "It's giving me the willies."

Emmit laughed; he didn't like the color much himself. "No, unfortunately I can see it."

"Then why in the hell are you using it? What's it called anyway?"

"It's called plumeria or something like that, some form of purple. And I'm using it because it's what Casey wants up here. She won the drawing."

"Drawing?" Evan wrinkled his brow.

"Oh, God. Not another one." Kyle sounded pained, and Emmit chuckled.

"This house is a blasted democracy. We vote on damn near everything. We voted on the color, but everyone wanted something different. So we did what we always do in this type of situation; we picked from a hat. Casey won." He shrugged. "I have no choice but to adhere to the demands of my daughters." His veto was often overruled by the majority.

"Where are those girls anyway?" Evan asked. "Awful quiet around here."

"Yeah. They're off with the Judge again this weekend."

"What are they up to this time?" Kyle wanted to know. "Hunting? Fishing? Hang-gliding?"

"No, they went shopping." He shrugged as he dipped his brush in the paint can.

"Fletcher too?"

"Yep. I think Charlie talked her into it. Seems she wanted some combat boots, and Charlie told her a store at the mall had them. Needless to say, that's all it took."

"That makes sense," Kyle said as Evan headed back downstairs. "Those girls know not to look a gift horse or Judge in the mouth."

"I guess," Emmit replied, annoyed at his friend's comment. He was on the defensive lately because of that damn woman. And her blasted pink mouth. Can't forget that, can you, Emmit? It was a good thing she was the girls' principal.

As if reading his mind, Kyle asked how the girls were doing in school.

Emmit glanced over his shoulder and grinned. "You mean, when they're not in the principal's office?

You know, I don't get it. Casey and Fletcher are both smart, but they can't stay out of trouble."

"Funny, that's what Savannah said too."

"Who?" Emmit asked, turning fully and taking his time recoating his paintbrush. Emmit knew damn well who Kyle meant. How did his friend, who was only here on the occasional weekend, know her?

"You know, Ms. Walker." Kyle adjusted the cuff on his sleeve. "The principal."

"That's who I thought you meant. How do you know her?" he asked, turning his back to finish painting so Kyle wouldn't see his eyes narrowing.

"Oh, I met her at Ida Mae's last month. We're dating actually," Kyle said and sat down on the floor with a sigh.

"Really?" he said flatly. That two-faced scrap of a woman. Here she had almost kissed him last weekend, and she was seeing one of his closest friends. Two-timing wench. He was about to tell Kyle the truth, when Evan stomped back up the stairs with a case of beer.

"You ain't dating Savannah Walker, Kyle. That's just wishful thinking," Evan said, handing out bottles.

"How do you know?" Kyle asked, twisting the top off his beer.

Evan took a swig and shrugged. "I just do."

"I just do," Kyle mimicked, then shook his head and grinned. "We're not exactly dating, but a guy can hope, right? I mean, you've both seen her. She's fucking beautiful. And that hair…" He put his fist to his mouth and moaned.

Emmit had relaxed, but he was wary. He loved Kyle like a brother, but his friend went through women like Evan went through quarts of oil. He had a feeling

Savannah wouldn't stand to be a notch in Kyle's bedpost. "The girls call her prissy-pants."

"Yeah, but damn, I'd love to get into those pants," Kyle said.

"It ain't gonna happen, buddy," Evan said, finishing his beer.

"You're probably right. Hell, I'm not even here half the time. A man can dream."

Emmit couldn't explain it, but he felt better.

****

Savannah opened the door to her home and rushed in. She had to pee and was afraid she wouldn't make it to the bathroom in time. She had gone out with Kyle again. They had taken a drive into the city to eat at his favorite restaurant, a fancy French restaurant. Savannah wasn't much of a fancy dining person. She had gone to similar places before, and she'd always felt uncomfortable.

Kyle was acting strange too. Okay, she admitted to herself, he had acted like a jerk. No, like the stereotypical male. This was disappointing because she liked Kyle. Unfortunately for both of them, she didn't like him the way he wanted her to. She had a feeling there were very few women who turned him down.

He had kissed her; it was a pleasant kiss, but she didn't kiss him back. He had been a perfect gentleman about it, Savannah remembered, as she washed her hands. But after she told him she just wanted to be friends, he had simply tolerated her, and *that* made him a jerk.

Then he'd patronized her at every turn. That made him typical. Savannah hadn't stopped to go to the restroom because she had just wanted to get home.

"It's a shame," she said to her reflection as someone knocked on her door. Her stomach knotted. Surely Kyle wouldn't have come back.

"Good evening, Savannah," Evan said, bowing dramatically when she opened the door. She pulled him inside laughing.

"What are you doing here?" she asked once they both took a seat on the sofa.

"Checking on yah." He smiled. "I was in the neighborhood and thought I oughta stop in to say hello. Actually, I'm surprised you're here. Thought you had a big date with Kyle." He wiggled his eyebrows, and she smacked him playfully.

"It wasn't a date, big or otherwise," she said, then mumbled, "but you aren't the only one who thought it was."

"That bad, huh?"

Savannah told him what had happened.

"Sorry things worked out like that. Kyle's a sore loser; don't take it personally. Trust me, he'll get over it."

"You think? I wish I did feel something for him, but I don't, you know?"

"You said before there wasn't a spark with Kyle," he reminded her. "Not like McKay."

She pulled back, her brow furrowing. "What are you talking about?" Was she that transparent?

"Don't worry; I don't think he suspects," he admitted, grinning. "I'd probably be bailing the girls out if he did."

"Evan, I like you, but you're being absurd," she scoffed.

"If you say so," he said, as his smile turned into a

deep frown. "I'd take a detour...if you ever get to thinking in that direction. McKay's not gonna return the compliment. He's never dated anyone but Gracie; never even looked at anyone else. So it's probably a good thing you ain't looking down that alley."

She just smirked at him.

"Seen any good school yard fights lately?"

"No, I rarely see anything, except the end results," she said, thankful he'd changed the subject.

They talked until it grew dark, and Evan excused himself. Savannah was about to turn on the lamp by the window when she noticed Evan hadn't left yet. She looked at the main house in time to catch Sadie opening the door and giving Evan a hug before ushering him in. Strange, Evan hadn't mentioned he was going to visit Sadie. She waited until after Sadie had shut the door to turn on the light, then laughed at herself for being silly.

Chapter Eleven

The banging would not stop. Savannah curled farther under the covers, trying to muffle the noise. She couldn't imagine what Sadie was doing. The banging continued. It was a Saturday and the first three-day weekend in November. She deserved some peace and quiet, didn't she? Absolutely, she did. It had been a bad week. No, it had been a terrible week.

The Thomas family came to talk to her about the school. Because Mr. and Mrs. Thomas were often away on business, most of their correspondence had been through clipped phone calls. And most of those had gone through Mildred. Savannah would compare the couple to Barbie and Ken, but she didn't want to insult Barbie. They had sat in her office all blond and fake expecting her to kowtow because they were the self-appointed "it" family in Blue Creek. Ha! That wasn't going to happen. The jerks.

Mildred had warned her, Savannah conceded now, but did she listen? No! She could handle it. And she could have, normally, but it had been a crappy week to start with. Her Jeep had broken down out of the blue, and she had to get Sadie to take her to school. Then the town mechanic, Ward "going to take a few days to get the part" Jessup, told her it looked like she was out of luck. Well, duh! She had asked for Evan, but Evan was out of town. Of all the weeks!

Then she had to deal with those pretentious people. Oh, Mr. and Mrs. Thomas were cultured and polished...but so were snake-skin boots. And when you take away the shiny veneer you're left with the same thing. The snake. This made sense because Ian Thomas was a venomous reptile. He actually hit on her, which was bad enough in itself, but his wife had been *right there*.

And that woman! Savannah pinched the bridge of her nose and got into the shower. If Savannah hadn't known the truth about the McKay girls' situation, all she would have had to do was wait to hear it from Beverly Thomas. That woman had the audacity to ask Savannah if she could see about getting those "McKay disasters" expelled.

"It would be so lovely if those disgraceful children were gone. Everyone could relax. They're all adopted, you know. And *that man* lets them run wild. Gracie is probably rolling over in her grave," Mrs. Thomas had told Savannah.

"Witch," Savannah said into the spray. The nerve! Savannah had expressed her opinion and asked them to leave. She had been polite and professional but barely.

By the time she'd gone to dinner at Ida Mae's, everyone had heard how the new principal had all but given Mr. and Mrs. Thomas the finger. Ha! She wished she'd given them the finger, but she simply asked them—politely—to leave. Savannah *could* have behaved shockingly enough to make that Thomas witch faint. She smiled at the thought and finished rinsing. Oh well, *they* couldn't fire her; she had a contract. The Thomas family might have weight, but they sure couldn't shove her around.

Then Kyle had shown up at Ida's while Savannah was eating. At least he hadn't ignored her. He had come over and spoken to her like a normal human being. But she could tell their friendship would never be the same. She added him to the list of things that were crummy about this past week.

Savannah finished her shower and blow-dried her hair. The thick honey-brown strands fell halfway down her back. She usually wore her hair in a bun or a twist, but today she decided on a braid. She put on jeans and a sweater. She was lacing up her boots when a noise came from the other room. She paused and closed her eyes for a second. Sadie was always coming and going as she pleased.

"Sadie, I'll be out in a minute," she called through her shut door. She walked out of her bedroom, but it wasn't Sadie she found.

"Hello, Ms. Walker...*err*...Ms. Savannah."

"What are you doing here, Alexandra?" Savannah asked, crossing her arms over her chest.

"The Widow Madison sent me over to ask if you would like to come to her home. We're having tea and would like for you to join us," Alexandra said as she studied Savannah.

"I haven't even had breakfast yet," she said, sidestepping the child and going into the kitchen to prepare a pot of coffee. Alexandra followed her.

"That's all right...it comes with it. You know, tea and cakes." Alexandra glanced at her purple watch, then back up at Savannah. "You sleep rather late, don't you? It's almost eleven now. So are you coming?"

"Why not?" It wasn't as if she had a choice. Sadie often asked her to have tea or coffee or dinner or whatever. The woman must think Savannah was incapable of taking care of herself. And Savannah had been up since nine, thanks to the banging, which had stopped.

"What was that noise earlier?" she asked, putting the coffee canister back in the cabinet.

"Daddy was fixing the Widow's porch railing."

And wasn't that perfect? Just what she needed to make her week complete, another encounter with Mr. McKay. Oh, he was always pleasant. But, as her students would say, he acted like she had cooties. Savannah bit her lower lip contemplating an escape.

"Daddy's gone into town for the rest of the day, so it's just us girls," Alexandra said as she peeked around the apartment.

"Where are your sisters?" Savannah inquired, relieved. She wasn't up to seeing that man today.

"They're with Granddaddy. It's the hunting and camping trip this weekend." Alexandra's small shoulders shuddered.

"You don't like either of those things?" she asked as she led Alexandra out the door and down the steps.

"Absolutely not! I am not some Neanderthal brute!"

"I don't blame you, Alexandra; I know *I* wouldn't like roughing it." Savannah wouldn't say anything about hunting. Mr. McKay knew how she felt about it. Alexandra gave her a big smile. "You look nice today," she said, knowing to this child it was important.

Alexandra wore a pink jumper with tights and a cardigan. It was a casual outfit for her. Savannah had heard Alexandra's sisters call her prissy and knew it was because she liked dresses and fixing her hair, which was in its normal bun today.

They walked across the yard from Savannah's apartment to the back of Sadie's house. Savannah inhaled deeply when they got closer. Sadie must have been baking all morning, she thought, smelling the air.

"Good morning, Savannah. I see Alexandra found you," Sadie exclaimed as she opened the porch door.

"Yes, she found me," Savannah said on a sigh.

Sadie had on beige slacks and a light pink blouse open at the collar to showcase a lovely string of pearls. Her gray hair was held back by a barrette, and Savannah was officially underdressed.

"Good, good. Come in, ladies, and let's get started. The pastries are fresh, and the tea smells delightful. Alexandra, darling, you serve," Sadie instructed as they took their seats in the screened-in porch.

The furniture was white wicker, with floral printed cushions, and a fresh flower arrangement had been set on the table. By the time they had finished, Savannah no longer felt like a weed among the roses. "You two outdid yourselves! Everything was excellent."

"Thank you; I'm so pleased you could join us," Sadie said. "Now, Savannah, be a dear and take Alexandra shopping for me. Something came up, and I can't go this afternoon."

"But Widow!" Alexandra cried. Sadie gave the girl a look, and Alexandra sighed. "Can you take me, please, Ms. Savannah? Tomorrow's Daddy's birthday, and I need to pick up his present. It's very important." Her young eyes pleaded.

"Sure, I can take you. I need to run some errands anyway," Savannah said. It was partially true, and she hated to disappoint Alexandra. "But wait, I forgot. I don't have my Jeep."

Sadie said, "Of course you do; Ward dropped it off this morning."

"Really? He told me it was going to take a week or so for the part to come in."

"Yes, well, he said Evan got home last night and had the part with him. Ward knew you needed your vehicle, so he hustled it over here. Ward's a nice man, really. You just have to get to know him." Sadie gave a sidelong glance to Alexandra, who ducked her head.

Savannah shrugged her shoulders and stood. "I guess we should go."

"Let me get you Alexandra's money, dear," Sadie said stepping into the kitchen, then quickly returning with her purse. "Here we are." She pulled out a small pouch and handed it to Savannah. "You girls go on…and have fun!"

****

It was late on Sunday when Emmit pulled into his driveway. His girls had been away for most of the weekend. Though he'd needed the quiet of the last few nights, Emmit was ready for things to be back to normal.

He'd gone out with the guys to celebrate his birthday the night before. It had been a good night. They'd gone to Shmittie's, the only bar in town, and had some beers. They played pool and talked about the old days. At one point, Savannah had been brought up in conversation, which made him tense. Savannah had turned Kyle down. Emmit could tell Kyle was disturbed by the whole thing, but for some reason, it made Emmit puff out his chest with victory. Strange.

He wanted Kyle to be happy, of course, but Emmit

didn't think Savannah was right for his friend. Evan had told him, when they were alone, that Savannah wasn't what she seemed. Evan was always saying shit like that, so Emmit didn't pay much attention. He didn't know how he felt about that particular topic. The woman had too much *advice* to give him about how to raise his girls, and that rankled. He had been glad when they started talking about their jobs.

Emmit hadn't mentioned to his friends that someone had vandalized the side entrance to the hardware store. Luckily, he was the only one who used that particular entrance, so no one else had to read the spray-painted obscenities marring his door. And if Ida had seen it, she would have told him—she would have told everyone, so that wasn't an issue. He'd filed a report with Sheriff Jasper Hart and took a few pictures before he painted the door and cleaned up the mess. These things rarely happened to anyone else in Blue Creek, but for some reason—Emmit shook his head. He wasn't going to dwell on it, not right now.

Tonight, all he wanted to think about was being with his girls, who he had missed these last couple of days. He would never admit it to them; they would only use it to their advantage, and he needed to keep the upper hand. God, he loved those girls. It was almost scary at times. He would die for them. He would do anything for them. A parent's love was like that, he reckoned. Consuming.

He smiled getting out of his SUV. His smile faded as he neared the porch steps. He was expecting shouts and loud voices, but silence greeted him as he opened the door.

"Surprise! Happy birthday!" the group shouted

once he hit the light switch. Each of his girls hugged him and wished him a happy birthday. He'd forgotten they hadn't celebrated it together yet. They were all dolled up; Charlie and Alexandra had on matching dresses while Casey and Fletcher had on jeans and matching sweaters.

"What a nice surprise," he said, touched.

"Fletcher and I made fried chicken, baked potatoes, rolls, and baked beans, and Alexandra fixed the corn on the cob," Charlie told him, winking at the end.

"Alex and me did the decorations and baked the cake," Casey said with a lift of her chin. Emmit bit the inside of his cheek when Alexandra cleared her throat and Casey ignored her.

He shook his head and looked around the room. "You girls did a great job and my favorite supper!" He patted his stomach. "You've outdone yourselves this time, truly." If he was grinning like an idiot, who cared?

"Girls worked real hard all day, McKay. Real hard," Judge J. T. Vaughn said, alerting Emmit to the presence of the other three adults.

"Your little ladies are talented. But you already knew that. Happy birthday," Sadie said standing on tiptoe to kiss his cheek.

"Ms. Savannah helped us too, Daddy," Alexandra said.

"Van's real good at this cra...uh...stuff," Fletcher said with a grin.

Emmit looked at Savannah; her hands were clasped and twisting. Nervous, was she? What had Evan said? Something about...oh hell, he couldn't remember. She was still beautiful, as if that was going to change anytime soon. Her neck was turning red at his stare, and he almost cursed.

"Happy birthday, Emmit," Savannah stammered.

"Thanks," Emmit said, then turned away. Something only had power over you when you let it. He wouldn't let her have any power over him.

"Let's eat," J. T. suggested, taking his seat.

Supper was an event all its own. The girls talked nonstop about their weekends. Cake was served, and the girls demanded Emmit make a wish. Then they insisted he open his presents.

J. T. stood. "This is my time to go I'm afraid," he said. "Happy birthday, McKay, goodnight, girls, Sadie. Nice meeting you, Savannah." After he'd received hugs and high fives from his granddaughters, he left.

"All right, Pops, open 'em," Casey decreed as each of the girls presented him with a gift. Casey and Fletcher had both gotten him action movies, which he loved. Charlie gave him a new coffee mug.

"It's supposed to keep the coffee hot for hours," she explained, pointing to the fine print.

Alexandra, not so demurely, shoved a small box into his hands. "Here, Daddy, open mine!"

Emmit laughed. He opened the package and was surprised to find the pocket watch he thought he had lost. His grandfather had given it to him years ago. Emmit had broken the face a few months back and then misplaced it. But here it was polished and unbroken.

"This is beautiful, Alexandra. Thank you," Emmit murmured. Alexandra laughed and threw her arms around him.

"I love you, Daddy."

Emmit smiled in her hair, inhaling her sweet smell.

"I love you too, sweetheart." Stepping back, he looked at all his girls. "I couldn't have asked for a better birthday. You girls simply amaze me."

"Ahh, it won't nothing, Pops," Fletcher said. "'Sides, we's had help from Van and the Widow."

"Oh, I'm sure you girls are more than capable of handling everything by yourselves. But I was glad to help," Savannah said.

"As much as I appreciate all of this, I know some girls who have to get up early tomorrow morning," Emmit said, waiting for it. Ah, there it was.

"We don't have school tomorrow, Pops. Sheesh, how could you forget?" Casey asked with her head cocked to one side and brows pinched behind her glasses.

"I didn't forget, Case, but if you girls want to go to the shop with me tomorrow, you still have to get up early. Unless, of course, you don't want to go?" He smirked. They all hopped up, said goodnight, and ran upstairs.

"I'll go tuck them in, Emmit, and then be on my way," Sadie said, moving hastily toward the stairs.

Chapter Twelve

Savannah started clearing away wrapping paper and tissue. She and Emmit cleaned together in silence, which he appreciated. He followed her into the kitchen and helped her dump an armload of trash.

"I wanted to thank you again for helping the girls. I know they're not the easiest to get along with," he said, and Savannah looked up at him.

"It's a pleasure. Actually, they're quite entertaining."

"Yeah, that's one way to put it, I guess." His lips quirked as he closed the trash can.

"You've done a great job with them, Emmit. They're more independent than anyone their age. In fact, they're more independent than some people my age. They work as a team. It's truly remarkable." Savannah slipped on her jacket and shouldered her purse.

"The McKays are definitely a team," he agreed. "I'll walk you out." Emmit followed her outside. She'd parked at the side of the house, so he wouldn't catch on to the surprise party.

"So..." she began as she opened the door to her Jeep and set her purse on the backseat. She turned around, giving him a great view of her ass, and pulled out a bag, handing it to him. "Happy birthday, Emmit."

The only people who gave him gifts were his

family. Females who weren't related to him didn't give him presents. He peeked into the bag, curious, feeling sheepish when Savannah laughed at him.

"There isn't anything in there that will bite. I promise. It's not much," she said, shrugging, but she continued to stare at him even when she shoved her hands into the back pockets of her jeans.

Emmit reached into the bag and pulled out a frame. The Jeep's interior light illuminated the pictures. The frame had four small boxes, each containing a picture of one of his daughters. He looked into Savannah's blue eyes.

"I sort of confiscated their school photos." She smirked. "Alexandra said none of the girls had brought their pictures home. Something about her losing a vote three to one. But they are good pictures, so I figured you'd want them."

"A vote, huh? That explains a lot. I asked, and they said they hadn't gotten pictures taken this year." He laughed. "Typical; I should've known." He looked back into Savannah's eyes and inhaled sharply. There was weariness but also desire. He bent his head and brushed his lips across hers. She froze, then let out a small whimper. He pulled back before he did anything they'd both regret. Her eyes were luminous when she opened them.

"Thank you," he said quietly and began to walk back toward the house. Her feet shuffled against the gravel behind him, and though he couldn't be sure, he thought she growled.

"Wait!"

Damn it all! He knew he shouldn't have kissed her, but he couldn't stop himself. God, he knew Kyle had wanted her, and Emmit didn't poach. What was he supposed to have done? Her mouth was pink and luscious, and damn it, he'd had to take a taste. Just once. Now he was going to hear all about it.

"I'm sorry. I shouldn't have done that," he said, and her eyes widened.

"Sorry, are you?" She circled around him and shoved him back toward her Jeep.

Emmit flinched as he backed up a few steps. He used to be real good at this man-woman stuff. Hadn't he? Hell, this was probably going to be the tongue-lashing he deserved.

"I'll show you sorry." And then she attacked him.

Emmit was taken aback for a second after she latched onto his ears and attached her mouth to his. Blood rang in his head, and his body reacted before his mind could.

Still holding the bag with one hand, he wrapped his arms around Savannah's waist as her arms slid around his neck. He lifted her up effortlessly; she wrapped her legs around his waist, and he walked them the few steps to the Jeep. When she moaned softly, he deepened the kiss, sucking on her tongue. His free hand found its way to her hair to hold her in place.

Somehow, he moved them to the hood of the Jeep, and he was between her legs moving against her. Her nails scraped against his scalp, and he tightened his hold.

Emmit was so hard he could feel the teeth of his zipper biting at him. He had never wanted someone this much. Never, and it scared the shit out of him. That cleared his muddled brain like nothing else. He started pulling away. Distance.

He exhaled a shaky breath, and Savannah rested her head on his chest. Her hands dropped from his shirt to her sides. Her legs were still wrapped around him, and it may have been his imagination, but he was sure he could feel her heat.

"I guess I'm not sorry," he admitted as he lifted her chin. Her eyes were glazed and her lips swollen. She was a wild cat; he needed to remember that.

"Thank you for small favors." She snorted. "Or not so small in this case," she said, looking down between them with a smirk.

Emmit broke contact and stepped back, rubbing his face with his hands. He had put the gift she'd given him on the hood of the Jeep behind her. He'd wait to get it.

"Look," he began.

"No, you look!" She held up a finger, jumped down, and shoved his gift into his hands. "We want each other; there's nothing wrong with that. We're both consenting adults, Emmit. Just because I work with children does not make me a child. I'm a big girl, and I know what I want. And for some stupid reason I want you!"

"Well, good. Great. How wonderful for you. But welcome to the real world, darling; we don't always get what we want. Trust me, this can't go anywhere. Dead ends and all that," Emmit said, tasting the bitterness of his words while gripping the bag.

"Do you know how annoying you are?" she said, pointing at him, then turning and stomping her foot.

"Yeah, maybe, but at least I'm not fooling myself here. What just happened—"

"If you dare say that kiss was a mistake, so help me I will get pissed."

"What about Kyle?"

"What about him?" she growled.

"He's one of my closest friends," Emmit reminded her.

"What does that have to do with anything?" She shook her head. "There's nothing between me and Kyle, and if he told you differently, then he's delusional." She tugged at her ponytail. "You want the facts, fine. We went out a few times; I was assuming it was just as friends. He apparently wanted something else. He kissed me, I didn't kiss him back, and then I told him what I thought had been clear. I didn't want a relationship with him, and all I had been offering was friendship. Is that clear to you? How's this…I. Do. Not. Want. Kyle. Ruthie." She stomped her foot. "Maybe I should print up a billboard for him, so he'll get the point."

"No, you made it perfectly clear. But even with Kyle not being an obstacle, I have four daughters, who in case you have forgotten are *your students*. And those girls up there are not stupid or blind. Hell, they know things before I do, and trust me, they would figure out something was going on between us. And if they didn't like it, there would be hell to pay." They would hate her; they'd be pissed at him too. Not to mention Kyle, but he wouldn't mention it ever again, not to her anyway.

"I didn't say you didn't have a point, Emmit. I had hoped…" She shrugged. "I don't know what I had hoped for."

"I'm sorry, Savannah, more sorry than I can say."

"Me too," she said and got into her Jeep with a shake of her head.

Emmit stood there until the taillights faded. He kicked the dirt with his foot. He wanted her; the evidence was still straining in his jeans. He'd been honest though; he didn't have anything to give her other than the physical. He knew Savannah deserved more, but he didn't have enough of a heart left. If sex was all she wanted, she could have had Kyle, easily. But she didn't want Kyle, she wanted him. It flattered him, and part of Emmit wished he could take the chance, but he couldn't.

He loved his girls, and that was enough, had to be enough. Even if he could afford to care about Savannah, he couldn't trust his emotions. Emmit felt like shit, but he knew things would be better this way. Gracie had left a hole inside him, and there were things he had to remember, truths he couldn't let himself forget. He gazed up at the stars and tried to find peace.

Chapter Thirteen

On Monday of the following week, Savannah was still trying to figure out why she couldn't shake her anger. She wasn't so blinded by lust that she wasn't aware a relationship with Emmit would not only be difficult but also a considerable lapse in judgment professionally. That didn't mean he needed to think so too…or shove it in her face.

She hadn't been in the man's presence for a week, and for lack of a better description, Savannah felt cheated. Being in the same room with Emmit made her heart beat faster and she tingled, for goodness sake! It was more likely than not a good thing they hadn't seen each other. Savannah would have punched him for breathing because as much as she wanted him, she knew he was right. The jerk.

Savannah may not have seen Mr. McKay, but she had seen his daughters. There was no avoiding them. First thing last Tuesday morning, Charlie came to her office with a basketful of muffins. Savannah couldn't help but smile; Charlie could make a guard at Buckingham Palace smile. The child was the definition of a mother hen. She wasn't capable of *not* taking care of those around her. And her culinary skills were superb.

On Wednesday, Alexandra had shown up. She wanted Savannah's advice on the new clothes she'd gotten when she went shopping with the Widow. She was told the outfit was meant to mix and match to make several different ensembles. The girl had a typed list cataloging all of her clothes to give Savannah a better idea of what she was working with.

Savannah shook her head. She was a principal, not a fashion consultant. But she hadn't wanted to hurt the child's feelings, so she made some suggestions. Alexandra had been pleased, so her recommendations couldn't have been all bad.

The strangest visit had come late that Friday afternoon; she had been home at the time. Fletcher showed up with twenty questions, asking about all of Savannah's favorite things, what she liked and what she didn't.

Fletcher walked around the apartment making note of everything. If Savannah didn't know better, she would have thought Fletcher was casing the joint, as they said on TV cop shows. She had focused especially on Savannah's movie collection. "Holy shit! You's gots the *Murder, She Wrote* shows!"

"Um, well, you probably shouldn't use those exact words, but yes, it's my favorite show."

Fletcher thought about it and nodded. "Hells bells, Van; you's gots 'em all!"

Savannah had controlled her laughter, but the child's enthusiasm was infectious.

"I's gots 'em all too," Fletcher had announced. "Yep, gots the VCR programmed."

"Really? Well, we can watch one if you like." Fletcher pursed her lips for a moment, and her excitement faded. As it happened, she had a previous engagement to attend to.

Even one of Emmit's best friends paid her a visit. Evan, the sweetheart, had come to see her. He had an uncanny sense of knowing when something was wrong. Evan said he'd been told he had a gift for listening, and people were drawn to it like wheels to an open road.

That being the case, she'd swallowed her pride and told him the truth. He hadn't even said, "I told you so." But he had hinted it was for the best. Maybe Evan was right, but it still irritated her.

So here Savannah sat, three days after her last visitor, and she was still pissed at Emmit. Not his girls though. She sighed and began packing her briefcase. The only McKay girl who hadn't visited her was Casey. The oldest McKay avoided her like the plague. Just like her father, Savannah mused.

"Are you leaving for the day?" Mildred asked from the doorway, shifting from side to side. Savannah looked up. There was a child behind Mildred.

"Yes, in a bit. Who's behind you?" Mildred was startled and narrowed her eyes as she turned around. Fletcher stood there trying to hide the tears running down her flushed cheeks.

"Well, Miss McKay, what's happened?" Mildred asked, her hands on her hips.

"Nothing. I's ain't done nothing. I's gotta talk to Van," she said, crossing her arms over her chest.

"Van?" Mildred repeated.

"Ms. Walker's what I's meant."

"Fine, go on in," Mildred said.

Savannah could hear Mildred mumble, "Van, is it?" as she turned to leave.

"What's wrong, Fletcher?" Savannah asked, squatting down in front of the child.

"Casey ain't talking to me. And I's swear I's didn't do nothing. I's swear on my underwear, I's didn't. But she ain't talking to me." Fletcher blinked back tears and chewed on her lower lip.

Savannah placed a hand on her shoulder, and the child shuddered. "Do you want me to find Charlie or Alexandra? Do want me to talk to her?"

"She ain't talking to them neither."

"Okay, so she's not talking to any of you?" Savannah asked, making sure she got it right.

"Her not talking to them's okay; she does that a lot. They gets on her nerves. But she ain't never not talked to me."

Savannah didn't even attempt to make grammatical sense out of that, instead she asked, "Did you two argue?" She shifted to her knees and dropped her hands to her side. Fletcher took it as an invitation and flung her arms around Savannah. She froze for a second, surprised by the action, then hugged Fletcher back. There were rules about showing affection toward students, but how could she not?

Fletcher said into Savannah's neck, "You's gonna try talking to Casey, ain't yah, Van? 'Cause Charlie said if I came to getcha, you's help."

She pulled back to look at Fletcher. "I'll try. Where is she?"

"She's in the bathroom," Fletcher said and pointed to the watch on her wrist as Savannah stood.

"What is it?" she asked, staring at the watch.

Fletcher gave her a funny look and said, "It's grown-up code for time's a wastin', right?"

Savannah bit her lip. "Right...well, let's go."

They started down the darkened hallway. It was

late in the afternoon, and most everyone had left the building. The school smelled like cleanser and the hotdogs they'd made in the cafeteria today. The art class had designed an imaginative new bulletin board, and she made a mental note to congratulate Mrs. Fields, the art teacher, on a job well done. The building itself was old but in good shape. Savannah didn't say anything, just concentrated on the squeak of Fletcher's rubber boots.

Charlie and Alexandra were guarding the door to the girls' restroom. These two always matched each other in some way. They were basically the same age. Charlie was a month or so older if one wished to be technical. They stood as a unit awaiting Savannah's arrival.

"Good, you found her," Charlie huffed as she checked her pink watch. "Savannah, you talk to Casey. I have to get home and start supper. Fletcher, Alex, you guys come with me."

"I's ain't leaving." Fletcher stomped her boot-clad foot.

"Fletcher, get over it," Alexandra said. "One of us acting like an ass is enough for one day. Ms. Savannah, you'll bring Casey home, won't you?"

Savannah noted that Alexandra wasn't really asking. In fact, she was taken aback for a moment. She had never heard Alexandra speak that way. Given there weren't any other adults present, she let the language slide this time. Charlie had once told Savannah there was an "Alex side" of Alexandra; this must be it.

Savannah cleared her throat and said, "Sure. You girls head home before your father gets there."

Fletcher tried to rush into the bathroom, but her

sisters grabbed her. Charlie had one arm, and Alexandra had the other. They dragged Fletcher away. Savannah waited until they were out of sight before taking a breath, then went into the bathroom. What did women do before they had restrooms to hide out in? She couldn't see herself holed up in an outhouse.

The profound smell of bleach told Savannah the pink tiles and gray stall doors had been cleaned recently. There were five stalls, and one of them muffled sniffles. She ducked down searching for feet. She wasn't really surprised when she didn't see any.

"Casey? It's Savannah. Can we talk?"

An angry voice came from the middle stall. "Those traitors! Why in tarnation did they get you?"

"You wouldn't talk to any of them, so they came and got me. They went home. Charlie had to start supper."

****

From inside the stall, Casey put her feet down and peeked through the cracks. She could see the tan slacks and burgundy sweater the prissy principal was wearing. Why did it have to be her? It didn't matter to Casey the Widow said she truly cared for this woman; what mattered was Savannah liked her Pops. Really liked him and wanted him for her own. Casey wasn't stupid; she could tell. Women always wanted to get their red claws in her Pops. He never noticed. But this one was different. She made Casey feel funny inside, not like she was going to puke, but like she'd been locked in the Ward's garage with all the fumes.

Sure, Savannah seemed nice and fair, but Casey knew you couldn't trust that. People were good liars, fancy women especially, women who wanted her Pops even more so. Casey had experience with liars. She wouldn't tell Pops though; she handled things her own way. But right now she felt like an idiot girl. How in the hell did Alexandra live like this?

Savannah was tapping her foot. "Casey? Do you want to tell me what's wrong? Do you want me to call your father?"

"Hell no!"

"If you don't want me to call him, you have to talk to me."

"Fine! I got my period. Happy now?" Damn, this was embarrassing.

"Oh, Casey, that's great."

"How the hell is it great? I'm bleeding like a stuck pig." Which just didn't seem right to her. "How am I supposed to go anywhere? Great, my ass!"

"You'll be fine, Casey. It's nothing to worry about. Women have been going through this since the beginning of time." There was a pause. "Do you have gym clothes here?"

"Yeah, in the girls' locker room," Casey answered. Her grade had lockers. The teachers said it was to prepare them for high school, but Casey figured it was because they gave them so much work it wouldn't fit into their desks. She told Savannah the locker number and combination.

"All right, sit tight; I'll go get them."

"Where the hell am I gonna go?" Casey rolled her eyes. This woman was a piece of work. It didn't take long before she came back.

"Your gym clothes are pretty clean," Savannah said as she handed them under the stall door.

"Alex makes us wash them twice a week." Casey

looked cross-eyed at the slim package she'd been given.

Casey sat there mortified while Savannah explained what to do with the maxi pad. Why had her sisters picked this woman—of all people? Sighing, she did what she'd been instructed to do.

Beet red, she came out of her stall holding her jeans in a roll. Savannah pushed off the wall she was leaning against and handed Casey a plastic bag. Casey put the jeans in the bag and washed her hands and face, watching the woman out of the corner of her eye.

"Thanks," she said tightly.

"You're welcome. I'll give you a ride home. It's starting to get dark, and the temperature's dropping."

Casey took a deep breath and closed her eyes tight. She felt like crying, and she never cried. Never. She didn't want this female thing. She didn't want to be a woman; she wanted to be a kid, to just be Casey. Most of all she didn't want to like this prissy principal. She wouldn't let herself like her.

"That's fine."

"Good, I'm going to grab my briefcase and meet you by my Jeep."

The vehicle was silent as they headed home. Casey stared out the window pushing her glasses up after a few minutes. Her stomach churned when Savannah stopped at Dot's drug store.

"What are we stopping for?" She wanted this day to end. Was that too much to ask?

"You're going to need supplies for the duration of your period. It usually lasts anywhere from three to seven days, but everybody's different. I thought it'd be easier to pick them up now." Savannah cleared her throat. "I figured it would be better for me to do it this time than your dad."

"Oh." Casey hid her gratitude with a shrug. She should have known. They had talked about this kind of thing in Family Life class. Casey hadn't paid attention because she never thought it would happen to her.

"Do you want to come with me or wait here?"

No way was she going into that store, Casey thought, as Savannah started to get out of the Jeep. No way in hell. "I'll stay."

It only took minutes for Savannah to come back. She handed Casey the paper sack. Casey held onto it as though it was a bag of snakes.

"You know, you're going to have to tell your father, Casey," she said softly when they turned into the driveway. "It's a fact of life; nothing to be embarrassed about."

"Damn it, I know that, it's just…well…oh hell, I don't know," Casey stammered, pushing her glasses up on her nose. "You don't understand." Savannah's fingers tightened on the steering wheel.

"Why don't you explain it to me then?" Savannah offered when they came to a stop.

Anger swelled inside her. "Do me a favor, and don't pretend you care. I know sure as shootin' you don't give a damn. You may have everyone else fooled, but not me. You get that? Never me!"

Savannah frowned. "What are you talking about?"

"All I'm saying is that you shouldn't act like you care about us when what you really care about is getting your claws into Pops," Casey shouted while pointing her finger at Savannah. "But go ahead and pretend. I'll make sure he sees you for what you really are." Casey grabbed the door handle, anger heating her cheeks.

"Truth is, you're a no-good lying bitch just like all the other whores," she spat and jumped out of the Jeep.

The driver-side door slammed, and the gravel crunched under Savannah's feet. Casey spun around when the woman grabbed her shoulder. "Excuse me?" Savannah shouted. "Do you want to repeat that?"

Casey narrowed her eyes, glancing briefly at her sisters, who had come out on the porch. She glared at Savannah, blood pumping through her veins. She tried to shrug off her hand, but the principal held firm.

"First off, you are twelve years old. Show some respect! I know for a fact you were raised better. Second, you don't know me all that well, Casey McKay, and if you think you can say those things to me, I'll tell you right now you have another think coming."

"What's going on?" Charlie asked.

"Yeah, what in tarnation is all the yelling about?" Fletcher put in, then, "You's best be unhanding my sister, Ms. Walker, 'cause we's don't like it."

"You three go back inside and stay out of this. It's between Casey and me," Savannah said with the same calm that Pops got when he was angry. That just made Casey more upset.

"You can't tell my sisters what to do! This is our property," Casey sneered at her.

"Savannah, I don't know what Casey said, but I'm sure she didn't mean it," Charlie said. Her brown eyes were wide and watchful.

"'Course I meant what I said. Every word. I wouldn't have said it otherwise."

"Fine! You two fight it out. Acting like ninnies. Alex and I don't want any part of it," Charlie said. She grabbed Alexandra's hand, and they headed for the door.

"I's ain't leaving," Fletcher announced, crossing her arms and widening her stance.

"Stay then," Savannah said, letting go of Casey's shoulder and rubbing her forehead. "I don't know what I ever did to you to make you feel this way, Casey, and I'm sorry you don't like me. But to tell you the honest to God truth, I don't like you much right now either." She started to pace.

Casey was glad Savannah didn't see her flinch, but by the way Fletcher's eyes went wide, she knew her sister had. She stood straighter and said, "That's fine, I don't care if you like me or not. You're not the first and won't be the last." She took a breath trying to get hold of the emotions that were threatening to overrun her. "You make sure you stay the hell away from this house," Casey whispered. She hadn't known Savannah saying she didn't like her would hurt. Her heart had pinched. She turned on her heel and started for the porch, lost in her thoughts.

****

Savannah stared at Casey's retreating back. She was shaking. She bent down and put her hands on her knees, trying to get control of her breathing. What had just happened? Things had been going well and then *wham*! She rubbed her temples as she straightened and faced the only child that remained.

Fletcher rocked back on her heels and let out a whistle. "Well, you's done it now!"

Savannah shut her eyes for a second, then looked at Fletcher and raised a brow.

"Yep, you's done stepped right in it." Fletcher

shook her head, bending down to pick up the paper sack Casey had thrown down. She straightened to look at Savannah.

"What? God, would somebody please tell me what I did?" Savannah shouted. Now she was asking a nine-year-old for advice!

"Huh?" Fletcher scratched her head. "I's don't rightly know whatcha did exactly. But Casey ain't ever been so disrespectful to an adult. Not countin' the Judge. But that was called for. I's reckon you's said something awful."

"But I didn't! And she called me…well, never mind what she said." Great, now she was whining. "Fletcher, please have your father call me when he gets home, okay?" She didn't wait for an answer; she just left.

Chapter Fourteen

"*You did what?*" Emmit rarely raised his voice, but he had not had a good day. Someone had thrown a rock through the front window of the hardware store. He'd spent all afternoon replacing the glass. After the break-in a couple years ago, there hadn't been another incident, but in the last three months, there had been a number of disturbances—too many for his peace of mind.

Sheriff Jasper Hart was looking into it. "Nothing we can do, McKay," he'd said. "No prints, no witnesses, no nothing. I think you should get that camera we were talking about."

The sheriff had offered to have patrol cars drive by more often, but that was as good as Emmit was going to get. He hadn't told Jasper he'd put in a camera after the break-in or that you couldn't make out anyone in the footage.

Emmit was a patient man, but three months of this ongoing crap was enough. He didn't think he could put up with it much longer, and he was seriously considering installing a security system.

Then, to top it off, Kyle had come by, and Emmit opened his damn mouth. He'd told his lifelong friend about Savannah. He had been shocked when Kyle laughed at him. "Emmit, don't let me stop you. She was right; there wasn't anything between us. I wanted it to be different. You know how I am when I get an idea stuck in my brain. Hell, I *am* a lawyer. We talk things to death."

Emmit was relieved, but to his mind, even having his friend's approval didn't change the situation with his girls. Now this. Home five minutes and all hell breaks loose. Apparently, Casey had had a knock-down drag-out argument with Savannah, which of course made no sense to him.

"She deserved every word. She's as fake as a three-dollar bill, Pops! Acting like she cares, trying to be nice to us, and it's all to get closer to you. I seen it. Don't you try to lie to me neither," Casey shouted, while pointing her finger at him.

He mulled over what she was saying. He didn't think Savannah was dishonest. In fact, he was quite certain she was the bluntest person he knew. He almost smiled, thinking Kyle could back him up on that. As for her trying to get closer to him, well, he hadn't thought they had been that obvious, but Casey had always been observant. Too much so.

"See, he isn't denying it," Casey pointed out to her sisters as she crossed her arms over her chest.

"What do you want me to say, Casey? You're acting like a two-year-old." That shut her up. Great. Now he was the bad guy. He stared at the ceiling and counted to ten. He looked back down to accusing violet eyes and shook his head. He would not back down.

"I told you your bad mouth would get you in trouble someday, and sure enough, it has," Alexandra told Casey using the door as a shield.

"What exactly did you say to Savannah?" Emmit asked again and was met with silence. "Fine! Casey, if you don't want to tell me what you said, that's your choice. Go to the guest room, and stay there until supper's ready. And you can go straight back there when you're finished and not come down, or go to your own room until you're ready to talk."

The guest room was empty except for the usual furniture, so sending her there was a far worse punishment than making her go to her own room. He had expected an argument and was surprised when his oldest daughter turned and went upstairs. Fletcher was hot on her heels.

"Fletcher, you stay down here, young lady," he said sternly. Fletcher stopped dead in her tracks. She turned and glared at him as if he'd grown two heads. He sighed; in for a penny…"You heard me. Casey needs to be alone to think about her actions."

Fletcher shifted on the steps, looked up the stairs, and then headed into the kitchen. Emmit went in the den and sat on the couch. Charlie crawled up next to him, whether to get comfort or give it, he wasn't certain. Alexandra stood studying him in the way that made uncomfortable, then turned to answer the door after someone knocked.

"You had to do it. I know you feel bad, but trust me she'll get over it," Charlie said. Emmit hugged her and kissed her temple. "I have to finish supper. It's running late tonight."

"I wish you'd let me cook once in a while, Charlie. I'm not that bad in the kitchen."

Charlie snorted. "I've got it under control, Pops." She patted his hand and went into the kitchen.

"Sometimes I wonder who the parent is," Emmit murmured, resting his head in his hands.

"She can't help it really. She's a mother hen."

Emmit's head whipped up, and there she stood, the bane of his existence. The cause of this ruckus. Her honey-brown hair was in the same kind of bun Alexandra always wore. Her face was scrubbed; she would have looked like a kid had her jeans and sweatshirt not been so snug. There was no denying she was a woman. He rose from the couch.

"Hello, Savannah. Heard you had a bit of excitement in my driveway this afternoon."

Savannah sighed. "Oh, that's an understatement and partly why I stopped by. I asked Fletcher to have you call me and got tired of waiting."

Emmit shot a quick glance toward the kitchen and caught the sight of a lone brown braid as it flew behind the closing door. "Did you?"

"Yes, obviously the message was lost." She took a breath and put her hands in her back pockets as she stood in the doorway. "Did Casey tell you what happened?"

"No, she wouldn't tell me. But I'm sure you will." He sat back down at her brisk nod. He didn't have a good feeling about this.

"She said and I quote, 'You're a no-good, lying bitch like the other whores.' End quote."

"Excuse me?" He didn't want to believe it, but the clenching of his gut told him she was telling the truth.

"You heard me, Emmit," she said, coming farther into the room. "As you can imagine, I was quite shocked."

"Savannah, I'm sorry. I don't know what else to say." Emmit held up both hands, then let them drop. "Casey's never acted like this before, I promise you. I don't expect you to understand when I don't." He had picked up on the fact that Savannah rubbed Casey wrong, but he hadn't known to what extent. Unfortunately, he was getting the idea.

"I believe you, but it's not you who needs to be sorry. Besides, that's only half the reason I came out here," Savannah said, sighing.

What now? He couldn't take much more.

"The other reason I wanted you to call me was because Casey started her period today, and I thought you should know. I picked up some feminine products at the store before I brought her home," Savannah said, trying to smile but failing. Emmit rose toward her when hurt filled her eyes.

"Savannah," he said gently. He wouldn't even think about the other. Periods and PMS were not his favorite topics.

She held up a hand. "Don't. You were right; those girls are observant. They could tell we were attracted to one another, at least Casey could. She has some wild idea I only pretend to care about her and her sisters to get to you, which is pretty twisted for a twelve-year-old. You might want to find out why she thinks that way."

Savannah took a deep breath and went on. "But she's wrong, you know, not about the attraction part, of course. But you knew that. Rather about the part where I would use them to get to you. You see, the truth is I like your daughters a lot. Probably more than I should, given I'm their principal. Even though I know there could be something good between us, I would rather have your daughters' friendship and respect than try for something that, as you said yourself, would never go anywhere."

She stood straighter. "I think it would be best if we end any relationship between us that's not professional. For Casey's sake and my own. If the girls want to see me, that's fine. They know where to find me."

"Savannah, I don't know what to say." And he didn't. He'd just lost something precious, but he couldn't define what. Emmit stood there, hands by his sides, staring at her.

"You don't have to say anything, Mr. McKay. I've said more than enough for both of us. As I've mentioned, I would appreciate it if, from this point on, our relationship is strictly parent-teacher…I mean, principal." She turned and started for the door only to stop and turn back.

Emmit swallowed, hating the absolute sorrow in her liquid eyes. His own eyes flared as she walked toward him.

Taking a breath, Savannah put her hands on his shoulders and stood on tiptoe to touch her mouth to his. He could feel the slightest wisp of her lips as she made to move away. Emmit caressed her cheek, using his fingers to hold her in place so he could kiss her back. Time stood still while their lips met and tongues savored. A choked sound came from Savannah's throat, and she backed away. She rested her head on Emmit's chest, not looking at him. Her breath was feather light against his shirt, and he closed his eyes until she shifted. She didn't say a word, just bowed her head, and walked quickly away.

Emmit stared after her, not moving until her tires pulled out on the gravel drive. He sat down and rubbed his hands over his face. He'd gotten what he wanted, hadn't he? She was out of their lives for the most part. Why did he feel hollow all of a sudden? It wasn't worth thinking about. He had a bigger problem…Casey.

He marched toward the staircase intending to confront his oldest. Emmit came to a halt. The girl in question was sitting on the stairs. Her glasses were fogged, and her nose was running, but no tears fell. His daughter never cried. He sat down next to her on the steps and waited.

"I guess you know," Casey said, avoiding his eyes.

"Reckon I do, Case. I've got to ask you, though, are you upset because of what you said or because of what you just heard her say?"

"Both, I guess." She wiped her nose on her sleeve, then took off her glasses and cleaned the lenses. "And I guess I feel bad for you too, Pops. I know you liked her," she said, still unwilling to look at him.

Emmit fixed that by turning and lifting her chin to face him. He gazed into her guarded eyes. "Casey, I didn't think I needed to say it, but I guess I was mistaken. Nothing and no one will ever come between us. No one could break up this family. No woman could ever mean as much to me as you and your sisters. I wouldn't let it happen."

"Except Gracie, right, Emmit?" she said, jerking her chin out of his grasp but still looking him in the eye. "You loved her more than anything. Even us." Casey's voice was full of venom. Emmit was shaken by her words. He took a deep breath and stood in front of her. She peered up at him.

"What Gracie and I had was different from the love I have for you and your sisters."

"She was a liar. I hated her. I'm glad she's dead!"

It happened too fast to stop it. Emmit's hand came up and popped Casey right in the mouth. It made a sharp smacking noise, alerting Emmit to what he'd done. He had never hit the girls. He hadn't even spanked them.

He stood stock still while Casey covered her mouth with a trembling hand. They both looked toward the kitchen when there was a small gasp. And there were the rest of the McKay girls. Alexandra's eyes were huge; one hand covered her mouth while the other clutched Charlie's arm. Charlie's mouth hung open, her lips moving but nothing coming out. Fletcher stood there trying to swallow.

"You three go back into the kitchen."

No one moved.

"Now!"

They tripped over each other to leave the room.

Emmit looked back to Casey, whose face was red and eyes filled with hurt. "I'm sorry, Casey. I didn't mean to hit you. You know I would never hurt you. It's just…damn it, Casey, how could you? How could you say those things to me? How could you be that cruel? To me and your sisters and Savannah too? Please explain it to me because I sure as hell don't understand."

Emmit felt like the lowest son of a bitch. She deserved reprimanding, but she didn't deserve to be smacked. He would grovel later, but right now he needed answers. If this was some kind of new PMS, he didn't think he could handle it.

"The truth hurts," was all she said before she walked back upstairs, leaving Emmit to his own thoughts and his other daughters.

Chapter Fifteen

Savannah drove around for hours. She had stopped by Evan's, but he wasn't there so, she continued driving. She was more angry than hurt one moment, more hurt than angry the next. She felt stupid for that, and she hated feeling stupid. She'd been desperate, too, which was embarrassing.

Why had she kissed him? "A bit dramatic, don't you think, Savannah Francis?" she said to the Jeep's interior. All in all she had done the right thing. She was twenty-eight, not some silly teenager.

She wanted him, but he was right, people didn't always get what they wanted. He wanted her too, physically at least. "Damn straight." At least he hadn't thrown what she had termed "the Kyle incident" in her face again.

Back home, Savannah pulled into her self-appointed parking space and slammed the door to her Jeep. It felt so good she unlocked it and slammed it again. But the tension didn't ease.

She had meant what she said. The girls did come first. How do you fall in love with children so easily? Savannah stopped in her tracks. She loved those girls. Damn it, she loved them as if they were hers.

It had torn her apart inside when Casey made those hateful accusations. She loved them. Charlie with her sweetness and peace-keeping antics. Alexandra for trying to always be a lady and for having the "Alex" side too. She loved Fletcher's spirit and loyalty. Though Savannah would never admit it out loud, she even loved the fighter in Fletcher.

And God help her, she loved Casey. Just admitting it to herself made Savannah either insane or a glutton for punishment, she didn't know which, considering Casey hated her. The eat-shit attitude and protective instincts were the very things she loved about Casey.

She loved them for who they were inside and out, even if she didn't understand all of it. The protectiveness, mothering, hair-trigger tempers, bad mouths, and prissiness were things she saw not only in them, but in herself. Savannah wasn't vain, but she liked herself; it was only natural to love people like herself. Right?

As she made her way up the stairs, she decided, yes, she was definitely a glutton for punishment. Instead of putting her key in the lock, she rested her forehead on the door, then began tapping her head against it.

"Sweet child, are you trying to give yourself a concussion?" Sadie asked, startling Savannah.

Embarrassed, Savannah turned around, and sat with a thump on the stairs. "No, just trying to knock some sense into myself. I've had a horrid day, Sadie."

"Yes, I know all about it. Now...come on, and we'll have a cup of tea," Sadie said, already heading for her house. Savannah hopped down the steps and quickened her pace to catch up with the older woman.

"How do you know what kind of day I had? Trust me, no one could have seen this day coming!" Savannah said once she was seated and had accepted a cup of tea. She added some honey, took a sip.

"Charlie called me after you left there. She wanted to make sure you made it home." She eyed Savannah over the rim of her cup, then shook her head.

Savannah's shoulders slumped, and she mumbled, "I should have known. Always the mother hen."

"To those she cares about, yes; that's an excellent description of Miss Charlie. Now tell me everything...from the beginning."

Savannah recounted the story from the first time she met the girls until a few hours ago. Sadie choked on her tea when Savannah repeated the things Casey had said, then gestured for Savannah to continue.

"...you see I must be insane, Sadie. After everything that happened, today of all days, I figured out I love those children. Of course, I generally love all my students, but this is different, it's more...I need a straitjacket," Savannah said, rubbing her temples.

"You're not crazy. News flash, you're human and a female one at that. It comes with a lot of baggage and not always of the more attractive variety, I'll tell you. And good for you not falling for Kyle Ruthie's ploy. The man is the use-them-and-leave-them type. It's a shame because he really is a nice person."

"Yeah, I picked that up too. But I put that behind me; it's Emmit who keeps bringing it up. Evan warned me about this. I should have listened to him."

"Evan is a wise man," Sadie said, nodding. "Emmit uses Kyle as an excuse. A form of protection, if you will. As for loving those girls, who wouldn't if given half the chance?"

"But I'm their principal, don't you understand? I'm not supposed to have favorites." Savannah fiddled with the handle of her teacup. "Unfortunately, I can't seem to stop myself."

"You can't help who you love; it's one of life's more distasteful truths. Trust me, I know." Sadie sighed. "I was married for twenty years to the man I loved. It wasn't always easy with Mr. Madison. He wasn't the lovable sort. Prickly, he was, and short-tempered. He was a good man, mind you, a kind man, but hardly likable. I loved him anyway."

"You never mention him," Savannah said, straightening in her seat. She had wondered what the story was behind the man who'd made Sadie "The Widow."

"Mmm. Sometimes, the past should stay there, and I can't bring him back. Besides, I'm selfish and like to keep my memories my own," she said with a small smile.

"I understand. I guess that's probably how Emmit feels. I know the girls are only part of the reason he won't take a chance. The other part is his late wife. I've heard people talk about them. Mainly how Gracie McKay was an angel, and poor Emmit was left all alone. He's only mentioned her to me once or twice, and I don't think it was on purpose. He can't let her go, obviously. I guess I'm selfish too. He's only had three years to grieve, and considering what I heard, that's probably not long enough for him." Savannah looked up at Sadie as she poured more tea for both of them.

After taking a sip of her tea, she studied Savannah. "I can see in your eyes, child, you want confirmation— need it, but I can't give it to you. Instead, I'm going to open a new can of worms. Grace Vaughn wasn't the princess this town makes her out to be," Sadie said with a bite to her voice.

"Explain?" Savannah asked, her brow furrowed.

"Didn't you wonder where Casey got her mistrust of women? It's partly from that awful home she was in for the first five years of her life. But mostly, I hate to speak ill of the dead, but Grace put that distrust in Casey."

"Was she cruel to her?" Savannah asked, clenching her fist.

"Casey overheard Grace talking once. The child's got a nose for these things and ears as well." Sadie sniffed and reached under the table and pulled out a small case. She pulled out a slim cigar.

"Sadie!" Savannah sat back with wide eyes as Sadie lit her cigar and inhaled.

"I'm sixty-seven years old—not dead—and I'm entitled to a vice or two. I have my secrets, which I assume are safe with you," Sadie said, her eyes twinkling.

"Yes, of course!"

"Good. Back to what I was saying," Sadie said, serious again. She pulled an empty saucer over to use as an ashtray. "Casey overheard Grace on the phone. It was about a year before the accident. Casey was about nine or so, I believe. She was watchful and wary even then. Grace was telling someone that Emmit was talking about adopting another child. That would have been Charlie, by the way. Grace said she didn't know why he wanted another one, when three was plenty, and she was already sick of them."

"Casey heard this?" How awful.

"Yes, but it gets worse, much worse." Sadie took a long drag and exhaled slowly. "You have to understand.

121

Grace was a spoiled child, unbelievably so. She always got what she wanted, which was Emmit in those days. Here, Grace was practically royalty." Sadie paused to add a bit of cream to her tea.

"The town thought she was a devoted wife, but there's a fine line between devotion and obsession. And Casey got an earful." Sadie put out her cigar after she'd described all that Casey had overheard that dreaded day.

Savannah swallowed the lump in her throat, then leaned forward. "Did she tell Emmit?"

"Goodness no! Who would have believed her? Grace was a masterful actress. She was the perfect daughter, wife, and mother. If you ask anyone in town, that's what they'd tell you. Everyone loved her, and everyone was fooled by her. Myself included," Sadie admitted.

"But Casey confided in you," Savannah pointed out.

"She did, but not until well after Grace had passed. One morning, there was a knock on my door. It was Casey. I remember it like it was yesterday. It was bleak and raining. Casey was soaked to the bone, and her small glasses fogged. It was if God himself had decided the rain should clean the mind's eye to see the truth," Sadie said, choking up at the end.

"Casey told you, and you believed her?" Savannah asked, wrapping her hands around her teacup.

"Yes, she told me, but not quite how you would think. She asked me if it was a ticket to hell to be glad Grace was dead. I was horrified. She told me what she had overheard, and I told her she was mistaken." Sadie got up from the table and went to a large cookie jar. She pulled out a small green book. "She shoved this into my hands and demanded I read it. This confirms what Casey said." Sadie shook her head. "Almost as though Grace was reading out an excerpt to the person on the other end of the phone. In my opinion, this is more damning than any conversation overheard or otherwise."

She handed the book to Savannah who raised her eyebrows and opened the book to the first page.
June,

What did I do to deserve this? I'm a good wife, am I not? I'm beautiful, thoughtful, and everyone loves me. So why must I endure three ghastly children? The oldest is odd, to say the least. The middle child, thank God, is beautiful and eager to please. But the last one is almost too much. She thinks she's a boy or a monkey. And Emmit encourages them! Two years I've had to play doting wife and adoring mother. I'm in purgatory. Everyone feels sorry for me, and they should. It's nice but annoying. I had cancer, I'm not an invalid! Just because I can't breed doesn't make me less of a woman. "Poor Gracie," they say. "Can't have her own children. Poor woman had to adopt." Well, hah! I didn't want any brats anyway. Emmit did though; sometimes I don't know why I put up with him. He was supposed to be different. But he's mine, and I will never let him go. If I have to raise these brats to keep him, then so be it...

"How am I supposed to react to this?" Savannah asked, holding the book up. "What kind of person could say these things? Write these things?" Her brow pinched. "Why did you tell me about this, Sadie?"

"Because it will help you gain perspective. Casey's

a smart girl, but she isn't about to let someone, *especially* a woman, just waltz into her life. She doesn't have rose-colored glasses. This is why she doesn't trust you."

"Does Emmit know about this? Has he seen this diary...read it?" Savannah asked, tossing the book down.

"No, I always say let the dead lie. He didn't see the truth because he didn't want to. I can't blame him." Sadie shook her head. "How could I? I wish I hadn't seen it. If you'd known Grace, you would understand. I loved her. I would have died for her; anyone in this town would have," Sadie said, twisting the napkin in her hands. "None of us knew the true person."

"No one except the person she was talking to on the phone that day."

"True, but we've never been able to figure out who it was. Grace had lots of friends. We'll never know. Until I read that, I never would have believed it. Never!" Sadie sighed. "But after I read it, certain events made sense. Things that had bothered me but I hadn't paid enough attention to. Once you take the blinders off, the truth can be a cruel and ugly reality."

"Do you think Casey told him? About the book, I mean." She sucked in a breath when the truth hit her. "She's protecting him too, isn't she? God, Sadie, they're living a lie."

"Yes, she's protecting him and herself. She knows if she continues to hide this, then her father won't have to face the truth."

"I always thought she was too strong for her age, you know? Too mature. I admire that and her, but she was wronged. They all were," Savannah said as tears started down her cheeks. "You know, they all act so tough, sometimes you forget they're just little girls."

Savannah rose and headed for the door. Sadie stood too, putting a hand on her shoulder and giving it a squeeze. She handed Savannah the journal.

"You keep it. Do with it what you think is right. Savannah, don't give up hope. Grace was wrong; those girls are more than worth fighting for…and so are you," Sadie said with a sheen of tears in her eyes.

Savannah waited for the door to shut behind her. She took a steadying breath and was about to go to her apartment when the deep timbre of a man's voice came from the other side of the door. Sadie had a man in there with her! She was torn for a moment, then headed to her apartment. She'd had enough of uncovering secrets for one night. As Sadie had said, she was entitled to a vice or two, and Savannah thought with a wistful smile, at least one of them should be having a secret love affair. The smile faded when she looked down at the journal she was holding. What the hell was she supposed to do with this?

Chapter Sixteen

Savannah was exhausted. She had been up all night and most every night this week. It was Friday again, and she didn't think she had gotten even twelve hours of sleep since she left Sadie's Monday night. She had been trying to process what she now knew. Even after dumping all her personal baggage onto Evan, she was still overwhelmed.

She was on her second pot of coffee, and Mildred was breathing down her neck. Mr. and Mrs. Thomas had come in again this week. They'd informed her that the school hosted a Thanksgiving play every year, and *they* wanted to know what *she* was doing about it. Honestly, the only thing she had been thankful for in that moment was that Mr. Thomas had another appointment he couldn't miss, and they had left quickly.

All Savannah wanted was a hot bath and a vacation. Her paperwork, much to Mildred's dismay, was forming a tower on her desk. How could she possibly concentrate on anything? What was she supposed to do? Forget what she'd read in Grace McKay's journal? Damn Sadie for unloading this crap on her, and damn herself for caring.

There was a brisk knock on her door. Savannah rolled her eyes. "What now, Mildred?" she asked, not lifting her eyes from her desk. She didn't want to see

Mildred and that I-know-what-you're-not-saying leer she had been giving Savannah all week. She was tempted to ask the older woman what the hell she was supposed to do, because Mildred seemed to have the answers to the universe.

"Testy today, aren't we?" Charlie asked, as she closed the door. The voice had Savannah's head snapping up from the cesspool that had once been her rather tidy desk.

"Charlie, why are you out of class?" Savannah asked, trying not to be affected when her heart lightened. There stood Charlie, grinning, her blonde curls tamed in two pigtails. She had on a beige jumper with a burgundy sweater and matching tights.

Savannah took an inventory of her own appearance, realizing she wasn't as put together as Charlie was. She wore a thick black sweater and wrinkled gray slacks. This was her go-to choice when she was in a hurry, and honestly she hadn't even cared this morning. She started to speculate on what had to be a bad hair day when Charlie spoke up.

"Class is over; it's three o'clock."

"God, where did the time go?" Savannah said. "And where's Mildred?"

"She left already. She said something about you being bad for her digestion."

Savannah made a ladylike snort, and then smiled—for the first time since Monday.

"There's a movie with your name. *Savannah Smiles,* I think?"

"Yes, I've seen it actually. You do know your movies!"

"Uh-huh. I watched a lot of movies when I was at

the home. It helped pass the time," Charlie said as she wandered around Savannah's office.

"I can imagine it did. What is it, Charlie? What's wrong? I haven't seen you or your sisters all week." Savannah sighed and pinched the bridge of her nose.

"I'll get right to the point!" Charlie said, turning from the bookcase to face Savannah. "You look tired."

"Thanks a lot!"

"Pops looks real tired too. But you wouldn't know that seeing as how you've given up on him."

Savannah frowned. That was certainly to the point—and salt in her wound. But ha! he looked tired too. Good, served him right. "Charlie, anything that happened between your father and me is our business. I'm sorry, but it's not yours," Savannah said gently, not wanting to hurt Charlie's feelings.

"Puh-lease! It is sooo my business. When my family is involved, it becomes my business. Did you know Casey hasn't eaten at the table all week? She and Pops haven't spoken since the night you left. She isn't talking to anybody, not even Fletcher. And Fletcher's going plumb crazy. Alexandra's hiding at the Widow's until supper, and Pops broods day in and day out. I'm at the end of my blessed rope. So it is my business. I want my happy home back." Charlie finished her rant by stomping her foot.

"What does any of that have to do with me?" She was arguing with a child.

"It's partly your fault."

"My fault, Charlie?"

"You just gave up," she said and shook her finger at Savannah. "You didn't fight back. You didn't make Casey see she was wrong. You should demand she see that you're *not* Gracie!" Charlie said, then smacked her hand over her mouth.

"You know?" Savannah asked stunned. Sadie said no one else knew about Grace.

"*You* know?" Charlie paused. "The Widow told you, didn't she?"

Savannah thought about denying it, but Charlie saw too much. "Yes, she did," she whispered around the lump in her throat. "Did Casey tell you?"

Charlie nodded. "I caught Casey burning pictures of Gracie. After we argued about it, she told me the truth."

"What about Alexandra and Fletcher?"

"Ha! Like we'd tell them!" Charlie shook her head and explained to Savannah why their sisters didn't need to know. "And no, we never said anything to Pops. The Widow always says to let the dead lie."

"I understand." Good grief, she thought, rubbing her temples. For a woman who claimed to want no part in the man's life, she was up to her eyeballs in it.

"Since you know the truth, maybe you could talk to Casey." Charlie held up a hand to finish speaking when Savannah opened her mouth. "Don't be afraid to talk to her. She's sorry for what she said; she probably won't come right out and say so, but trust me, she *is* sorry. I know it's a lot to ask, but I'm hoping if you say something to her, she'll apologize to Pops, and we can have peace in our house again."

Savannah was at a loss for words. Did she want to talk to Casey? Could she? Should she put herself out there again? What had Sadie said? "They're worth fighting for." And Evan had said second chances were a show not of weakness, but of courage. Did she have the courage? Yes, she would do this. She owed it to herself and Casey. Because they both deserved a second chance. She rose from her chair and went around the desk to stand in front of Charlie.

"I'll see what I can do. No promises, though."

"I knew you would!" Charlie cheered and hugged her, then skipped out and shut the door before Savannah could say anything. Sighing, Savannah went over to her desk and started packing up her things.

****

As Charlie headed out of Savannah's office, she ran smack dab into Fletcher and Alexandra.

"Why'd you's make me sound like a sissy? 'Plumb crazy,' my ass!" Fletcher hissed.

"And you made me sound like a scared pansy running to the Widow's," Alexandra accused, crossing her arms.

"You's are a pansy ass, Alex," Fletcher goaded, grinning when Alexandra shoved at her.

Charlie shushed them and herded them down the hall out of hearing distance. "I did what I had to do and said what I had to say. We agreed I would be the spokesperson, and I did my job," Charlie reminded them.

"Fine, but I wouldn't have done a thing for Gracie, and you know it."

"True as that may be, Alexandra, you didn't see through her either." Alexandra flinched and glanced away, making Charlie realize how cruel her words had been. She hugged her sister. "I'm sorry, Alexandra; I'm just on edge and took it out on you."

"Yeah, there's a lot of that going around, isn't there?" Alexandra sniffed.

"Hopefully not for long, if Savannah has anything to do with it."

"I can't believe Casey. How could she compare Ms. Savannah to Gracie? They're completely different," Alexandra said.

"All I's really worried about is Pops. I's don't want him hurt anymore," Fletcher said, shuffling her feet.

"None of us want to hurt Pops, Fletcher. Wait, you don't honestly think Savannah would hurt him?" Charlie asked.

"No! Goodness, Charlie, for someone who knows movies, you don't know much. Most of the time, it's the man who hurts the woman's feelings. Daddy is more likely than not going to hurt her before it's over," Alexandra declared, rolling her big blue eyes at Charlie.

"Maybe we should think about this some more. I mean, you didn't see Savannah. She looks bad. Not ugly, but she looks like she hasn't slept in days and days. I think Casey hurt her more than we thought."

"Get you'self together, Charlie. Jeez, don't be a sissy now. Van's tough, I's tell you's. Uncle Evan and the Widow both said so, remember? And she's smart; that's what we need to worry about. She could figure it out before we's done," Fletcher said, pulling her long braids around her neck and making choking sounds. "Then we's dead."

"All right, let's move on," Charlie said, looking down both ends of the hallway.

"You mean move on to phase two, Charlie?" Alexandra asked, straightening her dress.

"Yep, Savannah talks to Casey," Charlie said.

"Man, I's love to hear that! Casey's gonna be pissed." Fletcher snorted and smiled. Then the smile faded, and she said, "Hells bells, we's better run for cover." They looked at each other and started running down the hallway. Except for Alexandra, who skipped.

****

If I were a twelve-year-old tyrant, where would I be? Savannah wondered as she finished changing in the girls' locker room. She had put on her jeans and a black sweatshirt. Alexandra might think she was a lady, but if that meant not wearing comfortable clothes, then she was no lady. She had washed her face and brushed her hair into a ponytail. She had almost screamed at her own reflection. Linda Blair had nothing on her.

She walked down the hallway, which was perfumed with the pizza the cafeteria had served at lunch. Her shoes made the squeaking noise that was associated with sneakers and school floors. It didn't matter what school, the noise was the same.

If she were Casey, she'd probably be getting into trouble and enjoying every minute of it. Hadn't Casey said something about fixing cars? Yes, she could try Ward Jessup's. With that in mind, Savannah headed for the parking lot after retrieving her briefcase and keys. She didn't have to go any farther.

Sitting inside her Jeep was the object of her search. How convenient, it was now or never. She opened the driver's side door, stored her briefcase, and slid into the seat.

"Should I ask how you got in here? Because I know I locked the doors."

"I told you I know all about cars. I wasn't lying," Casey said. She pushed up her glasses and reached for the handle. Savannah put a firm hand on her shoulder, stopping her.

"I think we need to talk." Savannah let go of Casey's shoulder after Casey nodded.

"Okay then, you go first."

Why do I have to go first? "All right," she began, "you said some cruel things the other day." She rushed on when Casey opened her mouth to say something. "I said some things I didn't mean, and I'm sorry if I hurt your feelings. But no one has *ever* accused me of doing and being the things you accused me of. And that hurts, Casey." There, that sounded good.

"I kinda figured that out. Especially after I heard what you said to Pops," Casey admitted with a shrug of one shoulder.

"You were listening?" Savannah's face flamed with embarrassment.

"Yeah, I know it was private, but you sure as heck weren't whispering."

"Probably not," Savannah mumbled. She didn't want to think about it.

"I know you aren't like Gracie. The Widow told me she broke her promise and decided to tell you the truth. I trust her, and if she doesn't think you're like Gracie, then you aren't," Casey said, lifting her hands in the air, then letting them drop.

"I guess Sadie had her reasons, but she didn't share them with me. She's right. I'm not anything like Grace." I love you, Savannah thought, but bit her tongue.

"Charlie said you were different." She shrugged. "I should have trusted my sister. It was just hard to believe. I heard what you said...you know, choosing us over Pops and...well, I guess I felt..." Casey sighed. "I'm not exactly sure. I felt bad about what I said to you." Casey turned in her seat so she was looking directly at Savannah. "Do you love my Pops?"

How was she supposed to know? Casey's violet eyes narrowed behind their lenses, and Savannah knew she was being tested. "Honestly, Casey, I don't think I do. I...I..." What could she say? I want to have sex with your father? I want to make love to your father for hours and hours until I can't walk straight?

"You want to jump his bones." Casey smirked.

You could say that. Exactly. She let out a strangled laugh. "The truth?" she asked, looking at a twelve-year-old who saw way too much. "You're too young to understand." Savannah jumped when Casey let out a whoop.

"That's a yes!" Casey said, then opened the door and got out.

"Wait, am I that obvious?"

"Nah, Pops is." She turned to go, then turned back. "We're okay? Me and you? Right?"

"Yes, we're okay," Savannah assured her, trying not to think about how Emmit was obvious about it.

"Great, see you!"

And with that Savannah was alone in her Jeep. She started the engine and pulled out of the school's parking lot. She couldn't stop smiling.

Chapter Seventeen

He was sweating, but sweat did a body good. With every crack of the hammer, his frustration eased. And frustrated Emmit was. He was pissed at Savannah. Oh, *Ms. Walker*...his mistake. He was annoyed with Sadie because she was annoyed with him for some reason he couldn't understand. Even his girls were looking at him funny. The fact was, most of his aggravation came from within. He was a real ass.

Evan had even put in his two cents' worth. His old friend told him he was the biggest fool he'd ever known. Yeah, well, he didn't see Evan in a relationship; the man had no room to talk.

Everyone made mistakes, right? So when he did, why did the world tilt off its axis? If that wasn't bad enough, he hadn't the first clue as to what he'd done wrong. Emmit didn't understand why he was pissed at Savannah; she'd given him what he wanted. His solitude. Why wasn't he happy then? All his problems started the moment he met her. "Her fault," he muttered.

"Who's her?"

Emmit whipped around to face Casey. He was in his workshop at home, and as usual he hadn't heard her come in. She really was beautiful. He'd never tell her though. She would get defensive and probably bloody his nose.

But Casey was a sight with her long black hair in one lone braid and her mysterious violet eyes. He was going to be in trouble in a few years. Oh yeah, big trouble with a capital B. He wouldn't let any of them date until they were twenty-one. The idea lightened his mood.

"We talking again?" he asked nonchalantly, when in fact it was killing him. This was the longest she'd ever stayed mad at him.

"I reckon it's time," Casey said with a nod. "Besides, Charlie threatened to let Alex cook for a whole month." She kicked at the blanket of sawdust that carpeted his workshop. "It's either talk to you or die." She looked up at him, straight-faced.

"I see…" He put down his hammer to stand beside her and took a deep breath. He had faced criminals, but he couldn't talk to his daughter. He was not that pathetic. "I'm sorry for what happened, Case. I—"

She held up a hand and pushed her glasses up. "I deserved it. Charlie said I was lucky I hadn't talked to her like that because she would have broken my nose. I know it wasn't on purpose, and I'm…" She paused and swallowed. "I'm sorry about how I acted, with you and Savannah. I made up with her today too."

"Did you now? That's awful nice, Casey." He patted her head affectionately.

"You can hug me, you know. I won't mind."

He didn't answer her, just scooped her up off her feet and held her fiercely. To his surprise, she held him back just as tight.

"I missed you," he said into her braid.

"I didn't go nowhere, Pops."

"I know. I'm just being a dad, I guess." He gave

her one more squeeze before he set her down. "I love you, Casey, no matter what. You know that, right?"

"Yeah, I guess I just forgot for a time. I love you too, Pops."

He nodded and picked up his hammer again. "You headed in now?"

"Yeah...you?"

"Yeah, soon as I finish this bench for Ward Jessup," he said as she nodded and started walking away. "Hey, Case?"

She stopped and turned around.

He swallowed. "What did Savannah say?" He shouldn't have asked. Why did he care? What was it that killed the cat, Emmit?

"She said she was sorry, and she forgave me for what I said to her. And that we're on the up and up." She shrugged one shoulder. "You know, no hard feelings."

"That's good then." He nodded and went back to his project.

"Hey, Pops?"

He turned. "Yeah, Case?"

"She wants to jump your bones!" she shouted, then was out the door like a rocket.

Emmit smiled and went back to hammering. He was midswing when what she'd said dawned on him. "Holy shit!" he mumbled, then jumped when the hammer came down on his thumb. "Damn it!" he shouted and went back to work. But he was smiling.

****

"Let's go over this again, Fletcher."

"We's done been over the damn thing five flaming times, Alex. Whatcha wanna fix?"

They had been in the attic since after supper, telling Pops they were having a sleepover. They'd hauled their sleeping bags and flashlights and radios and a whole bunch of other stuff up here. It wasn't a lie.

Fletcher knew they were sleeping up here, but it wasn't for the fun of it. Nope, they had a plan they needed to go over. They each had a part to play. She knew her damn part. Why Alex wanted to go over it again and again was beyond her.

"How hard is it to say 'Alexandra'? Hmm?" Alexandra asked with her face in her hands, then looked up as Fletcher stuck out her tongue and rolled her eyes. Casey and Charlie laughed, but Alexandra gave a dramatic sigh and said, "I don't want to change anything else if that's what you mean, Fletcher; it's just important that I know what to do. If something goes wrong…then—"

"We're screwed," Casey put in, laughing when Alexandra gurgled a scream.

They were all lying on their stomachs, each looking at a copy of "Operation Chance." Charlie had come up with the idea, and Casey had devised the battle plan.

"Fletcher, Alexandra has the biggest part in this op, and if she needs to get a better idea of what she needs to do, then let her. Her ass is so hog-tied if she gets busted, and you know it," Casey reminded her, then shook her head and said, "Give her a break. You're acting like a jackass."

"Enough," Charlie said when Fletcher attacked Casey. "If you two don't keep it down, Pops will come up here."

Charlie unfolded the "blueprints"—notebook

prints, actually. Fletcher had everything detailed to the letter. It was risky, the whole damn thing, but the end justified the means in this case. She pointed to the paper, and they ran through everything again.

"Everyone got it now?" Fletcher asked, and they all stared at Alexandra.

"I've got it. I don't have to like it, do I?" she said, then grinned. "Let's do it!"

Four McKays piled their hands together, let out a collective whoop, and dropped back to their sleeping bags.

"We're the flipping Goonies," Fletcher told her sisters.

"I couldn't have said it better myself," Charlie said, and Casey threw the first pillow of the night.

****

The chill in the air prickled his skin, but Emmit ignored it. He was sitting on the porch steps admiring the stars and thinking about the letter he'd received today. He sipped his decaf coffee, enjoying the way the steam danced across the rim. His daughters' laughter drifted down from where they played in the attic. It should have made him happy, but it didn't; he was on edge.

He had been having such a good day. Casey was speaking to him, and his girls were all happy, healthy wiseasses. All should be right in his world. But the letter in his pocket was spreading ice through his veins.

The porch door creaked open, and he glanced over his shoulder at Charlie. She had on her thick socks, flannel pajamas, and her blonde hair was in pigtails. He took another sip of his coffee, then set the cup aside.

"Pops, you're going to catch a cold sitting out here

without shoes on," Charlie informed him. She came and sat beside him when he didn't answer her right away. "What are you brooding about now?"

That made his lips twitch. Charlie always knew when something was bothering him. Uncanny talent, that. "I have some business I need to take care of out of town."

"Is everything okay?"

"Everything's fine. There's a meeting I need to attend; just business," he lied without blinking.

"Are you going?"

She said "you," not "we," and he was relieved. "Maybe." He shrugged. Emmit was going, no question. Charlie moved to sit in his lap. He hugged her to him resting his chin on her head, and they sat studying the sky.

"We could stay with the Judge or the Widow so we don't miss school," Charlie said after a while.

"I was thinking about that. I'd be gone for four or five days."

"We can handle it. Really. No sweat." Charlie turned in his arms and gave him a hug. She glanced over her small shoulder as she went to the door. "Don't worry, Pops, everything will work out perfectly, I promise," she said, then left him alone.

He snatched the letter out of his pants pocket and read it again. The warmth Charlie had brought to him receded, and his insides churned. He crumpled the letter, gazed back at the stars, and picked up his coffee again. He'd call Sadie and ask her for a favor.

****

"Would you mind repeating that?" Savannah asked.

"I asked if you wouldn't mind taking care of the girls for me. When I told Emmit I'd watch them, I got my weeks mixed up; I have to speak at a convention this week," Sadie said, worry etching her features.

"I don't think it's a good idea, Sadie." Nope, definitely not good. Closer to horrible. The kind of idea you avoid. Like jumping out of a plane. "What about their grandfather?"

"He's out of town on business. Please, Savannah, I can't let the committee members down. This has been in the works for months." Sadie paused, then said, "It's for *Southern Living* magazine. They're doing an article on our group, and I'm the spokeswoman. If I'm not there, we may lose our chance to be included in the article."

"Damn it, Sadie!" Savannah had a bad feeling, one that screamed she was being set up. But Sadie's eyes were both pleading and desperate. She needed her head examined. "I'll do it, but I swear, Sadie—"

"Good, good, I must get going before I'm late." She grabbed her suitcase and headed to the waiting car. "The girls are in your apartment already, dear. Have fun!" And she was gone.

Savannah stood there for a second; she had no doubt she had been maneuvered. She turned from Sadie's porch to stare at her apartment, ran her fingers through her hair, and closed her eyes. She could do this. She loved those girls, and this was a chance to have them all to herself. She smiled at that. She could do this! She was a principal, for goodness' sake. With that in mind, she headed for her home.

****

Fletcher pulled back from the window and looked

at her sisters with a cheesy grin. "Hook, line, and sinker!" she exclaimed.

"Good. The Widow did her part," Charlie began, brown eyes shining. "Now, it's our turn. Everyone remembers what they're supposed to do, right?"

"We know what to do, Charlie." Casey sneered. "I don't know why I'm going along with *this* plan. I still say stick with the original plan. I don't like surprises, and I hate changing mid op! 'Sides, I still think she might be too prissy."

"You, my dear sister, are a Neanderthal and have absolutely no taste," Alexandra said with a roll of her eyes.

"Says you, the prissiest of prissy pants." Casey smiled when Alexandra made a face at her. "I just don't like surprises. And Pops is a grown man..." Casey shut up when Charlie sat down next to her on Savannah's plush couch and looked her straight in the eye.

"We agreed. For this part of the plan, we push a little. Like the fairy godmother in *Cinderella*. Except we're like fairy goddaughters." Charlie clapped her hands.

"I's ain't no flipping fairy," Fletcher spat, and Casey pinched her.

Chapter Eighteen

Savannah found them huddled around her sofa when she walked in. They appeared to be plotting something. Her demise, perhaps? She had an urge to eavesdrop, but four turning heads chose for her.

"So, girls, what's the plan?" They gave her a suspicious glance. What had she done wrong now? "What's the plan for the next few days?" she asked, the girls relaxed.

"The Widow said this is a pull-out couch," Charlie said, patting the cushion. "Alexandra and I will sleep here."

"Me and Fletcher set up our tent in your office," Casey said. "We'll be fine in there."

"That was fast," Savannah said, glancing over her shoulder toward the office and wondering how they'd fit a tent in that tiny room. Oh well, what's done is done. "Okay, what's next?"

"We's could put in one of your *Murder, She Wrote* movies. I's know I's like that," Fletcher told Savannah.

"I know I'd like that," Savannah corrected, and Fletcher rolled her eyes.

"I refuse to watch that show again," Alexandra said. "Goodness, Fletcher, you've seen every episode and can recite every line. I'm not watching it!"

Fletcher crossed her arms and mumbled, "Fine." Charlie and Casey both rolled their eyes.

"What would you suggest, Alexandra?" Savannah asked.

All eyes on her, Alexandra sat up straighter. "We could do makeovers. It would be fun."

"No way you're touching me with that prissy paint, Alex. No way in hell," Casey said while Fletcher, white-faced, bobbed her head in anxious agreement.

"*Alexandra*," Alexandra hissed.

"My name is Alexandra," Casey mocked, holding out her hand with her pinkie up as if she were drinking tea. Savannah's eyes widened, and she clamped her lips together to keep in her laugh.

"You wish," Alexandra said with narrowed eyes.

"Girls, girls," Savannah said. "We've established no *Murder, She Wrote* and no makeovers. How about a board game?" Four girls, four very different ideas of fun. Thank the Lord, she had kept her board games.

"What games you got?" Casey asked, sitting up straighter.

"My personal favorite's Clue—"

Loud whoops cut her off. Charlie gave Savannah two thumbs up.

Alexandra held up a finger. "Only if I get to be Ms. Scarlett," she said.

****

One more day. Emmit would be back tomorrow, or at least that's what the girls had told her. She hadn't spoken to him. Savannah figured if he wanted to talk to her, the ape of a man could ask to do just that. She would have wanted to speak to the person watching her children. Obviously, he didn't feel the need. Should she be insulted or flattered?

Sadie had called and told Savannah that Emmit had

left a message on her answering machine. He'd given the name of the motel he was staying in and the room number. The girls each took about ten minutes every evening speaking with him, and he was always there when they called. Savannah didn't know what they talked about, but they were smiling when they got off the phone. She, no doubt, would be smiling too.

Tomorrow, Sadie would be back, and she'd said she would take the girls home. But damn it, Savannah didn't want to give them back. I knew this would happen, she admitted to herself while shoving papers into her briefcase. She'd known she would get even more attached to them. So much for self-preservation.

"Stupid," she muttered. "Stupid, stupid man."

"Fools! The lot of them," Mildred agreed.

Savannah's head whipped up so fast her hair fell out of its bun and tumbled down her back. "How long have you been standing there?" she asked as she pulled bobby pins out of her hair and ran her fingers through it.

"Long enough," Mildred said, rocking back on her heels.

"Well?" Savannah was annoyed enough not to care if she was short with Mildred.

"Nothing, missy. Just came to say 'bye."

"Oh…'bye, then." She sighed when Mildred didn't make her usual clipped exit. "That wasn't all?"

Mildred's lips pursed. "The girls are waiting in the hall."

"Okay, thank you." Savannah waited for Mildred to leave, but she walked to the front of Savannah's desk and put her hands on her hips.

"I know you've been doing the Widow a favor by

watching the McKay girls, but it's got tongues wagging."

"Mildred, I don't care."

"I know you don't care! But you need to start. Look…" Mildred's voice dropped low. "In other places, this situation may not make anyone blink, but you're in Blue Creek now."

Savannah sat back hard in her chair. "Why does it matter, Mildred?"

"It doesn't matter to me! I couldn't give two hoots and a holler, truth be told. I like the McKays, and when *you're* not being snippy, I like you too." Mildred huffed. "But you've already stepped on some toes."

Savannah gave an unladylike snort. "This is about the Thomases?"

"Yes," Mildred hissed, "it's about the Thomases! Ian Thomas is a vile pest, but he's a vile pest with clout and connections."

"I'll take that under advisement, Mildred."

Mildred gave Savannah a curt nod and said as she headed for the door, "See that you do, Ms. Walker. See that you do."

Mildred left the office, leaving the door open behind her. Savannah drummed her fingers on her desk. She didn't want to pollute her brain thinking about Mr. Thomas or his clout. She was worried enough about the emotional aftermath of the girls going back home. She leaned forward and rubbed her temples.

"Gots a headache, Van?" Fletcher asked from the doorway. She was leaning against the frame studying the end of one of her pigtails.

"No, sweetheart, just thinking." Heartache was what she had. Savannah stood and picked up her

146

briefcase. Fletcher hit the lights as they left the office. The others were waiting in the hallway. Savannah shrugged into her coat and helped the others get into theirs.

"I was thinking we should eat out tonight," Savannah suggested.

"Sounds good to me!" Fletcher said, racing to the door, a peculiar smile playing at her lips.

"Where?" Alexandra asked as she and Charlie held hands going out the door.

"I was thinking Ida Mae's," Savannah said. On one hand, it was the only place to go, and on the other, Savannah felt good when she was there...at home. What a silly thing to cross her mind. Savannah shook her head as she unlocked the doors on her Jeep.

"Ida Mae's the biggest gossip in town," Casey said as she climbed into the passenger seat. Strange Casey would be worried about people seeing them out. Just as Mildred had been.

"Yeah, but she's an ace in the kitchen," Charlie said. "Besides, it's right next to the store. We have to make sure Uncle Evan didn't burn it down," she added as she buckled her seatbelt.

"Like I's said before, sounds good to me," Fletcher said.

****

The diner wasn't crowded. They were seated and served almost immediately. Savannah sat back and watched the girls. *Her girls*, a voice whispered in her head. Casey and Fletcher were at the counter talking about mechanics and things Savannah didn't understand. Alexandra sparked up a conversation with Trixy about the latest styles, while Charlie went back into the kitchen with Ida Mae to talk about the apple cobbler they'd had for dessert.

The McKay girls were well known, and everyone who happened to be at the diner would tell someone else they had seen the McKays at Ida's, and guess who they were with? The news would fly to those who hadn't already heard. Just as Mildred had warned her it would.

"You look like you lost a puppy," Evan said, making Savannah jump when he sat down.

"You've got to stop sneaking up on people," she said, laughing.

"What's wrong, Savannah?" Evan sighed.

"Don't you mean what's wrong *now*?" she asked with a tight-lipped smile.

"However you wanna put it is fine by me, as long as you answer."

"Mildred told me the town was whispering about my relationship with the McKays and that I should be more careful."

"People will always talk; you just have to live your life."

"I agree." Let people talk; she wasn't doing anything wrong.

Evan cocked his head to the side. "There's something else though, am I wrong?"

Savannah sat back. "No, as usual, you're right." She leaned forward and motioned toward where the girls were now gathered around the counter. "I've had them all week," she whispered.

He nodded.

"I don't want to give them back."

Evan rubbed his jaw. "I feel the same way

sometimes," he confided, then dropped the subject when the girls came back to the table.

"Uncle Evan! What a wonderful surprise. How's Daddy's business?" Alexandra asked with a smirk.

"Ha-ha...it's fine, smart ass. What, did you think I'd burn the place down?"

"Nope. But Charlie did," Fletcher said, punching him in his arm. He glanced at Charlie and raised a brow.

"There was that one time, Uncle Evan. You remember, Casey," Charlie said, gesturing to Casey. Savannah's interest was piqued when Casey turned beet red.

"It was an accident. And your dad put it out before anything bad happened," Evan said in a rush. He turned to Savannah. "See, Emmit has a small stove in the back of the store, and I didn't realize when I left the towel near the range that I'd left the stove on. You can imagine my surprise when I heard Emmit holler and grab the extinguisher. Seems the towel caught on fire. But there was no harm done. Accidents happen all the time," he said as Casey choked on her tea.

They talked for a while more about the crazy misadventures of Uncle Evan, and then it was time to head home. Something Savannah was personally dreading.

On the way back to the apartment, Casey sat up front while her sisters curled up in the back. "Daddy's coming home tomorrow," Alexandra said around a small yawn. Savannah glanced back into the darkness looking at the girls.

"Yes," Savannah said, though she didn't need reminding.

"I miss him," Casey said, then looked out the window. No one said anything more. Savannah figured there wasn't anything else to say.

****

It had been five days. Five mind-numbing days since he'd seen his daughters. Questions he had tried to ignore now had answers, and it was worse than he could have imagined. It just goes to show you, watch who you trust. Both he and the Bureau had missed this.

Emmit had been young when the FBI approached him, but they hadn't cared about his age, only his expertise with a rifle. He wouldn't lie; he'd loved his work. Being part of a team that worked together to take down criminals had been rewarding. Emmit had had close calls before, but that last time, he'd gotten shot in the chest and hadn't been willing to risk another brush with death. At twenty-nine, he turned in his badge, ending his seven-year career.

The Bureau had investigated, and he'd agreed with their finding that what happened had been a fluke accident. Apparently, they shouldn't have made such hasty assumptions because he'd been shot by a hired hit man who called himself Mr. X.

Emmit glanced at the envelope on the seat next to him. He hadn't been able to resist the chance to make sense of a past that still woke him in the middle of the night. All of this because of a fucking letter.

Do you want to know who tried to kill you, Mr. McKay?

Come to the Marble Park Motel, fifty miles south of your town on Tuesday, and you will find your answers.

He'd gone. He'd arrived Saturday afternoon, checked in, and spent two days familiarizing himself with the area. First thing Tuesday morning, an envelope had arrived at his door. Emmit had done as Mr. X requested and gone to the library to do some "necessary research."

He'd gone inside and talked with the librarian. Mr. X had the entire thing set up because when he said his name, she perked up and said she had something for him. She'd handed him a box of microfiche and pointed him to where the microfiche readers were. And there he'd spent the day going through film after film.

He'd found what Mr. X had wanted him to find. Proof. Not about what had happened with Emmit himself, but proof that Mr. X was indeed who he claimed to be. A hit man. Because the commonality throughout the stack of microfiche was each slide contained an article about someone who had died mysteriously, each a freak accident without explanation. The lack of evidence and the unexplainable events themselves were Mr. X's signature. Leaving Emmit without doubt of the man's claims.

On Wednesday, a package arrived, sending him on a twisted scavenger hunt to find clues. Two days of running around town without a clear idea of what he was getting himself into had set Emmit on edge. He'd found himself wondering if obtaining answers was worth playing this game, and what was the ultimate cost of finding out the truth? More importantly, did he want to?

When the last clue on Thursday afternoon was a key to a safety deposit box, he hadn't hesitated in his decision to get what he came for—answers. He'd waited until Friday afternoon, as requested, to go to the bank. The box was in his name, reminding Emmit once again of the kind of man he was dealing with. Inside that box was the envelope sitting next to him now.

On top of the envelope had been another letter from Mr. X. It said Emmit was free, of course, to send his findings to his old colleagues at the FBI if he so wished. But the point was moot as the note explained. Mr. X had spent the last year clearing the skeletons from the closets of the people who had hired him. Purging his soul, it would seem. Emmit was the last loose end to be tied. Mr. X wrote that, by the time Emmit reached the safety deposit box, he would already have taken his own life before the Parkinson's disease could. For some reason, Emmit didn't doubt the hit man had done as he claimed.

The contents of the envelope gave the particulars of the event in such a way that Emmit couldn't dispute the fact he had been one of Mr. X's assignments. The paper said there were two people, who together, had hired Mr. X. He hadn't been asked to kill Emmit, only to wound him enough to have to leave the bureau. But the silent partner had had another idea and offered to pay extra for Emmit's elimination.

Luckily for Emmit, Mr. X hadn't felt compelled to be disloyal to the original agreement. Here he now sat, knowing what he knew. Mr. X only had one name. He'd never seen nor spoken to the silent partner, and he hadn't cared enough at the time to find out the person's identity.

Emmit was aware someone had wanted him dead. But who? On the surface, he'd told himself it hadn't been true because that's what he'd wanted to believe. Having the physical evidence in front of him now,

Emmit was resigned to the fact that he'd been deluding himself for a long while. Mainly because he was at peace; it was as if he was letting out a breath he hadn't realized he was holding.

Knowing a second person was still out there made Emmit feel like his skin was too tight. Was he capable of handling this situation? There wasn't a choice.

He rubbed his hands over his face. Was he or his family in danger? Mr. X said the silent partner hadn't been happy with the results but *had* conceded. The hair on Emmit's neck stood up. It had been seven years...he was still alive.

He couldn't think about it now; he wanted to see his girls. Emmit collected his things, shoving the envelope into his suitcase. The familiar sounds of pots banging and laughing children drifted toward him. He was home, and nothing else mattered. Emmit would protect his children.

As soon as Emmit opened the front door, he called out, "Where are my favorite girls?" There was a moment of silence, then an uproar. Suddenly, he was engulfed by four girls and one group hug. They clung together. This was life; this was truth, goodness, and what was right. These girls were his everything. Letting go and stepping back, Emmit took inventory. They were all here and healthy, just the way he'd left them.

"How did your week with Sadie go?" he asked, as they went back to what they were doing. No one answered him. Curious, he asked again and caught the quick glances. "Girls?" he said in the I-mean-business tone that scared the shit out of most men. Then they looked at each other again. He turned to Fletcher. She couldn't lie to him or anyone. Bless her heart, he hoped she never changed. "Fletcher?"

"We didn't exactly stay with the Widow," Charlie admitted first.

"We stayed with Van," Casey and Fletcher said in unison and put on that and-whatcha-gonna-do-about-it? stare that annoyed him. He had known. Somehow he had known. Damn Sadie.

"Really?" It came out calm though his blood pressure spiked.

"We stayed with Savannah," Alexandra said. "The Widow had a prior commitment she'd forgotten about when you asked her to watch us. Savannah said she didn't mind if we stayed with her, so we did. We had a wonderful time too."

"Savannah, is it?" he groused. When had Alexandra stopped calling her "Ms. Savannah"? What did that mean?

"And before you ask, the Judge was away on business," Casey said.

"Why didn't you girls tell me when I spoke with you on the phone?"

"We didn't want you to worry about us when you had to be focused on your meeting," Charlie said matter-of-factly.

"Thanks, but next time don't withhold information from me. What if something had happened, and I couldn't find you?" Emmit swallowed. God, what if someone still wanted him dead and went after his girls? He couldn't live with that.

His fear quickly morphed into anger, and he was about to blast his daughters, but Sadie walked in. "Why the hell didn't you tell me you weren't with the girls?" he shouted loud enough to make Sadie jump. All five females were staring at him. He needed to clear his head, and fast. "Maybe this time you could *actually* stay with them, so I can get some damn air!" He slammed out, taking his keys with him. He didn't stop when Sadie called out saying she'd stay until he got back.

Chapter Nineteen

Savannah had just gotten out of the shower when someone started pounding on her door. She threw on her light pink silk robe and wrapped her hair into a towel.

"Just a second! I'm coming." She was not in the mood for rudeness. She flung open the door, and her jaw dropped open. There he stood, Mr. Dangerous-to-a-Woman's-Sanity. Hers in particular. She tried to shut her mouth, but he looked like he was about to kill someone.

He stood in faded jeans, a white tailored shirt, and a tan leather jacket. His jaw had a dark shadow of beard, and his blue-gray eyes looked like a stormy sea. She stepped back and let him in. It was that or be knocked over.

"Why the hell didn't you call me and tell me you had my girls?" he hollered at her the minute she shut the door and leaned back against it.

"First off, I thought they told you, and secondly...don't yell at me!" Sexy or not, no one took that tone with Savannah Francis Walker.

"What did you plan to do? Use it as leverage? Huh, Savannah? Did you think I'd be so grateful I'd fuck you? Is that what you thought? Because it ain't gonna happen, sweetheart."

Savannah choked on her own tongue and stepped

away from the door pointing at him. "Listen to me, you bastard; I did Sadie a favor, not you! I didn't and don't want a thing from you." Except your girls, her mind taunted. She smartly ignored it. "You can leave here and go screw *yourself* for all I care!" she shouted and went past him only to turn around when he kept talking.

"Why so defensive, Savannah? Does the truth sting?" Emmit asked with narrowed eyes.

"What truth? You arrogant ass! You come here picking a fight with me, throwing words like 'fuck' at me, trying to get me rattled. Please, get over yourself."

Some emotion flickered in his eyes, but she was too upset to guess its meaning. He pinched the bridge of his nose and whispered, "Why do you have to be so goddamn beautiful?"

Savannah's eyes widened for a second, then narrowed. "What, now you want to get on my good side? Well, it won't work. You can just get the hell out."

She tried to shove past him to kick him out, but he grabbed her arm and jerked her against his body. Savannah reached out to grab the towel as it fell from her head, but she was unsuccessful, and her wet hair tumbled down her back.

"I've never seen your hair down before. It's…" He didn't finish his sentence, just ran his hand through her hair, making Savannah swallow.

Emmit was staring at her as if he would devour her. Oh no, he wasn't getting off that easy. She pulled back her hand intending to slap him. He caught that hand and the other when she tried it. He started backing her up against the closed front door. She was staring at his chest.

"Let go of me, you overgrown ox," she demanded between clenched teeth. Her heart was about to pound through her ribcage. She wouldn't look up at him. She didn't want him to know she was turned on. Her own body was a traitor.

"No, I don't think I will, Savannah, not tonight anyway," he said as he bent his head.

Emmit's lips were mere inches from hers when she met his gaze. Savannah figured he'd seen desire in her eyes because he brushed his mouth ever so slightly against hers.

"Let me go," she said. His brow furrowed, but he let her go and backed away. She glanced down, seeing the proof of his need.

"Savannah, I'm sorry. That was uncalled for." He shook his head but wouldn't look at her. "I thought..." he stammered with his back to her.

"Emmit, sit down," she said, none too gently. He took off his jacket, laid it across the back of the sofa, and sat. He rubbed his hands over his face, then laid his head back against the cushion and closed his eyes.

Savannah had two choices: talk and...well, talk was overrated. Or...she untied the knot holding her robe together and walked over to where Emmit was sitting on the sofa, eyes still closed. She let the robe fall down her arms. Her wet hair was cool against her overheated skin. Savannah took a moment to study him, then made her move. The cushions dipped beneath her knees as she straddled him. His head came up, and his hands caught her. He caught his breath when he realized she was naked.

"Savannah," Emmit croaked. Then after a moment, he ran his hands along her ribcage.

Savannah bit her lip. Feeling bold, she took his hands and guided him to her breasts. She gasped when his rough hands brushed against her sensitive nipples.

Savannah adjusted her position, so she was on top of the straining bulge in his pants. She rubbed herself against him, and he inhaled sharply as she moaned. Using her fingers, she traced her way to his ears, where she then held firm and attacked his mouth with hers, using her lips to show him that she wanted it hard, fast, and now. She shoved her tongue into his mouth when he gave her entrance.

Emmit's hands traveled roughly down her spine, grabbing her backside. He kneaded it softly—the opposite of their hungry mouths—and then pressed her against him. She rolled her eyes behind her closed lids at the deliciousness of it.

Savannah released his lips and started unbuttoning his shirt. Her fingers trembled, but she was able to undo each button, exposing Emmit to her. She ran her hands over his muscled chest, through the mat of hair which led a path down to bigger, better things. She sat back wanting to look at him, and that's when she saw it—round, puckered, and right above his heart. She met his eyes.

"Not shy, are you?" he asked, cupping her cheek.

She leaned into his hand. Looking up from his chest, she smiled. "Obviously not." She smirked and rubbed against his erection. He pulled her hair.

"What do you want, Savannah?" he asked. She wrapped her arms around his neck and hugged him. His arms went around her and tighten.

"Honestly?" she asked, nipping at his neck.

He nodded.

"I'd say you, but I don't think that's what you want to hear tonight." She pulled off his lap. Standing in front of him, she held out her hand. He took it and stood. She reached for his jeans and undid the button. "I want…" she said, pulling down his zipper.

He removed her hands and kicked off his shoes, jeans, and boxers. She stared at his erection, which bobbed between them. Savannah stopped thinking in a moment of worry. He was huge. Not just big. The man was hung. She tried to swallow, but her mouth had gone dry. Well, what to do? Emmit lifted her chin and raised an eyebrow. "Umm, where was I?" Savannah mumbled.

"You were going to tell me what you wanted. You got up to 'I want.' " He smiled and shrugged out of his shirt.

She reached down and grabbed his erection. It was hot and silky, and when she gave a gentle squeeze, it throbbed. He groaned low in his throat. Now or never, Savannah.

She took a breath, then moaned when he bent down and sucked on her nipple. His arms wrapped around her, and he bit gently down. Savannah wanted to scream at the intensity of it. Emmit lifted his head, replacing his mouth with his callused fingers.

"What do you want, Savannah?" he asked, again taking her bottom lip between his teeth and tugging. She pulled free and licked her lip.

"Make me come, Emmit," she whispered.

"Is that all you want? You're almost there now. Is that all you want?" She shook her head. "Then tell me." He pushed his erection against her stomach.

Savannah whispered into his ear what she wanted. "Happy now?" she hissed, heat sweeping up her cheeks.

Emmit growled and lifted her up. Savannah wrapped her legs around him, and he attacked her mouth. He backed her up against the front door. Their tongues tangled in a battle of wills. He whispered that he wanted to see if she was ready, and his fingers trailed down to her most sensitive spot. Savannah knew he would find her more than ready. She moaned against his mouth when he slid two fingers inside her and used his thumb to send chills down her legs.

Savanah tightened her inner muscles around his fingers and moved against him, but it wasn't enough. Not nearly enough. She tore her mouth away. "Emmit, please. I need *you* inside me," she said, her voice raspy. Emmit nodded against her throat, then shifted. He flexed, then entered her, moving mind-numbingly slow.

"You're killing me, McKay," Savannah confessed, then rammed her pelvis down, taking all of him. She was grateful his mouth caught her cry when she came.

After she got her breath back, Savannah lifted her head from his shoulder to study him. Her back was against the door, and she could feel a tremor run through his body as he held onto her. Savannah clamped her inner muscles tight and swiveled her hips. Emmit groaned; she grinned, then did it again and again until she'd broken his tight control.

Emmit moaned low in his throat and began thrusting into her. Savannah dug her nails into his back and clung to him. He held her hips in a biting grip as he moved faster. Harder.

Emmit tensed as he got closer to his own climax. He pulled back, then he plunged forward, throwing his head back as he came.

Emmit carried her to the sofa and sat down. She

collapsed against him. He was still inside her, but she didn't want to move. They were both slick with sweat, their scents mingling together.

"Still wanna fight?" Savannah asked, stifling a yawn.

Emmit sighed. "I guess not."

Savannah could have stayed this way forever or at least until her leg started to cramp. She laughed when Emmit maneuvered them, so that they were lying on the sofa and she could stretch out her leg.

"Better?" Emmit asked, and she nodded, resting her head on his chest and listening to the beat of his heart while he rubbed her back.

Maybe it was the gentle way he was touching her or the fact she was worn out that had Savannah's eyes closing. She wasn't sure how long they slept, only that she woke to the demands of her bladder.

Emmit's breaths were even beneath her cheek as she opened one eye, then the other. Slowly, so she wouldn't disturb him, she got up, grabbed her robe from the floor, and put it on as she headed to the restroom. She watched him sleep for a few minutes when she came back into the room. She'd brought a blanket from her bed and was about to lie down with him when he stretched. She laughed softly; he was too tall for her sofa.

"Hi," she said when his eyes opened.

He rubbed his hands over his face. "What time is it?" he asked, his voice thick with sleep.

She glanced at the clock in the kitchen. "After one." Sheer joy shot through her, she could live in this moment forever.

Emmit swung his legs around and sat up. Savannah

wasn't sure what to do, so she dropped the blanket on the sofa and tried not to fidget while he got his bearings. She bit her lip when he stood. She'd been too involved earlier to appreciate the sight before her. Emmit McKay naked was not something one should take for granted. She sighed, and he gave her a sheepish smile when he looked up from where he was putting his pants on.

She walked over to him then, and he held her. Savannah's hands slid up his chest, finding the scar she'd seen before, and she rose up on tiptoe to kiss it. His entire body went rigid, and he stepped away from her.

"What's wrong?" she asked. She had just experienced the most amazing sex of her life and here he was…what was he doing? Leaving?

"What is this?" she asked. He continued buttoning his shirt. She grabbed his arm. "Emmit?"

He jerked out of her hold. "This was a—"

"If you say 'mistake,' I will not be responsible for my actions," she said only half joking. She looked into his eyes, and her stomach lurched. She had known of course. She took deep breaths.

"I'm sorry, Savannah. God, what we just did, it was never…" He shook his head. "I don't want to hurt you."

Savannah let out a bitter laugh, making Emmit pause.

"I…"

"Emmit, leave," she said, handing him his jacket. He took it and slipped on his shoes. She tightened the knot at her waist and opened the door. Emmit stopped in front of her.

"Please, just go," she whispered, unable to face him. She shut the door after he walked out, then rested her forehead on the cool surface. A single tear slid town her cheek, followed by another and another. She'd seen it in his eyes...regret. She let out a strangled laugh.

Savannah walked to her sofa and sat down, only to jump back up. His scent still lingered—their scent. She picked up a music box from the counter just to hold onto something. Her emotions flooded her, overwhelmed her, and she threw the box against the door. The shattering of the glass echoed through the room. But it wasn't the only thing that was breaking.

She knew the answer to the question she had asked her mother when she was eight. Yes, hearts could break, and it *did* hurt. It hurt like hell!

Chapter Twenty

"What in the hell were you thinking?" Evan demanded, his head following Emmit as he paced.

"Keep your damn voice down. The girls are on the other side of those doors," Emmit hissed, pointing to the house.

"Sorry. Jesus!" Evan ran one hand through his buzz cut, then shook his head. "I don't know how you could let this happen. You at least thought to use protection, right? Emmit, tell me you did," he said when Emmit dropped his hammer.

"Oh shit," Emmit murmured. He rubbed his hands over his face. "I told you, I wasn't thinking last night. This proves my point." He sat down with his hands between his knees.

Sadie hadn't said a word to him when he'd come through the door last night. No, she collected her purse, gave him one long disapproving look, and left. Emmit had laughed in the empty kitchen, thinking if Sadie had known what he'd done, he would have gotten a whole hell of a lot more than disapproval.

Over breakfast, he'd explained to his girls he had been under a lot of stress last night and hadn't meant to take it out on them. They understood and were sorry if they made it worse. Charlie suggested he come out here to his workshop to help relieve any more stress he may have because they didn't want a repeat of last night's performance. Or so they said. Then Casey had called Evan, and here he stood.

"What the hell set you off anyway?" Evan asked around his coffee cup.

Emmit swallowed his own coffee to wash down the bile that rose in his throat. He thought about what Mr. X had revealed. Emmit could tell someone and get it off his chest. "I found out that it wasn't an accident that I got shot all those years ago."

Evan jumped up from where he was sitting. "What the hell are you talking about?"

"That's where I went. I got a letter." Emmit explained what he'd found out, but he didn't give names. Some things one took to the grave.

"Who? Damn it, Emmit, tell me."

"All Mr. X said was that it was someone close," Emmit said, feeling some relief after confiding in Evan.

Evan grabbed him when Emmit shook his head. "How can I help if I don't fucking know what you're not saying?" He let go of Emmit's shirt and shot Emmit a pained look. "How can I help protect the girls if you don't give me answers?"

Evan sped away, spitting gravel everywhere. Emmit winced. Evan knew now; it would take his friend a while to get over it. Then again, he didn't know the entire story.

"Good luck," he said to the dust on the driveway and went back into the workshop. His thoughts went to Savannah. What must she think of him?

With a sigh, he returned to his work and ignored the ringing telephone. The girls would get it. They liked to answer the phone almost as much they liked recording the outgoing message for the answering machine.

"Dad!" one of his girls called out.

Emmit stopped what he was doing and headed for the house.

"Daaad!" He recognized the voice and started running.

He caught Fletcher as they both came onto the porch. His heart was pounding. She never called him Dad. He inspected her quickly.

"What is it, Fletcher? What happened?" She shook her head and pointed as his other three daughters came running outside. He set her down.

"Dad," Casey began, "someone tried to burn down the store." She panted and pushed her glasses up. "They've put out the fire, but Sheriff Hart wants you down there now."

Emmit's mind went blank for a moment. Their store. "Let's go." He ran inside and grabbed his keys, then they piled into the SUV. "I'm going to drop you off at Sadie's; then I'm going to check out the damage." His driving was erratic, but his hands were steady.

They reached Sadie's in a matter of minutes. Emmit was out of the SUV and banging on the door before his girls had even unbuckled their seatbelts. He pounded on the door. "Sadie!" He pounded harder. "Answer the goddamn door."

"She's not there." He turned around, Savannah was walking toward them. "She had to go to the city," she said, crossing her arms over her chest.

"Someone's done set fire to the store, Van," Fletcher told her in a small voice.

"What?" Savannah looked at Emmit for confirmation, and he nodded.

"Someone tried to burn down our store. They've put out the fire, but I need to go down there." He looked back at Sadie's empty house.

"Girls, go on up to the apartment. I'll be there in a minute," Savannah said, surprising Emmit. They both waited while the girls crossed the yard to the apartment, then turned to face each other once the door closed.

Savannah cocked her head to the side. "What are you waiting for? Go!"

"Savannah…" He stopped; this wasn't the time for explanations. "I don't know how long I'll be."

"That's fine. I don't have anything better to do anyway." She turned to walk away and flinched when Emmit grabbed her arm.

"There were reasons; I don't have time to explain right now."

"I don't want your explanations, Emmit," she said and removed her arm from his grip.

"You may not want them, but you deserve them," he said, then kissed her. I am an asshole, he thought, until she kissed him back. He wrapped her up in his arms and held on.

****

Across the lawn, a curtain shifted. "Uh, guys? I's don't think we's need to worry about the op," Fletcher told her sisters cheerfully. Her sisters crowded behind her to see what she was talking about. Man, Pops was gonna suffocate Van for sure!

"I'll be damned," Casey whispered, pushing her glasses and leaning closer to the window.

"That's no surprise!" Alexandra said, giving Charlie a high five.

"Do you think we should break them up?" Charlie

asked, her cheeks turning pink. Then she closed the curtain.

"That was the easiest mission ever. We's didn't even do nothing." Fletcher spoke more to herself than to her sisters.

"Yeah, I don't like it either."

"You just don't like it because you didn't have a hand in it. You should be glad though," Alexandra said. "Daddy made the decision for himself."

"Maybe," Casey murmured.

"Let's turn on the TV and see if there's any news about the fire," Charlie said.

Fletcher found the remote and hit the button.

****

Outside, Savannah pulled back first and rested her head on his chest. "You should probably go."

Emmit hugged her close again, then let her go. "Yeah, but we'll talk later, right?"

"There's nothing to say," she said and straightened her spine.

"I think there is. What's between us, for one thing."

"I can't keep putting myself through this with you, Emmit. I'm a strong woman, but I'm not a saint. Last night, as amazing as it was, did not end well. I'm not willing to go through that every time you think you've made a mistake. I'm worth more than that. Go check on your store, Emmit, and don't worry about the girls. I'll take care of them." She walked away before he could say anything.

And what could I have said, Emmit wondered, as he drove into town. The moment he had seen her, he wanted to get down on his knees and beg her to give him another chance. His world was upside down, and along with his girls, Savannah was a bright light in his life. He just didn't think he could keep her. When she'd kissed his scar last night, it had been as though she'd hit a switch flooding his mind with memories. Things he couldn't afford to forget. But standing there watching her walk away from him didn't sit well. In fact, it tore at the remains of his tattered heart.

Chapter Twenty-One

The smell of smoke overwhelmed him the moment he stepped out of his vehicle. He was thankful only the left side of the building was hit, because Ida's was on the right, and this could have been a whole hell of a lot worse. As he started digging around, Emmit concluded that even the damage done wasn't as bad as he'd feared.

"McKay," Sheriff Jasper Hart called out. He was standing by the fire chief, Todd Mae. Emmit shook hands with both men. Why did they look so uncomfortable?

"Do we know what happened? You told Casey someone tried to burn down the place. But it seems premature to guess arson. Unless you have someone in custody." Emmit narrowed his eyes when Jasper lost all his color.

"We found something just as incriminating as a man with a gas can," Todd Mae said, then gestured to the sheriff. "Jasper."

"Damn, McKay, those vandalisms were just the beginning. Someone is after your tail," Jasper said, and Emmit's blood turned cold.

"How so, Jasper?" he asked calmly, when in fact his mind was racing. Jasper pulled out a plastic baggie. Inside it was a note.

"This was stuck to the door." Jasper handed Emmit the evidence bag. "Read it and see for yourself."

Tick, tock, goes the clock,
whose time has reached its limit,
No place to go, nowhere to hide,
because time's run out for Emmit!

"Any ideas?" Jasper asked when Emmit handed the bag back.

"Not one, Jasper. Damn," he lied. He knew as his heart started thumping this was too much of a coincidence. The break-in a couple years ago, the vandalism—this was what Mr. X had been trying to tell him. Someone out there was still playing games, goading him. Perhaps the unknown accomplice had decided *almost* dead wasn't as good as six feet under. But why now? Why after all these years? What had set the bastard off?

"Just what I need," Jasper said under his breath, but it brought Emmit out of his thoughts.

"What?" Todd asked, then grunted.

Emmit couldn't help his own grimace when Ian Thomas continued walking toward them. The McKays and the Thomases had never been friends, and that still held true. Ian was a jackass, and that was on a good day.

"What have we here?" Ian Thomas drawled.

"Nothing for you to worry about," Jasper said, crossing his arms over his chest.

"Perhaps," Ian said as he squinted his hazel eyes and took inventory, "you should be more careful, Emmit."

"How so?" Emmit said through gritted teeth.

Ian gave a long, hard look. "This is yet *another* situation in which you have neglected your responsibilities."

"Oh?" Emmit said, his blood starting to boil.

"I'd be more than happy to explain to you all your failures—"

"That's enough!" Jasper cut in stepping between Emmit and Ian. "Todd and I have an investigation to run, and unless you have information about what happened here—"

"How dare you," Ian hissed.

"Then you best be moving on," Todd finished for Jasper.

"Very well," Ian said, jutting out his chin as he walked away.

"What the hell is that guy's problem?" Todd asked as Ian got into his BMW.

Jasper shook his head. "You never know with that one."

"My girls would say he's got his boxers in a bunch," Emmit said, smiling.

"I think it has more to do with the stick up his ass," Todd said, and they all laughed.

People were running up behind him, and Emmit turned; Evan and Kyle were coming his way. They stopped in front of him, looking back to the building, then to him again.

"What the hell happened? How'd it start?" Kyle asked. "Was anyone hurt? My God, Emmit, the girls?"

"Looks like arson. The fire took out the side wall. No one was here, and the girls are fine. They're with Savannah," Emmit said and ignored Evan when he raised a brow. He shrugged.

"Do we know what started it?" Kyle asked Jasper.

"Yeah, some firebug tried to burn the place down with gasoline. As far as Todd can tell at this point, anyway." He turned to Emmit. "I'd watch my back and be real careful if I was you, McKay, real careful." Then he and the fire chief left.

"What's he talking about?" Kyle asked, shoving Emmit when he didn't answer right away.

"Seems someone's after me; left me a note telling me my 'time's run out.' I pissed someone off." He didn't want to tell Kyle all of it. His old friend would call Jasper back, get the authorities involved, and try to put Emmit in protective custody. Kyle was a do-it-by-the-book type of man, and Emmit wanted to handle this his own way.

Emmit looked at his store; it would take a few weeks to clean up and make repairs. Thank God for insurance, he thought, as he started toward his family store to take stock of what needed to be done.

****

Savannah poured another cup of decaf and headed for the door when Emmit pulled into the driveway. She met him on the small landing and handed him the cup she'd made for him. She sat down and sipped. He sat next to her.

"Thanks," he said, saluting her with his cup after he'd taken a sip.

"It's not as good as Alexandra's, but it does the job," she told him, making him chuckle.

He was filthy. Soot covered him from the top of his head to the tips of his boots. She could smell smoke on his clothes. She spied him out of the corner of her eye. He was deep in thought.

"How bad was the damage? The girls and I saw it on the news so I have some idea, but…"

"The left side of the store will have to be torn down

and rebuilt. There's water damage, but that's not too bad. It could have been a hell of a lot worse. No one was hurt; that's a blessing. I owe Ida Mae; she saw the smoke and called the fire department before it could reach the diner." He rubbed his dirty face on his shirt.

"Was it arson?"

"It was." He sipped his coffee.

He was too calm, and it was making her uneasy. "What aren't you saying, Emmit?" She sensed there *was* something else; she didn't know how she knew, but she did. Her suspicions were verified when he gave her a quick glance.

"Where are the girls? We need to get going."

"They're sleeping, and you're not waking them up this late. You can either stay here too, or come get them in the morning."

He ran a hand over his face. "I think the best idea would be if I came and got them tomorrow. Don't you?"

"Yes," Savannah agreed. "Now that we have that covered, I'll ask you again to tell me what you're not saying."

"You don't need to worry about it."

"There *is* something to worry about, though?" she asked, then stood after he did. He handed her his cup and started down the steps. She set the cups down and followed him.

"I'll pick the girls up in the morning," he told her.

"Emmit? What is it? Maybe I can help." She followed him to his SUV. He swung around.

"Don't you get it? I don't want to talk about it, okay? Especially not with you." He winced. "I didn't mean it like that. Look..." He rubbed his neck.

"There's a lot of shit going on right now, Savannah. I don't want you to get hurt."

"It must be pretty bad for you to think I'd get hurt. What about the girls? They can't help but be involved. Could they get hurt?" She glanced up to where the girls slept.

"I don't know. I just don't know," he whispered, looking in the same direction.

She swallowed her pride and grasped his arm.

"I'm not trying to start anything with you right now," he said, "but would you mind hugging me?"

Savannah stared at him for a moment, and her chest tightened. Weariness was not only in his eyes but also lined his handsome face. She wrapped her arms around his waist and rested her head on his chest. His arms tightened around her, and he held on. She didn't know how long they stood together like that, and she didn't care. He relaxed and took a cleansing breath, then kissed the top of her head and let her go.

"Thank you."

"You're welcome." She reached up and brushed the hair on his forehead to the side.

He took her hand and gave it a squeeze. Then he turned to leave. "I'll see you in the morning."

She nodded and headed back inside, picking up their coffee cups on the way.

****

A knock came at Savannah's door around nine the next morning. She had called Mildred and told her she wasn't coming in until noon and that the McKays weren't coming in at all today due to the fire. They were finishing up breakfast when Fletcher answered the door.

"Hey, Uncle Evan. Whatcha doing here?" Fletcher moved to the side to let him in.

"Hey, squirt. I've been dubbed the personal chauffeur of the McKay sisters." He gave a curt bow. "At your service."

Savannah smiled when he gave her a wink. "Come on in, Evan. Would you like some breakfast or some coffee at least?"

"I'll take a cup of coffee, Savannah, if you don't mind." He came to the kitchen table, plucked Casey out of her chair, and sat down, resetting her on his knee. She playfully punched his arm and finished her French toast.

"Where's Pops?" Casey asked.

Savannah glanced up, wanting to hear Evan's answer. He shifted in his seat under the girls' scrutiny.

"He's at the store with the insurance adjuster. It'll probably take all day for him to go through everything, so you girls are coming with me to the garage. Hurry up and finish because we need to get going."

Casey jumped down, and they all hustled around washing their breakfast dishes and getting their things. They had taken showers, and Savannah had washed their clothes last night. The girls still had extra belongings there from the last time they'd stayed, so they were all clean, fresh, and ready to go.

"Evan, are you all right? You look like you're about to hit something," Savannah said. Then she gestured to the cup he was gripping. "I won't be happy with you if you break that." She smiled at his sheepish grin.

"You break her cup, and you get two days' suspension," Casey said. "Trust me, it isn't worth it.

Plus, Pops would probably kick your butt, and he's got enough problems."

"Thanks for pointing that out," he told Casey, but he was laughing. "Girls, head 'em up and move 'em out."

They raced to the door, saying good-bye and thanks to Savannah. Evan tossed his keys to Casey and motioned for them to go ahead. He turned to Savannah and cleared his throat. "Emmit, ah, told me, ah…" He shrugged, then hid a smile when she turned red. She knew what he meant. "Oh, never mind, it ain't my business anyway." He rocked back on his heels.

"No kidding," she choked out, then sighed. "I probably would have ended up telling you myself." She smacked him, when he grinned. "Oh, hush. Who asked you anyway? It was a lapse in judgment." Savannah shrugged one shoulder. "Like you've never made a mistake in your life, Evan Jessup."

"That's true. I myself have made many mistakes." Evan nodded.

"See. No one's perfect."

"Hell no, perfection is a deceptive little shit," he said as he stared out the window.

Savannah eyed him curiously. She had a feeling he wasn't talking about her situation. No, she thought, noticing the shadow that came across his face, he was talking about something else altogether.

As if sensing her thoughts, Evan turned to look at her. "You be careful, all right? Try to stay outta trouble," he said before opening the door and racing down the steps.

Savannah rubbed her arms when an icy wind blew across her doorstep. She had the most peculiar feeling.

She just couldn't put her finger on it. She was about to turn around when Sadie popped out of her house. Savannah rushed down her steps at Sadie's request.

"Why was Evan picking up the girls from your house? And why are any of you home on a Monday morning?" Sadie asked with a furrowed brow.

"When did you get home?"

"Late last night. Now come in out of the cold and have some coffee. Then you can tell me what's going on." Sadie led Savannah to the kitchen. Savannah waited until the coffee was poured and Sadie was in her seat to begin.

"Someone tried to burn down the hardware store yesterday," Savannah said.

Sadie gasped. "Was anyone hurt? Emmit?" she choked out, hand to her throat.

"Oh, no, no one was hurt," Savannah assured her, then recounted the events of the last twenty-four hours. "That's all I know." She sipped her coffee. This made cup number four. The caffeine was welcome, though, since she hadn't been able to sleep; she had sat watching the girls as they slept. The girls appeared almost angelic in their slumber, which was absurd. Savannah knew they were little devils, every one of them.

"Good Lord, poor Emmit; he must be going crazy." Sadie shook her head. "His great-grandfather built that store. It's a family tradition—wait...you said someone—it wasn't an accident?" Sadie twisted the napkin in her hand.

"No, as far as I can make out it was intentional. What's more, Sadie, whoever did this has Emmit worried. If you could have seen him last night..." She rubbed her temples. "Something's terribly wrong. I can't explain it, but I have this feeling. This...I don't know, it's just...something bad is happening. Emmit said there was a lot of stuff going on and he didn't want me hurt. He's worried. The girls might be in danger too." Savannah glanced out the window as the wind tossed leaves about on the driveway. "I think he believes the same thing. But he wouldn't come right out and say it." She looked at Sadie. "And I think Evan knows too, but neither man's talking."

"Now *I'm* worried. If you're right, which I unfortunately believe you are, then we all need to be on our toes. Emmit won't ask for help; he never does." Sadie went to one of the kitchen drawers and pulled out what looked like an address book. "If that man refuses to tell us what's wrong, then we'll just have to find another way to help him."

Savannah nodded, then glanced at her watch. "Sadie, I've got to go get ready."

"Yes, dear child, you go, and I'll start making some calls."

Savannah waved good-bye to Sadie, who had already begun dialing numbers.

Chapter Twenty-Two

The next month went by in a blur of activity. Emmit didn't know why he'd been surprised when most of the town had come out to help him put the store back together. So many people had shown up, even Trixy Mae, who would rather die than mess up her nails. It had taken weeks, but here he stood in his store. Blood and sweat had been put into rebuilding, and it looked better than it ever had. He and his girls had celebrated the grand reopening just this past week.

Emmit closed up for the night and set the new alarm. He had called an old friend from the Bureau who ran a security business and had him install this state-of-the-art system. Charlie had gotten him a new bell to hang over the door for Christmas last weekend. He smiled, thinking how she always gave the most practical gift.

His girls had invited Sadie, the Judge, Evan, Kyle, and Savannah over for Christmas supper. The house had been filled with laughter and fun, which filled him with peace. Everyone had had a nice time. Kyle and Evan got in a playful argument about lawyers only getting coal for Christmas. The girls had laughed until they cried.

But the biggest news came by way of J. T. "I have an announcement," he'd said at supper while clinking his fork against his glass. The older man had actually been blushing. "As you know, Sadie and I took a trip to the city last week—"

"You had us all wondering about that, old man," Kyle had said, grinning sheepishly when J. T. glared at him for interrupting.

"Lawyers never know when to keep their mouths shut. As I was saying, we went to the city." He stopped to take Sadie's hand. "The Widow Madison has renounced that title once and for all. She is now Mrs. Sadie Madison Vaughn." He puffed out his chest, joy etched in his features.

Emmit smiled at the memory. You could have heard a pin drop until his girls had started shouting, jumping out of their seats, and calling Sadie "Grandma." The woman had cried her happiness then, and Emmit had made a toast to the newlyweds.

Blue Creek had been abuzz the next day when the news broke. No one knew what to call Sadie. Emmit himself was glad that she didn't insist on being called the Widow anymore. But she said she had liked the title and was flustered to see it go. Sadie had told him she'd come up with a few choices to replace it but hadn't made her final decision yet.

The night had ended late. Savannah hadn't said much to him though; in fact, she'd ignored him. He tried to walk her to her Jeep to get a moment alone with her, but his girls had made that impossible. They hadn't wanted her to go. Even Casey had asked her to stay the night, claiming that the road was a bit icy. But Savannah said she wanted to sleep at her own place.

She had spent more on the girls' gifts than he would have liked. The woman had gone overboard, almost outdoing him—but not quite. He had furnished the attic. He had *absolutely* gone overboard, as was his right.

Emmit remembered the girls tearing up the steps when he said their biggest gift was in the attic. They had been speechless, a moment he would always treasure, as they looked around. He'd been extra careful on Christmas Eve. He'd had Kyle take the girls to look at the lights around town, while he and Evan had moved all the furniture upstairs.

He'd bought a couch, stereo system, bean bag chairs, rugs, and lamps. He'd built two end tables, a coffee table, and a large bookshelf. Between building the furniture and rebuilding the damage done to the store, Emmit had hardly slept in the last month.

Seeing their faces had made it all worth it. Even having to get the saleswoman to help him pick out the colors to match the plum walls had been worth his embarrassment. The girls hadn't wanted to leave the attic the rest of the day, until absolutely necessary. He had truly outdone himself this time, but Savannah had come close too. He still couldn't believe it.

"Jewelry," he said into the empty cab. Who would have thought his girls would want jewelry? Alexandra, yeah, that was a no-brainer. Even Charlie he could understand. But Casey and Fletcher? He would have bet against it and lost.

Savannah had gotten them all specific pieces, each as unique as his girls were. She'd given Charlie a heart-shaped gold locket with a diamond in the center.

Charlie had squealed with delight. "Just like Annie's," she had told him, smiling brightly enough to blind him.

Alexandra had gasped when she opened her small

box to find a charm bracelet. It had little charms too. Ballet slippers, a rose with a diamond in the center, and a small cross with opal flecks, were the ones he could remember her pointing out to him.

Savannah had gotten Casey a pair of earrings, which would have been a problem if *Uncle Kyle* hadn't taken them all to get their ears pierced as an early present. Emmit still didn't know how he felt about that, but he couldn't take Kyle's gift back. Savannah had known what Kyle was going to do because she had gotten Casey earrings to replace the studs. The earrings were unique—tiny wrenches, each holding a small diamond between its teeth. He didn't know how Savannah had found something like that.

He remembered Casey's confused expression. "I don't know what to say," she had whispered and then shocked everyone by hugging Savannah. It had been quick but spoke volumes. Later, Casey told Emmit she didn't think she deserved them because of how mean she'd been to Savannah. He'd told her Savannah had forgiven her a long time ago. The woman didn't know how to hold a grudge. Unless, of course, it was against him.

Fletcher had the funniest response. She didn't even want to open her gift, saying she wasn't a sissy. She had gotten her ears pierced only because Casey had called her a coward. But she looked almost ill holding that small box, watching it as if it might come alive and bite her. He laughed and told her no one would call her names. Casey, of course, asked Fletcher if she was calling her a sissy because she planned to wear her earrings. After thinking about it for a moment, Fletcher proceeded to open her gift.

It was a thick chain of white gold with a small round locket attached to it. Fletcher had sat there turning it over in her small hand for a long time not saying anything. She then mumbled her thanks and left the room. Savannah had looked a little worried, but smiled nonetheless.

It still had Emmit shaking his head that they'd loved the jewelry. He'd seen Fletcher wearing her necklace and would have thought he was outdone had his girls not dragged every one of their guests, including Savannah, to the "lions' den" to show them what his present had been.

He was smug when he pulled into his driveway. At least, he was until he saw Sheriff Hart's SUV parked in his spot. Emmit sped up and hit the brakes. He shut down the engine, none too gently, and would have jumped out the door if his seatbelt hadn't gotten in the way.

Nothing had happened in the last month. No notes, no threats, no petty vandalism. Nothing. God, the girls! He started running.

Jasper was sitting at the kitchen table when Emmit ran into the house. The sheriff was sipping his coffee and talking to the girls. Emmit stopped on a dime. "What in the hell is going on?" he shouted, making everyone jump. Hadn't they noticed him storm into the house?

"Seems there was a bit of trouble," Jasper said.

"What kind of trouble?" Why was the man so calm when Emmit's heart was racing? He glanced around the kitchen. All his girls were there. They didn't appear to be hurt, but they did look guilty. Emmit took a deep breath and almost laughed. He'd thought...no, he wasn't going to think about it right now. Instead, he crossed his arms over his chest and looked at his girls. They squirmed. "What did you do now?" His gaze swung to Jasper when the sheriff laughed.

"They didn't do nothing, McKay," Jasper told him and sipped from his cup. "No wrongdoing *this* time."

"If you four didn't do anything, why the guilty faces?" he asked, he knew from their expressions something was amiss.

"They called me out here because they lost something. I was just telling them making false claims to the police is against the law." He finished his coffee and got up. "I'll leave you to them. Good luck! And remember our talk, girls." Jasper's chuckle echoed as he left the house.

"What was misplaced?" He was dying to know.

"It won't misplaced, dagnabbit!" Fletcher shouted and ran out of the room, all eyes following her. It was then he noticed her hair. It wasn't braided. The long brown strands were loose and running wild. Then the three remaining girls looked back to him.

"What was that about?" he asked. Fletcher never left a room without having one of her sisters "trap her hair" for her.

"She can't find the necklace Savannah gave her. She only takes it off when she takes a bath. And even then, she leaves it on the dresser in her room," Alexandra explained, biting her lip and fingering her own charm bracelet.

"She accused us of taking it! We told her we couldn't have because we were in the attic when she was taking a bath this morning. She didn't believe us," Charlie told him glancing at the ceiling and wringing her hands. "She started trashing our rooms searching for it. We didn't take it, Pops, I swear. We were all in the attic together. We wouldn't take it!" Charlie's small voice was thick with tears.

"How long was she in the tub?" he asked. Fletcher and Alexandra were the only ones who actually took tub baths. It was one of the only things Fletcher did that he considered feminine.

"About half an hour, I'd guess," Casey said with her arms crossed tightly.

Emmit took a good look at his oldest. There was a bruise forming around Casey's right eye, and she was wearing her spare glasses. He went over to her and lightly brushed her cheekbone; she winced.

"Hit you, did she?"

"She sucker punched me and broke my glasses too. She's lucky Alexandra held me back 'cause I woulda gotten her just as good," Casey said, gingerly patting her eye, and Alexandra nodded. "Then she went into your room and locked the door. I guess that's when she called Sheriff Hart, because she didn't come out until he pulled up."

Charlie sniffed and continued the story. "She told him what happened and he listened; then he told her she probably just misplaced it, and she got real quiet. He'd only been here for about ten minutes when you got here."

"I've only seen Fletcher this upset when her favorite video was ruined, and even then she had another copy to replace it. She doesn't have another necklace," Alexandra reminded him.

Emmit nodded. "I'll go talk to her."

"Might wanna take a weapon, Pops. She isn't

thinking too clearly," Casey warned, tapping one finger to her temple.

Emmit sighed and began climbing the stairs to find his youngest girl. What must Jasper think? Last summer, the sheriff had sat at the same kitchen table white-faced and told Emmit he'd caught Fletcher taking an unguided tour of the sheriff's station. Jasper said he wouldn't have believed it if he hadn't caught her himself. Since then, Emmit had paid closer attention to what the girls were up to. Or at least he tried to.

Finding Fletcher's bedroom empty, he went up to the attic but found the same. He went back downstairs to search all the girls' rooms. "Trashed" didn't convey what Fletcher had done to her sisters' rooms. She had torn them apart. He ran downstairs again and began searching the house. He started calling her name. She didn't answer. Then everyone joined in. They couldn't find Fletcher. She was gone.

Chapter Twenty-Three

Savannah rubbed her temples and checked the calendar again. She was pretty sure she had missed her period, but she'd never been regular. Plus, she had been under a lot of excess stress lately. Ha! That was an understatement.

Mildred had called her this morning to let her know she'd heard, from an undisclosed source, that Ian Thomas had gotten his hands on a copy of Savannah's contract right before winter break. Savannah couldn't say she was surprised after the Christmas pageant fiasco. She winced, remembering.

Marylou Thomas had been picked to give the solo during the pageant's grand finale, which would have been fine if Savannah hadn't seen her shove another student hard enough to make her fall. And yes, it could have been an accident as Marylou's parents had claimed, if it weren't for the fact Marylou had then pointed at the child and laughed. Savannah believed that kind of behavior deserved punishment. Marylou lost her part in the pageant, and the solo had gone to another student. Needless to say, the Thomases caused quite a scene in her office. Again.

If knowing Ian Thomas was scrutinizing her contract wasn't unsettling enough, Mildred informed her the entire town knew who she'd spent Christmas with. That particular gossip had inspired Mr. Thomas to hold a meeting at his home. "I warned you about that man," Mildred had reminded her. Yes, she'd been told this might happen, but she hadn't thought he would stoop to this level.

Savannah was beginning to think her position wasn't as secure as she'd assumed. What worried her was that she wasn't as upset about the possibility of losing her job as she should be. Mildred had suggested Savannah ask the Widow for advice, but she wasn't going to bother her friend.

"She's Mrs. Sadie Vaughn now," Savannah said with a laugh. Wanting to keep that warm feeling instead of contemplating what Ian Thomas was after, Savannah decided to make some tea. She put the kettle on the stove and looked at the clock. The mailman should have come by now, Savannah thought, and headed out to the mailbox.

She smiled at the pile of mail as she took it from the box and went back up the stairs. She sifted through it—nothing of any real importance. There was a small package; Savannah shook it and shrugged. She was about to open it when the tea kettle whistled. Savannah got out a cup and placed a tea bag in it. She added the boiling water and let it steep. As she waited, her thoughts went back to the former Widow Madison.

Sadie had asked Savannah to help her pack because she was moving into the Judge's home. Savannah had had a moment of panic when Sadie told her. She'd asked if she needed to look for a new place, but Sadie had assured her she could stay in the apartment for as long as it suited her. She'd even offered the option of staying in the main house, but Savannah turned her down.

Savannah asked her friend why she wasn't going to put the house on the market, and Sadie informed her that she planned on giving it to whichever of her new granddaughters got married first. She had laughingly told Savannah that Kyle had almost had a heart attack when she'd had him draw up her new and improved will. Sadie told Savannah the late Mr. Madison had made sure she was taken care of, so financially she didn't need to sell.

After Christmas, Savannah spent the remainder of her break helping Sadie pack her things. Sadie had decided to take only her clothes, books, silver, and fine china. She told Savannah emptying the house would be akin to taking away her memories completely, and she wasn't ready to do that. She would make new memories in her new home, and that would be enough.

The older woman had divulged to Savannah she had been having a secret affair with J. T. for years, and no one had ever suspected. Sadie had actually blushed. Savannah knew it was J. T. she'd overheard in Sadie's kitchen, but she kept that to herself; she didn't want to spoil Sadie's fun. She was happy for her friend. She was, to be honest, a tad jealous, but she stomped that out while she put honey in her tea and savored its warmth.

Yesterday, they had said good-bye. The Judge had arranged a honeymoon for the two of them. They were going to Hawaii for an entire month, and Sadie had been in a tizzy to get things ready. Savannah smiled, then sighed. Without Sadie, she was alone.

Savannah jumped when a knock came at her door. She was surprised when she found Fletcher standing there. The child was wearing a short-sleeved shirt and jeans. It was freezing outside; Savannah herself had on two shirts and a sweatshirt. Fletcher didn't wait to be asked in; she just threw herself into Savannah's arms. Savannah held her while she pulled her inside and shut the door.

"What's wrong, Fletcher?" she asked, stepping back and sitting on her knees to look the girl in the eyes. Fletcher's hair was swirling in disarray, and Savannah swallowed a lump in her throat. She lifted Fletcher's small face. Tears tracked her wind-flushed cheeks. "What is it, Fletcher?"

"Someone stole my necklace," Fletcher whispered as fresh tears fell. "I's only took it off to take a bath. It won't even an hour...Sheriff Jasper told me I's shouldn't call the police when I's misplace something. Then Pops came home, and I's don't think he believed me either." She gulped. "I's didn't misplace it, Van; someone stole it. I's swear."

Savannah hugged her again, tears in her own eyes. "It's okay, Fletcher. I'm sure whoever took it will see how upset you are and give it back, honey." She sat back and looked at Fletcher. Who would do such a thing?

"You's believe me, don'tcha, Van?" Her voice wobbled. "I's know I's acting like a ninny crying and all, but I's know you's won't tell nobody. 'Sides, Van, I's been wronged." Fletcher took a breath and nodded. "Big time!"

"Yes, honey, I do believe you, and you're not acting like a ninny at all," Savannah said as she rubbed her hands up and down Fletcher's small arms. "Goodness, you're freezing. Come on, I think I have an old sweatshirt you can wear."

She took Fletcher's hand and headed toward her bedroom. She found the sweatshirt, pulled it over Fletcher's head, and rolled up the sleeves, which swallowed the child's arms. "I think we need to do something about this, don't you?" she asked, pulling Fletcher's hair out from beneath the collar.

Fletcher nodded.

She walked the child to the bathroom, then lifted her onto the counter. Fletcher was a lot smaller than her personality portrayed. Savannah grabbed her hairbrush from the drawer. It took about ten minutes to get the knots out, but she kept going until the brown strands were shining. Then she grabbed two bands and braided Fletcher's hair. The girl hadn't said a word, but she was studying Savannah in the mirror. She got a warm washcloth and washed the tears from Fletcher's face. She kissed the top of her head when she was done.

"I's love you's, Van," Fletcher whispered, meeting Savannah's eyes in the mirror.

"I love you too, sweetheart," Savannah said around the lump in her throat. She hugged Fletcher again, tighter this time. "I love you very, very much." They both jumped when someone banged on her door. Fletcher hid her head. Savannah winced. "You didn't tell anyone you were coming over here, did you?" When Fletcher shook her head, Savannah sighed. "Your dad's probably going to tear my door down! We better go show him that you're fine."

****

Emmit glanced down to where three of his daughters were waiting in the SUV, then banged on Savannah's door again. They had searched everywhere for Fletcher, and he'd been ready to call Jasper back to

193

the house when Charlie had suggested they come here first. Not to Sadie but to Savannah. Emmit wasn't sure how he felt about the possibility that Fletcher had come here. But he'd never know if no one answered. There was movement on the other side of the door, and he lifted his fist to knock again when the knob turned and Savannah opened up.

"What the hell took you so long to answer the damn door? Have you seen Fletcher? I can't find her!" Emmit didn't care that he was yelling. He automatically stepped in when she backed up. He was about to continue his rant when he noticed a tiny person. Almost knocking Savannah over, Emmit scooped his daughter up into his arms and held her tight. Kissing her forehead and rocking back and forth.

"Fletcher, if you ever do this to me again, I'll make you wear dresses for the rest of your life. God, I was so worried." He put her down and squatted on the floor still holding her hands. "What in the hell were you thinking leaving like that? You took ten damn years off my life, and you're going to tell me why." He shook her at the end.

Savannah made her way to the kitchen, probably to give them some privacy.

"I's knew you's wouldn't believe me about someone taking my necklace," she accused, stomping her foot.

"Why not?" He knew better than anyone Fletcher wouldn't lie. He believed she truly thought someone had stolen it.

"Because my own sisters didn't believe me! But Van does." She pointed to the kitchen. "*She* believes me, and *she* loves me. She told me so."

Emmit's chest tightened. "You don't think I love you?" How could she think that? He was stunned when she kissed his cheek and hugged him.

"Course you's love me, Daddy." Fletcher snorted. "Don't be a ninny." She shook her head against his neck and stepped back. She made a big production of rolling her eyes, and he smiled.

"Okay! Then you'll know I'm grounding you for your own good," he said and stood. She'd called him Daddy; that lightened his heart. Her braids were in place, and Emmit held one out with a raised brow.

"Van trapped it for me," Fletcher told him smiling and snatching back her braid to study it herself. They both turned when Savannah sucked in a sharp breath.

"What is it, Savannah?" Emmit asked, coming to stand beside her. He glanced down where a small box containing red rose petals lay discarded. He looked back to Savannah, who was clutching something to her chest with one hand while the other held a small piece of paper.

Savannah's mouth moved, but nothing came out at first. "I was just opening the mail...and..." Her fist clenched.

"What is it?" he asked, again studying her.

"It's Fletcher's," she whispered, opening her palm to show him the locket.

"How do you know?" Emmit asked, squinting to try and see what she saw.

"The...the inscription. I had Fletcher's locket engraved."

"That ain't his business," Fletcher hissed from the doorway. She snatched the locket out of Savannah's hands and was putting it around her neck before anyone

195

could stop her.

"There's a note with it, Emmit. Someone put it in my mailbox." She shook her head, eyes wide. "I didn't even check for a postmark when I opened it," she said as she reached out to hold onto Fletcher and handed Emmit the slip of paper.

How close is too close?

Emmit read the words and locked his knees when they threatened to give way. He felt like he'd just been sucker punched. "Sick bastard," he said more to himself than anyone else. His girls weren't safe. And neither, it would seem, was Savannah.

"Someone's threatening us, huh, Pops? I's guess Casey was wrong," Fletcher told him, still caught in Savannah's embrace. She paused, pulled away from Savannah, and covered her mouth with both hands.

Emmit spun around toward her. "What do you mean Casey was wrong? Wrong about what?" What had he missed? His mind began to race. He had to keep his girls safe. Should he send them away? But where? He could send them to stay with his parents in Florida—no, they were in Europe.

"Fletcher, sweetheart, you need to tell us. It's very important," Savannah said, taking Fletcher's hand.

"We's got phone calls when Pops was at the store. We's voted and decided it was just pranks. Pops has enough to worry about."

"Damn you and your flapping mouth," Casey said from the kitchen doorway.

At the same time Charlie said, "We got tired of waiting."

And Alexandra nodded twice.

"Don't yell at your sister, Casey!" Emmit shouted.

"You tell me what was said in those phone calls. How dare you four keep this from me?" He was angry, and damn it, someone was threatening his family.

"Emmit, calm down; there's no need to shout at them," Savannah said, then backed up a bit when he turned to glare at her.

"How I talk to my girls is my business."

"Don't you yell at her! She didn't do nothing! It was my idea to not tell you about the calls," Casey shouted, then raised her chin. "Anyway, all they ever said was 'I'm watching, I'm waiting.' It didn't mean nothing. Just someone trying to scare us is all. I'm sorry we didn't tell you."

"Girls, go in my room for a few minutes. Your father and I need to talk privately," Savannah said, and Emmit pulled out a chair to sit down.

"Will you please tell me what's going on?" Savannah asked once they were alone. She took a seat across from him. "First, tell me what we're dealing with, and then we need to call the police."

"In that order, huh?" He rubbed his hands over his face, groaning. He hadn't wanted the police involved, but he wouldn't risk his girls. "About seven and a half years ago, I had what I thought was a near-fatal *accident*," Emmit said, starting at the beginning. "Then I got a letter." He went on to explain to Savannah about Mr. X. "And now I know the undeniable truth." He studied Savannah's face for a reaction.

"That was where you went. And that's why…" She looked up at him, not finishing what she was going to say as her face grew pink.

"Yeah," he said, "then someone set fire to the store, leaving me a note, but not as to the point as this."

He motioned to the paper on the table. "But the meaning's the same. Whoever it is wants me to know they're still out there, and time's running out."

Savannah stared at him.

"I didn't tell Jasper. I guess I didn't want to believe it. But now..." He shook his head and sighed. "This person was in my house. Inches away from my girls. Close enough to take Fletcher's necklace, and smart enough not to get caught. They could have..." He didn't even want to think about it. But he knew. His girls could have been killed. Tears filled Savannah's eyes before she turned her head. "Whoever it is knows about you too, Savannah. You're not safe either. I'm sorry." He reached out to take her hand, but she used it to briskly wipe the tears from her cheeks.

"Why are you sorry? Is it your fault some lunatic wants to harm you? You're to blame for these things happening? I don't think so, Emmit. I refuse to let you think so, either. As for me being in danger, fine. I'll handle it one way or another." Savannah stood, palms against the table. "What you need to do is call the sheriff, while I go talk to the girls."

Emmit got to his feet as she went to pass him. He caught her arm and looked into her luminous eyes. He sought refuge in her kiss. Understanding. And when she kissed him back, he found what he needed. Savannah pulled away first, and he closed his eyes when she stroked his cheek.

"Make your call," Savannah whispered and headed for the other room.

Emmit waited for the door to close, then picked up the phone. "Jasper? Yeah, it's McKay. Uh...Jasper, there are a few things I may have forgot to mention."

Chapter Twenty-Four

"I can't believe you didn't say a damn thing," Sheriff Jasper Hart said. "I'm madder than hell at you, McKay! Here I've known you all your life and you being former FBI—withholding information from a police investigation. What the hell do you think I should do about that? Hmm?"

Emmit sighed, all too familiar with Jasper's indignation. "I'm sorry, Jasper."

"Sorry, are you?" Jasper huffed. "Now, I know you probably have more experience with this kind of situation than I do, but I'm the sheriff, McKay. *I'm* the damn law, and I need to know what the hell's going on in my own damn town!"

Emmit held up his hands in mock surrender. His girls had been following every move Jasper and the deputies made, and he knew Jasper well enough to know it was making the sheriff uncomfortable. The more he felt his authority was being questioned, the more ornery he became.

"You're infuriating, McKay! When a crime is committed, I, not you, will be the one to bring about justice! We've got us a criminal running around, and I don't have any idea who the hell it could be. Do you?" Jasper asked as he handed one of his deputies the last evidence bag and sent them back to the station.

"If I had any idea who it was, I wouldn't be sitting

here," Emmit said, annoyed. Bad enough someone was out to get him, now everyone would be talking about this. About Savannah and her relationship with his family—with him.

"And that's exactly the attitude I don't need from you! Vigilante talk's what that is."

"Damn it, Jasper!" Emmit shouted but stopped when Fletcher came closer to their conversation.

"I's told you's someone stole my necklace. I's don't lie," Fletcher told Jasper and guilt swathed the sheriff's face.

"I see that," he said, then sighed and pointed to Fletcher's neck. "Miss McKay, I'm gonna have to confiscate your necklace. I'm sorry, but it's now part of this investigation."

Fletcher held her hand to her throat and shook her head. Emmit motioned for her to come to him. "I's don't wanna give it to him. Please don't make me," she whispered in his ear.

"I'm sorry, Fletcher, but he'll give it back. I promise."

Fletcher slowly took off her necklace and walked toward the sheriff. She handed it to him and ran from the room. Casey hot on her heels.

"Sorry, McKay, rules are rules, and some of us got to follow the letter of the law," Jasper said. He turned the locket over, then glanced at Savannah. "Guess what people's saying's true. You got the McKay girls jewelry for Christmas."

"How did you know?" Savannah asked, her face turning red.

"That's probably my fault," Charlie explained. "I told Ida Mae and, well…" She shrugged her small shoulders.

"I said something to Trixy," Alexandra confessed.

"Well," Jasper said, then snickered. "Everyone knows the Mae women like to talk."

"No worries, I wasn't trying to hide anything," Savannah said. "Come on, girls, let's check on your sisters."

Emmit gave Savannah a small smile. She was trying to put on a brave front, but she couldn't hide her unease. He rubbed his hands over his stubbled jaw as Jasper spoke his own thoughts.

"What a mess!" Jasper said, shaking his head. He held up the bag containing the necklace. "I'll run prints, but I doubt I'll find any."

"I don't think you will." No, whoever was doing this was way too careful.

"What are you going to do?"

"Put my girls somewhere safe. Try to convince Savannah to go somewhere else as well." He shrugged.

"I would ask you to let me know what you're planning, but I have a feeling I wouldn't like the answer! As far as the girls go, if you need help or if Ms. Walker needs something, you can always call my wife. For some reason, Laura doesn't care how infuriating I think you McKays are," Jasper said with a smirk. "Now, I'm headed out. I'll warn you though; if you don't tell me the truth from now on, I'll arrest you for obstruction. Got it?" He didn't wait for Emmit to answer; he just left shaking his head.

****

"They're all asleep," Savannah told Emmit as she stepped out onto the porch to join him. Sitting this close, she could feel his heat. They had left her apartment, Emmit insisting she come home with them. He told her they would be safe tonight because today had been about the warning, setting up pieces for the next move. Tomorrow, they would have to make plans. But she'd already made hers. "What a day," she said, and he gave a sarcastic laugh.

"I *am* sorry, Savannah," he told her, turning so they were face to face. He touched her hair.

"I'm not," she said honestly. Savannah had admitted to herself she loved him, and she felt foolish for doing so. Love wasn't what she thought it would be, nor what she had mistaken it for in her youth. It was complicated, and…and…her heart was broken because she knew he couldn't love her in return.

Savannah wasn't naive enough to think she could love enough for the both of them. She deserved more than that. Would she tell him how she felt? No. Why cause herself more pain, or admit out loud what a fool she was? No, she would keep it to herself. Now, for the hard part. "I'm going to go back to Maryland."

His eyes may have darkened, but there wasn't enough light to be accurate. He did turn away from her though.

"I see. What about your job?" Emmit asked, his voice tight.

"I called in my resignation when I was on the phone earlier. It wouldn't have been possible to keep it anyway. Ian Thomas already wants my head on a platter, and when this gets out, he'd have all the ammunition he needs to ruin me."

"You're going to let him win?"

"Leaving on *my* terms isn't letting him win. In fact, I think he'll be disappointed not to get the chance to burn me at the stake."

"Maybe."

"Think what you want, Emmit, but I know I'm right." About Ian Thomas at the very least.

"When are you planning on leaving?"

"Tomorrow," she said, glad it was dark to hide her tears.

"What about your stuff?" Emmit asked.

"I'll send for it once I'm settled in."

Emmit got up and walked into the yard. "What should I tell the girls?" His tone was demanding. Was he upset? No, she knew better than that.

"You won't need to tell them anything. I plan on telling them in the morning." It was going to kill her.

"I guess I should thank you for that." Emmit sighed.

"I'd never leave them without saying good-bye." Or telling them I love them. "I'm going back inside."

****

She had taken over his room. Emmit was getting some clothes, and then he was going to the guest room upstairs. He could smell her. He closed his eyes. Savannah was in the bathroom getting ready for bed. He stared at the door. She was leaving; he'd seen the suitcases in her Jeep. The shower turned on, and on impulse, he went in.

Savannah's eyes widened when he opened the shower door, but she stepped aside so he could join her. He bent down and kissed her, closing his eyes only after she'd closed hers. His tongue came out to taste her, and he tried to be gentle, so very gentle. He was pleased when she kissed him back with the same care.

Emmit stepped back to gaze into her blue eyes,

squashing the thought that he would not see her again. He wouldn't think about it. Not now. He reached for the shampoo. Pouring some in his hand, he began to wash her hair, and she turned to give him better access. He loved her hair. Emmit savored each moment, as he made sure they were both thoroughly cleaned. He took his time drying her off once they'd finished. Dropping the towel on the floor, he scooped her up into his arms.

He carried her to his bed and laid her down. Emmit stepped back to take her in. She lay there, amongst the shadows cast from the bathroom light. Seeing Savannah like this made it difficult to keep his sanity, and he took a steadying breath as he joined her on the bed.

Emmit lay beside her half on, half off her. Her hardened nipples pressed into his chest, and he kissed her softly. Then his fingers took a journey to her breast, kneading the fullness and using his thumb to graze the sensitized flesh. Savannah arched into his hand, and he squeezed, making her moan. He dipped his tongue in and kissed her deeply, still molding her breast. He left her lips to find her nipple with his teeth and tongue.

"Emmit, please..." Savannah pushed at his head and then his chest, making him roll over. She kissed him then, first on his lips and then downward. She nipped at his neck where his pulse spiked. Emmit groaned when she repeated the action. Her soft lips and sharp nails made their way down his chest. He sucked in a breath as she reached down to squeeze his erection. And he clenched his jaw when her trail of kisses led her to his most sensitive spot. He squeezed his eyes shut at the pleasure of her mouth on him, but he had to stop her before...

Emmit reached down to pull her up, his cheek

twitching. He kissed her, tasting himself on her mouth. He didn't think it was possible, but he got even harder. He then rolled them over so she was under him.

Her nails bit into his back, making him groan once again. Savannah was a wildcat, no question. He laughed and lifted up to meet her gaze. "I was trying to be gentle and suave."

"I'm not made of glass, Emmit," Savannah said, rolling her glittery blue eyes at him and giving him a seductive smile. He kissed her again, and she pulled his head tighter against her lips to deepen the kiss.

Releasing her, he sat up and rolled her onto her stomach. He kissed her shoulder gently. "Rise up on your knees," Emmit whispered into her ear. She was trembling beneath him. "It's okay," he soothed, running his hand along her spine. "You're so damn sexy, Savannah," he murmured as he maneuvered himself behind her. She sucked in a breath as he slipped inside her wet heat. He had to close his eyes as she contracted around him. He moved once, then twice, groaning.

"Are you okay?" he asked, slowing his strokes.

"Yes," she whispered. He ran his hand along one side of her body, and goose bumps rose on her soft skin.

Taking a breath, he brought her up with him so he was on his knees and inside her to the hilt. He pulled her arms over his head to wrap them around his neck. He was as deep as he could possibly get. Emmit moved gently at first, swiveling his hips, and as he increased his pace, her grip on his neck tightened. Her breathing quickened, and she started to move faster, harder until stars danced behind his eyes. His hand had come up to her mouth to cover her moan as she convulsed around him.

Emmit squeezed his eyes shut as her inner muscles contracted. Making her so tight her body was milking him. He pumped into her once, twice, and finally one last long hard stroke, and he held firmly onto her shoulders as he climaxed. He wanted to brand her as his in this moment.

Slowly, he released her shoulders, catching her when she slumped forward. He kissed her flesh where his hands had left marks, then wrapped his arms around her. Savannah's hands squeezed his forearms as her head rolled back against his chest. Emmit turned over, dislodging himself, then turned her into his arms. He brushed her hair out of her face and kissed her closed eyelids. Savannah smiled and opened her eyes. He turned into her hand when she reached up to cup his sweaty face.

"Sleep here with me," she said. "We can set the alarm, so we wake up before the girls." She looked at him with pleading eyes. He nodded and set the alarm but didn't get up to turn off the bathroom light.

Emmit wrapped his arms around her, and she spooned against him. No one spoke of the future because there was none to speak of. Emmit was almost asleep when one of her tears rolled down his arm.

Chapter Twenty-Five

She woke to an incessant buzzing. Savannah rolled over Emmit to shut off the noise. He was sleeping soundly. She stared at him, his chest rose and fell. He was still naked, but then so was she. They had made love twice more during the night. The soreness of her body reminded her. The second time had been slow and gentle, while the third had been just as intense as the first. She had been tempted to tell him she loved him, but she decided it was best to keep it to herself.

Savannah slipped out of the bed and hurried to take a shower. She didn't want to say good-bye to him. Or more accurately, she didn't think she would be able to. She was showered and dressed in five minutes flat.

Her hair was still wet and soaking her sweater as she snuck out of his room. She left her bag of clothes and her shoes by the back door, so all she'd have to do was grab and go. She headed up to where the girls slept, being extra careful because it wasn't yet dawn and the hallway was dark. She crept up the attic stairs, trying to keep her breath steady.

Savannah was surprised to find a light on and even more surprised the girls were awake. They were sitting in a circle sifting through papers. When she cleared her throat, they scrambled around. Her heart jumped in her chest.

"Good morning, girls," she began. "I've got

something to talk to you all about." Then she came fully into the space and sat down between Casey and Charlie, who moved over to give her room.

"This about Pops sending us away?" Casey asked with a frown.

"No. I don't know what your father's going to do about that. But I'm sure wherever it is, it will be safe." They all nodded. She took a deep breath. "I wanted to tell you I turned in my resignation as principal. I quit."

"You quit your job 'cause of us, huh?"

"No, Casey, not because of you girls. Honestly, that was part of it, but not all. I'm not cut out to be a principal in a small town. Marylou's parents were driving me crazy," she admitted, making them laugh.

"Who will be the principal then?" Charlie asked.

"I don't know, honey. But you'll be fine."

"What are you going to do?" Alexandra asked, and the group stared at Savannah.

"I'm not sure yet." She shrugged and smiled weakly. "I'll figure it out, so don't worry."

"Where are you going?" Casey asked, narrowing her eyes behind her glasses.

Savannah swallowed. "Maryland." She was surprised when Casey flinched, then asked her why. "Because I can't stay here. I have to move on," she choked out.

"You's leaving me?" Fletcher accused with tears running down her cheeks. "You's leaving me?"

Casey grabbed her and held her tight. Charlie also had tears in her eyes. Alexandra's face was flushed, and she was staring at Savannah, silent.

"It's not you I'm leaving, sweetheart. It's…" Her voice broke, and she reached out to take Fletcher's hand.

"Who you's leaving then? *Who*? You's told me that you's loved me! You's lied to me!" Fletcher's voice was so tortured, Savannah's heart broke again.

"I didn't lie, Fletcher. I swear I wasn't lying," Savannah said, ignoring the tears that fell. "I do love you. I love each of you more than anything." She glanced around the small circle. "That's why I have to go."

"You love us?" Alexandra asked with an edge to her voice that Savannah didn't understand. "You love us so much you're going to leave us?" Charlie grabbed Alexandra's hand, but she snatched it back.

"Look at her, Alexandra. She isn't lying," Charlie whispered.

"Of course, I love you." Too much. Savannah wiped her cheeks and covered her eyes. Arms came around her, and she hugged the child. She opened her eyes to find Casey holding her. Casey gave her a squeeze and backed away. She ducked her head and sat next to Fletcher, who was rocking herself.

"It's because of her, isn't it?" Casey asked, and her sisters looked up. "It's cause of Gracie. He can't see past her. He sure as hell never saw through her. That's it, isn't it? You love Pops and us, but he doesn't love you?" Everyone was waiting for Savannah's answer, but she couldn't find her voice so she nodded. Her girls were smart. *Her* girls!

"We love you back. But that's not enough, is it?" Casey whispered, taking off her glasses and reaching up to touch her cheek. She stared at her hand when she pulled it away.

"Case? Oh shit, Case," Fletcher whispered.

"I'm sorry." Savannah rose to her feet. She had to leave. She couldn't do this anymore.

"Wait, Van!" Fletcher yelled, stopping Savannah before she could make it to the steps. Fletcher pulled Savannah down to her level and hugged her tight. "I's will always love you's forever," she whispered in Savannah's ear, then kissed her cheek. She backed away letting Charlie and Alexandra through. They hugged her, their bodies trembling.

"We love you, too, Savannah," Alexandra said and Charlie nodded. Then they backed away, leaving Savannah to face Casey, the child who didn't cry, who had tears running down her cheeks. Her eyes were pure violet.

"I never loved anyone like a ma before," Casey began, making Savannah's heart stop. "I guess this is as close as I'm ever gonna get." With that she hugged Savannah. "I love you."

"I know," Savannah whispered back. She let Casey go and stood up. "If you ever need me, I'm just a phone call away." She pulled out the small scrap of paper she'd written her cell number on and handed it to Casey. Fletcher snatched it away and put it in the pocket of her shirt right over her heart.

Instead of reaching out for one more hug, Savannah rushed down both flights of stairs and grabbed her stuff. Someone was calling her name, but she didn't dare stop—she hadn't even bothered to put on her shoes. She ran to her Jeep, opened the door, and threw everything into the passenger side. She didn't pause, just started the engine, and took off without looking back.

****

Emmit stood on the porch until the Jeep turned the corner. Savannah was gone. She hadn't even said good-bye to him. He had heard her running down the stairs, so he knew she'd said good-bye to his girls. He'd called her name, but she hadn't heard him...or didn't want to. He walked out of the cold into the warmth of the house, but the chill didn't leave him. He hadn't bothered with a shirt, but that was the least of his worries. Emmit hit the lights because it was still dark out and turned to make himself some coffee. It was going to be a long day.

He wasn't prepared for the sight that presented itself before him when his daughters made their way into the kitchen. Charlie's blonde hair was coming out of its braid, and her face was both red and wet. Alexandra was next. Her face was white, and her eyes cold. Emmit swallowed hard. He looked at Fletcher, but she refused to meet his gaze. That left Casey; her violet eyes were red, swollen, and filled with tears. He dropped his coffee cup and jumped as it shattered. It was like a bomb in the silence.

"Casey?"

"Like you never seen a body cry before," she sneered at him.

"I've never seen *you* cry, Casey," he said. Charlie had started sweeping up the broken glass. "I'll get that, sweetheart." He reached for the broom to take over, but Charlie flinched and jerked away from him, tears falling down her cheeks.

"I got it," she whispered.

"Will someone tell me what the hell I did? Please?" His chest hurt, and it was hard to breathe. "Girls, please talk to me."

"She's gone," Alexandra answered in a voice as icy and biting as the winter wind. "She's gone, and she isn't coming back."

There was a whimper, and Emmit looked in Fletcher's direction. The child had curled into a corner of the kitchen holding herself.

"I'm sorry Savannah had to go. I didn't want her to go either." And God help him, he hadn't. If she had stopped, he would have asked—hell, he would have begged her to stay. He didn't know if he could trust himself to love her, but could he live without her?

"Whatcha say?" Fletcher asked, finally speaking. She crawled out of the corner and stood up in front of Emmit.

No one saw it; no one heard it until it was too late. The window exploded, and Fletcher was slammed forward. She tried to block her fall with one hand, but her wrist gave way and her head smacked hard against the linoleum. Emmit was by Fletcher's side within seconds. Everyone else was on the floor scrambling for cover.

Alexandra crawled on her belly to where the phone hung. She plastered herself against the wall and rose up slowly until her fingers found the cord. She gave it a hard yank and caught the phone with the other hand.

Emmit rolled Fletcher over onto her back with great care to inspect her wound, looking up as Charlie scooted across the floor. He could hear Alexandra speaking to the emergency dispatcher.

Emmit called Fletcher's name a few times and about died of happiness when she opened her eyes. She was grinning at him, the little shit. He checked her pulse, which was beating hard and steady.

"Oh, baby," he whispered, kissing her forehead. Emmit couldn't see how bad the wound was, but blood was soaking through her shirt and onto the floor. Charlie handed him a towel. He covered the top of Fletcher's shoulder and put pressure on it. She flinched and stopped grinning.

"Hells bells, Daddy, that hurts!" she whispered.

"I'm sorry, kiddo," he whispered back.

Fletcher rolled her eyes, then she actually *tsk*ed at him. "Grown men don't cry, you's know," she said as her head lolled from one side to the other.

Yeah, his tears were flowing freely, and who would say anything about it. Emmit took inventory of the room and noted where the bullet had embedded itself in the one of the cabinets. Charlie was holding Fletcher's hand and whispering in her ear. Alexandra, still on the phone, was staring at him. She gave him one sharp nod letting him know help was on the way. He checked where Casey had been. She wasn't there.

"Charlie, keep pressure on the wound," he said, replacing his large hands with her smaller ones. "Keep it tight." She nodded. Emmit got to his knees and crawled, hitting the light switch on his way so that the room went dark.

The porch door was open, so he went out and sure enough there she was. His oldest girl was on her belly with a rifle trained between two porch rails. She was waiting, calm and steady. Just like she'd been taught. Emmit didn't want to scare her, so he made a slight noise. She didn't move. She didn't even look at him.

"She alive?"

"Yes, and she should be all right. Alexandra called for help." He hoped they would hurry the hell up.

Emmit scanned the lawn and the surrounding woods for movement, but with the sun still low on the horizon, he couldn't see much. He closed his eyes and exhaled a shaky breath as sirens pierced the quiet. Casey moved then, sitting up, then standing slowly, never taking her eyes away from the yard. He snatched the rifle out of her hand and grabbed her. She had guts, but in this moment, she had too much for his peace of mind.

They went back into the kitchen, and Emmit traded places with Charlie again. Fletcher was still conscious, which was a damn good sign. Charlie went over to Alexandra, and Casey held Fletcher's hand.

And that's exactly how Sheriff Jasper Hart and the paramedics found them.

****

They were sitting in the waiting room of the hospital. The doctor had come out and told Emmit Fletcher would be fine. He said the bullet, though it had taken a chunk of flesh and caused profuse bleeding, had only grazed her shoulder. Her wrist was fractured, and she had a concussion. They had stitched her up and given her a transfusion to replace the lost blood; considering what could have happened, the doctor said, she was one lucky little girl.

Emmit had been so relieved, he sat down in the middle of the hallway. Now he paced the waiting room needing to see her with his own eyes. His other daughters sat together on the floor. They were whispering and glancing at him. Evan and Kyle sat in chairs staring at him. Both were pissed off. Evan was angry because Emmit hadn't called him yesterday when the package came to Savannah's. God, was it just yesterday? It felt like an eternity. And Kyle was pissed that Emmit had kept him completely in the dark. He'd read Emmit the riot act, literally.

"Mr. McKay?" a nurse addressed the group. They all stood. The nurse blinked and then pointed to Emmit when he raised his hand. "You can see your daughter now." He took a step down the hall, and Casey was right behind him.

"I'm sorry, but we can't allow her to come in with you," the nurse said, motioning to Casey.

"What in the hell are you talking about, lady? I *am* going in, and you can't stop me. You—*oomph*—" She was cut off when Evan scooped her up and covered her mouth. She was squirming, but he held tight.

"Go on, McKay, we'll be fine," Evan assured him with a nod as he carried Casey back to the waiting room.

"Is she Savannah?" the nurse asked. "She's been asking for Savannah or Van. One or the other. Was that her?"

Emmit shook his head and followed her down the corridor. It was a small private room. Fletcher looked like a doll lying there in the big hospital bed. She had an IV in her small arm. She smiled at him when he walked in.

"Hi, Daddy," she said sheepishly and narrowed her eyes. "You's mad at me?"

He tripped over himself to get to the bed and took her hand carefully, not wanting to hurt her. "God, no. Why would you ask that?"

She shrugged, then winced. "I's went and got shot," she said, sighing.

"That wasn't your fault, kiddo," he said, kissing the top of her head.

"You's ain't mad then?"

"No. I am not mad at you." He shook his head. He was so happy she was alive. There was nothing she could do to piss him off at this moment.

She nodded. "Good, 'cause I's ain't leaving here or talking to nobody until you's bring Savannah back." Fletcher narrowed her eyes. "She gave us her phone number; it's in the pocket of my shirt. Call it and bring her back. I's ain't leaving or talking till you's do," she declared, then shifted. "I's still love yah, Daddy. Now that's the last thing I's saying." And she made a zipping motion across her lips with her fingers.

"Fletcher, Savannah isn't coming back," he said, and she crossed her arms. "Be careful; don't pull out your damn stitches!"

Her eyes brightened.

"It'll hurt like hell if you do, Fletcher."

She grinned.

"Fine, I'll try. If she's not here in a week, we go. That's the only deal I'll give you." The doctor had said that due to her age—and the insistence of the sheriff—a week of inpatient observation was advised; Emmit figured Fletcher didn't need to know that.

She shook his hand in agreement. He kissed her forehead and left the room. He had to find where they'd put Fletcher's clothes…and then figure out what the hell to do next.

Chapter Twenty-Six

She was pregnant. Savannah shook her head for the millionth time as she pulled up to the room she was renting. She had called her old landlord before she'd left Blue Creek to see if they had anything available. The furnished one-bedroom apartment was hers on a month-to-month basis until she decided what she wanted to do. Almost a week had passed since she left Blue Creek, and she hadn't heard anything from anyone. Savannah let out a deep breath, not wanting to go down that road; she knew it was a one-way ticket to a crying jag. She was going to have a baby, and that was her number one priority.

Savannah bit her lip not knowing if she should let her smile escape. Her heart felt lighter. She'd called her old gynecologist and made an appointment after she'd taken a home pregnancy test. She remembered feeling the overwhelming rush of emotion when her doctor confirmed she was pregnant. Once she'd finished crying, she'd been instructed to lay off the caffeine altogether and take prenatal vitamins.

She was going to have Emmit's baby. She was almost two months along, which told her she'd gotten pregnant the first time they were together. Savannah rested her hand on her flat stomach as she shut the front door behind her. She was floating all the way to the kitchen where she put on a kettle to make some herbal tea. She stood by the stove as the water heated and let her mind fly.

Though she knew she shouldn't, Savannah let herself think about the girls and Emmit. She'd spent five absolutely miserable days here trying to come to grips with what had happened and a future she couldn't see clearly. Especially now. So many times she had picked up the phone to call them just so she could hear their voices, but she had never finished dialing. She had given them her number, but she figured Emmit had sent the girls away and was trying to deal with the situation. Maybe he didn't know what to think.

"Oh, just stop it, Savannah Francis!" she berated herself. She was making excuses because she didn't want to believe they didn't want her in their lives, that they could move on so quickly; she, on the other hand, wondered about *them* with every breath she took.

She sat staring out of the window and sipping her tea. As the snow fell, she couldn't help but wonder how everyone was in Blue Creek. She hoped Sheriff Hart had everything under control. It was only when she went to refill her cup that the light blinking on her answering machine caught her attention.

"Maybe the doctor's office?" she thought aloud and pressed the button. Savannah listened to five hang-ups as she sipped her tea. She froze when the sixth message played.

"Savannah? Damn it, it's taken me forever to find your number! I need you here." There was a pause and then a heavy sigh. "Look, I hate to tell this to a machine, but Fletcher's been hurt..."

Savannah didn't listen to the rest of Emmit's message. She ran to her bedroom, grabbed her suitcase, and started throwing in clothes.

****

Savannah arrived at the McKay home around ten that night, but there were no lights on. Where could they be? She had packed her things, loaded the Jeep, and once again made the long drive from Maryland to North Carolina. She'd only stopped when she absolutely had to. She should have called someone, but she wanted information face to face, not over the phone.

Savannah went to the hospital thinking she should have gone there first. She raced for the door, stopping only to find out where Fletcher was. She'd tapped her foot impatiently while the nurse at the front desk checked to make sure her name was on the list. Once she was cleared, Savannah took the elevator, pacing around the other people occupying it with her. It stopped at the floor she needed, and she jumped out and ran down the hallway. And there he was, standing in the corridor talking to Sheriff Hart. She didn't stop to think, just headed his way.

Emmit stepped away from the sheriff in time to catch her. He kissed her before she could say a word. Savannah sighed and leaned into him. They parted only when Sheriff Hart cleared his throat. Emmit kissed her cheek and inserted her under his arm. He started walking them down the hall, ignoring the other man.

"How is she? What happened? I didn't even listen to the entire message, I just came." Savannah pulled away from him, craning her neck to meet his eyes.

Emmit stopped. "She's going to be fine, Savannah." He grinned and explained Fletcher's vow not to speak. "Now that you're here, maybe she'll talk."

Savannah relaxed and laughed as the tears started coming. Emmit wiped them away with his thumbs, then guided her toward the room.

"When did this happen?"

"The day you left," Emmit began and rushed on when Savannah took an outraged breath. "Fletcher had put your phone number in her shirt—the same shirt she was hurt in—and we couldn't find that slip of paper and…trust me, I looked."

"Then how did you find me?" He'd been trying to reach her all this time; she was ashamed of herself for the things she'd been thinking.

"Mildred finally thought to call the school board and get your information from your application. Which they wouldn't give her." Emmit smiled. "The old girl nearly came off her hinges when they told her no. Luckily, Jasper stepped in and helped us out." He sighed and gestured toward the door. "Here we are."

Savannah took a deep breath and put her hand on the knob. She looked at Emmit over her shoulder. "Could you give us a few minutes alone, please?"

He nodded.

Savannah entered the room slowly. The small light made Fletcher appear tiny and pitiful. Savannah walked over to the bed and sat on the edge. Fletcher was sleeping. She looked so sweet up close. She leaned in and whispered in Fletcher's ear, "Sweetheart, you have to get better. I'm going to make you a big sister—*ouch*!" Savannah jumped back and rubbed her forehead after Fletcher's head came up and smacked into hers. Her blue-green eyes were wide open, and she was grinning like a fool.

"Really?" Fletcher shouted. Savannah laughed,

seeing with her own eyes that Fletcher was going to be back to normal in no time. She made a shushing gesture with her finger.

"Truly. But we can't tell your dad just yet, okay?" She had known the minute her eyes had landed on Emmit talking to Sheriff Hart that she'd been deluding herself. She loved Emmit too much, loved these girls too much, to just give them up.

"I's cross my heart. I's won't tell, and neither will they," Fletcher said, pointing to her sisters who had come out of hiding. Savannah gasped.

"Cross my heart," Charlie said.

"Hope to die," Alexandra added.

"Stick a needle in my eye," Casey finished, and they all crossed their hearts.

"I's glad you's came, Van," Fletcher said after Savannah had hugged everyone.

"Me too, sweetheart. Now, someone tell me what happened." They all rushed to tell her, but Casey held up her hand. It was the signal only she could use, being the oldest, and everyone stopped talking so she could tell it. Savannah listened after grabbing Fletcher's hand and holding it tightly.

"Oh, my God, you were shot!" she squeaked when they were finished. "Oh, my poor baby." She hugged Fletcher to her.

"I see you found the stowaways," Emmit said, walking into the room.

"Something like that," Savannah said, and then the girls broke into a fit of giggles. Savannah smiled when Emmit raised an eyebrow, then shrugged.

"Thanks for getting Van, Daddy," Fletcher said and looked at Savannah. "I's sick and tired of going from this bed to that bed and back again. I's been poked at, pulled on, and policed. All I's can do is sit here all day. And it don't even hurt." She lifted her arm to show Savannah, then winced. "Okay, maybe it hurts some, but that's 'sides the point." Fletcher pointed to Emmit. "The point is, when are we's bustin' me outta this joint?"

"Tomorrow morning is what they're telling everyone," Emmit said, "but we're breaking you out of here tonight."

"Where are you taking them?" Savannah wanted to know.

"*You* and the girls are going to hide out at the apartment above Ward and Evan's garage. Apparently, Ward and Evan have a termite infestation, and the garage will be closed until it's taken care of." Emmit winked and then shrugged. "It's not the Ritz, but Evan fixed it up a bit so it'll be more comfortable."

"That's fine." Savannah wouldn't argue about going with them; she had planned on it. She cocked her head to the side. "And where are *you* going to stay?"

"At the house." The girls started complaining. "You keep going on like that, and you're going to get us all in trouble," he warned.

"But, Pops, we haven't been back to the house all week," Casey said.

"Then where have you been staying?" Savannah wanted to know.

"We were going to stay at Granddaddy's, since no one is there, but Daddy couldn't remember where he put the key," Alexandra said with a haughty sigh.

Savannah pursed her lips to keep from smiling. "I see."

"We've been staying at the hotel next door," Emmit said.

"But now it's safe for you to stay at the house?"

"Yes, Savannah, it's safe. A security system was installed this morning." He gave a heavy sigh. "I've never needed one living in Blue Creek, but...desperate times and all that. Jasper's got some guys patrolling our property. And I'll be armed." Savannah knew he was waiting for a reaction from her, but to be honest she was relieved.

"We're going to miss an awful lot of school," Charlie grumbled. "I've only ever missed one day, and now I've missed a week!" She cupped her face in her hands. "I'll be so behind."

"That's not a problem. I'm more than qualified to teach you. I'll have Sheriff Hart get in touch with Mildred to register you all for home schooling."

"How long we gonna be at Uncle Evan's?" Casey asked, crossing her arms over her chest.

"As long as it's safe there. It's either that or Uncle Kyle takes you to a safe house. We've spread a rumor I'm sending you all to stay with my parents in Florida. And no one in Blue Creek knows you've come back yet, Savannah. If people see you, they won't be suspicious."

"That sounds reasonable. Do you have a plan to catch this person?" Savannah asked.

"Yeah, but none of you need to worry about it," Emmit said just as Evan and Kyle walked in.

****

The apartment above the garage was cramped and musty. Savannah wrinkled her nose for the twentieth time. There was a small bathroom that Evan said he'd spent most of the day repairing so they could use it. The small kitchenette boasted a minifridge, microwave, and small sink to do the dishes. It wasn't five-star, but they would be safe.

The girls had been in awe of the room. Apparently, it hadn't looked this good the last time they were here. She smiled. Evan had gone out of his way for them. The man went out of his way for most people. Savannah wondered, not for the first time, if he was seeing anybody. He could tell you just about anything you wanted to know about the people of Blue Creek, but he wouldn't say anything about his personal life. Savannah shrugged. Let him have his own life; he deserved it.

Kyle had been here as well. He had brought groceries, books, a VCR, and movies. Lots of movies. He had also gone by the house and picked up the girls' things. Then he picked up some of the things Savannah had left at Sadie's, including her board games.

The girls had laid out their sleeping bags on the air mattresses and crawled in. They were sleeping soundly. Savannah let out a heavy sigh.

"Been a rough week...a rough month for everybody," Evan said, coming in the door. He was wearing black sweats that only made him appear more intimidating. His buzz cut glistened from the shower he'd taken. He was drinking a can of soda, which looked ridiculous in his hand. He came and sat on the sofa with her.

Savannah had put on long flannel pajamas. Charlie had braided her hair, then twisted it into a bun. She was tired but smiled at Evan anyway. "You could say that. An adventure of sorts, I suppose." She brought her knees up and rested her head on them.

"An adventure? You are nuts, lady," he said, laughing a little. They both kept their voices down. There was a small lamp, but the room was dim. Evan was watching the girls sleep as he took a sip of his drink.

If Savannah hadn't seen it, she never would have believed it. His hand trembled. This big man was trembling. She glanced away.

"Are you gonna leave again after this is over? Or are you gonna stick it out?" he asked her, sitting back against the cushions.

"I'm not going anywhere. Besides, I was back within a week."

"Yeah, but Fletcher had to get shot." There was a bite to his voice.

"You're angry with me?" she asked, brows puckered.

"More disappointed, I guess. I thought you were a fighter." He shrugged as she lowered her legs and turned to face him fully.

"Why do you care so much, Evan? What does it matter to you if I go or stay?" His anger was obvious, and it fueled her own.

"I only want what's best for those girls. I thought it was you, but now I'm not so sure." He shrugged. "You were quick to leave them."

"Where do you get off saying that to me? Weren't you the one who warned me off Emmit? Are you not the same man that basically told me Emmit was a lost cause?" She was so offended, she was having a hard time whispering.

"You didn't listen though, did you? Now we have

to adjust to the changes. Are you strong enough to stay and stick through this? You gonna fight for him, Savannah?" Evan's eyes scrutinized her, and Savannah straightened her spine.

"I'm strong enough, and I will fight for him...and them, even if it kills me." She had let Emmit down. For a week, he had been trying to reach her, and her pride, her stupid *pride*, hadn't let her pick up the phone and call him herself. If she had, she'd have been here sooner.

"You left once. What's to stop you from doing it again?" he asked.

"I left because I was confused and scared. But I have more information now. There's too much at stake to leave again." Evan followed her as she rose to go to the kitchen. She faced him. "I'd gladly die for them, Evan. In a heartbeat!" she whispered and then ducked her head.

"Oookay, this has gots to stop!" Fletcher said from the air mattress on the floor. She rose taking extra care not to hurt herself as Savannah reminded her for at least the eightieth time.

"Uncle Evan, please leave her alone. You're going make her cry and really piss me off," Alexandra said, sitting up with a sniff.

"Yeah, and there isn't nothing worse than a pissed-off lady. Leave her alone, Uncle Evan," Casey warned from her position on the air mattress.

"She isn't going anywhere, are you, Savannah?" Charlie asked, rolling her eyes as she sat up.

"I told you, I'm staying right here," Savannah said, giving Evan a dirty look for waking the girls. She was glad he had the decency to wince.

"I's wasn't talking about Uncle Evan. Sheesh, he's just being a ninny. I's was talking about this 'dying for us' business. It ain't gonna happen, Van. You's can't die; you's made me a promise, remember? I's gonna hold yah to it. 'Sides, getting shot hurts like hell." Fletcher pointed to her shoulder, then narrowed her eyes. "You's go and get hurt, and all bets are off."

"She's got you there, Van. You did promise her. And us. We're holding you to it too," Casey chimed in.

"Remember the big bad wolf?" Charlie asked Savannah, who couldn't help but smile and nod. "He's got nothing on us."

"It's unanimous. You go back on your promise, and the hounds of hell won't be able to track you down where we put you," Alexandra said, getting an approving nod from all her sisters.

Casey gaped at Alexandra. "What the hell's gotten into you?"

Alexandra lifted an eyebrow. "What? Being a *lady* is hard. Being a Neanderthal brute like you is easy."

Evan laughed. "I don't know what the hell they're talking about, but that's good enough for me." He hopped up on the counter when the girls moved into the small kitchenette. "Now that you're staying, what are you gonna do? Job-wise, I mean. I know you resigned as principal. What are you gonna do now?"

Savannah's brow furrowed. "I have no idea. I have a master's in education. I have a bachelor's degree in business." She shrugged when everyone stared at her. "I liked school and figured, why not?"

"Okay, well if you're staying here, the master's is out. We'll focus on business." Evan brightened. "I think I've got an idea."

He explained it to them, and Savannah nodded. It sounded good to her.

Chapter Twenty-Seven

Emmit sat at the kitchen table alone. Hell, they didn't even have a damn dog. Evan was with Savannah and the girls. Lucky bastard. Kyle had to go back to the city for work and wouldn't be back for a couple days. Lawyers, apparently, were always employed, and Kyle was exceptional at his job.

Emmit had spent a good hour fixing the window, then spent what seemed like an eternity cleaning the stain from his daughter's blood off the kitchen floor, finally deciding to replace the whole damn thing. He had moved the table out and unhooked the fridge. He felt a sort of bliss when he tore into the floor. He had taken it out and moved the table back in. And here he sat at a kitchen table that rested on an unfinished floor.

It was almost dawn. He should be sleeping, but he hadn't been able to; hence, the renovations. Sleep wouldn't come easily when he knew someone was out there waiting…watching. Emmit wanted to get the son of a bitch who shot Fletcher. The fact they had been aiming at him didn't matter. No, the bastard could have killed his baby. That alone, in Emmit's mind, warranted a death sentence.

He started wondering again about who it could be. Someone who was close to him way back then might not be now. He had lost touch with this town, Emmit admitted to himself. He was close to a lot of people before he had gotten shot. Then his group of friends dwindled considerably after Gracie died.

Emmit hadn't wanted to deal with people. Furthermore, the town hadn't exactly opened their arms to his girls. That hadn't only pissed him off, it hurt him. He'd known these people all his life. Hell, his family had been part of the founding of Blue Creek. But one of them wanted him dead. The question was, who?

The sun rose, brightening the kitchen. The room resembled Emmit, ragged and dirty. Well, that's what happened when you rip up linoleum. He needed to get at least a few hours of sleep if he was going to be worth a damn.

****

The house was silent at noon when Emmit woke. He took a shower and headed to town. He ignored Jasper's deputies, sitting in their squad cars. He needed to get some flooring for the kitchen. There had been a print that had caught his eye in the shipment a couple weeks ago. It was a creamy yellow in a pattern that resembled terracotta tile. Charlie would love it, which made it perfect.

He pulled in behind the shop and entered through the side door. He knew no matter where he went he'd be a target, so he turned on the lights, unlocked the front entrance, and flipped the sign. Let the perpetrator come after him directly. Better him than the girls.

The sheriff was the first person to walk in. "McKay, the report just came in, and as we suspected, there were no prints on the envelope Ms. Walker received." He scratched his chin. "We didn't find anything around your property, neither."

"We didn't expect to find prints, Jasper," Emmit

said as he straightened a display of paint brushes.

"True, true. But answer me this. If this person is so damn good, why hire a killer? Why didn't he just do it himself?" Jasper put his hands on his hips.

"I've thought about that. I can only guess they didn't want my blood literally on their hands." Emmit shrugged.

"I can see that. Then I think, maybe he ain't too good with a rifle neither 'cause that bullet, which we assume was meant for you..."

"It was. Fletcher just got in the way." He would never forget that. Never. What sleep he'd gotten this morning was haunted by the memory...as it had been every night for the last week.

"Knowing that, the shooter missed your head and heart by a mile."

"Jasper, you know that getting shot in the gut is a painful, agonizing way to die. He was aiming lower."

Jasper chewed on the information and grew pale.

"The bastard wanted me to suffer."

"I see...unfortunately, I see." Jasper glanced around, and his eyes narrowed. "Where are my deputies?"

Emmit ignored him and moved behind the counter.

"Damn it, McKay, how am I supposed to help you if you don't take my help seriously!" Jasper shouted, then stormed out of the store when Emmit once again remained silent.

****

After discussing the risk and deciding it was minimal, Savannah headed into town. She was excited and nervous. Evan had had a wonderful idea. She just hoped it worked. She'd been waiting all morning and most of the afternoon for Evan to get back to the apartment.

He had gotten a call from a *friend*. Savannah smiled to herself. She was almost positive it had been a woman. He had been fidgety and somewhat agitated when she had asked him about it. Whoever it was, she was a lucky woman. Evan was a gentle giant.

Savannah had, while waiting for Evan, had the girls open their school books and study. She held a small class, really more like a long lecture. The girls seemed to enjoy themselves, though. They had done history, math, and English. Casey was better at math than at English. Charlie loved history. And Alexandra, well, Savannah had been surprised. She had glanced over Alexandra's test scores once before and found them impressive, but the girl retained knowledge and understood it. That left Fletcher, who, if you could get her to stay still, was eerily intelligent. And they had worked on her grammar until Savannah's eyes had crossed.

She had the feeling Casey's memory was almost photographic. The girl, not surprisingly, knew how to use it to her advantage. Her test scores hadn't been as high as Alexandra's, but they had been above average.

Charlie could recite mathematical equations and historical documents. She said it was like reciting a recipe. But the key was she understood what they meant. Savannah sighed, knowing they were bored in school for the most part.

She had a feeling the scores she had seen didn't even skim the surface of their potential. When they were together, their knowledge combined was uncanny. She was surprised she hadn't noticed this when they had stayed with her before, and she wondered if Emmit was aware. The girls were experts at keeping secrets. In fact, they'd probably voted to keep their aptitude hidden. Knowledge, after all, was a weapon.

Savannah pulled into the parking lot behind Ida Mae's and got out. This was it. She laughed to herself as she headed for the door. She was shaking with nerves. The smell of coffee hit her as soon as she walked in, making bile rise in her throat, and she swallowed hard. Not now! she told her body, surprised when it obeyed her. Savannah tried to go unnoticed while she headed for the back corner booth.

She sat down just as someone else walked in. Of all the people! Ian Thomas. She might actually throw up at the sight of him. She made herself small, hoping he didn't see her as he picked up his to-go order. Of course, the moment the thought crossed her mind, he glanced over, and his eyes widened when they met hers. The look he gave her was scorching, to say the least. Savannah straightened her spine. She would *not* cower to this wretched man. He narrowed his eyes at her, then snatched a bag from Ida's hands and left abruptly. Ida was shaking her head when she looked over to where Savannah was sitting and jumped, startled. Savannah waved her over.

"Girl, what are you doing back in Blue Creek?" Ida whispered, glancing around. "The whole town is buzzing about what's happened with the McKays. I'm worried about Emmit, myself. And Lord help that little Fletcher. I can't imagine if that was my Trixy."

"I've heard—"

"That's why you're back, right?" Ida pointed to Savannah. "Everyone knows about you and Emmit, missy. No use trying to fool old Ida Mae."

"I...I..." Savannah stammered.

"Are you gonna go to Florida to stay with those girls? This is the craziest thing to happen in Blue Creek in my lifetime. I'm damn sure it isn't one of us!" Ida shook her head. "Nope, it's one of those FBI most-wanted people."

"I'm not sure what my plans are yet," Savannah began once she was allowed to get a word in edgewise. "I came because I have a proposition for you. Why don't you have a seat?"

"Business?" Ida sat down. "Talk, missy!" And as Ida listened, her face crinkled into a grin.

****

Emmit was about to close up when Charlie's bell rang. He walked to the front and stopped. "What in the hell are you two doing here?" He regarded J. T. and Sadie speculatively. "You"—he pointed at the two of them—"are supposed to be on your honeymoon."

"We would be, but I called Mildred last night when I couldn't reach Savannah. Mildred filled me in, and we came right home," Sadie explained, an edge to her voice. "I knew I shouldn't have left. I wanted to wait, didn't I, J. T.?"

"She did," J. T. said.

"I had this feeling something bad was going to happen. Of course, I thought it was about flying. As you know, Emmit, I hate planes. But this time it wasn't in the air; oh no, the evil is on the ground." She had tears in her eyes.

Emmit winced. "Sadie...I'm sorry—"

"Boy, I can't believe you didn't call us," J. T. said. "What if Fletcher hadn't..." He didn't finish, just ran his hands through his silver hair and cleared his throat.

"I would have called you, but it's been hectic around here. Threats and bullets kind of cloud a man's thoughts," Emmit said, then grimaced at how harsh he sounded. "Sorry. It's been a rough week."

"Where are my grandbabies, Emmit?" Sadie asked as she shifted her purse strap.

"They're safe." The fewer people who knew the better.

"Ha! You may have everyone around here fooled," Sadie said, lowering her voice to a mere whisper, "but I know your parents are in Europe. You must move them into my house."

"Now, Sadie…"

"That's Granny Vaughn to you, young man," she snapped.

J. T. snickered, knowing Emmit wouldn't dare argue.

"All right, Granny Vaughn, then. Your place isn't exactly the safest."

Sadie took a deep breath. "Actually, Emmit, it's the safest house in this town. My late husband had a problem with paranoia." She lifted her shoulders and sighed. "He spent years rebuilding the inside of the house. He put in secret passages and hidden rooms. You remember what you've always said about my attic?"

Emmit was staring at her. "I said it was built all wrong. The measurements of the original plans didn't coincide with the actual layout. Especially in the attic."

"Yes, that's because there are two small rooms up there. They lead into the passageways. Jonathan was a bit obsessed. As I said, my home is the safest place for *our* girls to stay."

"She's right, Emmit. I've been through the house. It's bizarre, but it does give you the upper hand. And no one knows about it but us, of course." J. T. motioned between himself and Sadie.

"All right," Emmit said after he thought for a moment. "We'll move them in tomorrow." He looked up when the bell chimed again.

Savannah came in, grinning. Her hair was up in its tidy bun. She was wearing a navy-blue skirt and jacket with a cream sweater; her heels clicked on his floor. She stopped, noticing his other guests.

"Sadie!" she shouted and hugged the other woman. Pulling back, Savannah's smile faded. "What are you doing back?" she asked, glancing between J. T. and Sadie.

"What did you think, child—Granny Vaughn would let her grandbabies come to harm?" She *tsk-tsk*ed and scowled at Emmit. "We know they aren't in Florida, dear, so don't fret...or try to lie."

"I wouldn't dream of it!" Savannah said only after Emmit nodded. "I'm glad you're here, Granny Vaughn." She winked at Sadie. "And you too, J. T. I'm sure the girls will be happy to see you."

"Speaking of my daughters, who's with them?"

"Oh, I left them by themselves," she said with a tight-lipped smile. "You know, because I'm an idiot and no one's out there making threats...Evan's with them," she finished on a huff.

Emmit rubbed his forehead. "Sorry."

"As you should be; you ruined my good mood." She crossed her arms and tapped her shoe. "Since you're all so interested in *why* I'm in such a good mood, I guess I'll just have to tell you."

"What's your news, Savannah?" J. T. asked.

"Yes, tell us," Sadie said.

"I can't take all the credit because it was Evan's idea. You know how Ida is always complaining she'll never be able to retire?" Everyone nodded. "Well, I bought her out!"

"What?" Emmit asked, because surely he hadn't heard right.

"I bought Ida out. I thought I was going to have to wait because Kyle isn't in town, but Ida had another lawyer."

"Duncan Lawrence, Mildred's cousin, he's the only lawyer who stays in town. Everyone else lives closer to the city," J. T. said with a smile.

"That's the one. Ida called him, and just like that"—Savannah snapped her fingers—"we had a contract drawn up and signed. I take over at the end of the month!" Her excitement was palpable.

"Congratulations, Savannah!" Sadie and the Judge said in unison. Emmit followed a few seconds later.

J. T. put his arm around Sadie. "My bride and I need to go get the house ready. We'll see you tomorrow, McKay, Savannah."

After the couple left, Emmit turned to Savannah and stared. She wasn't leaving, not after buying a restaurant. "Where did you get that much money? I know Ida, and she's a shrewd businesswoman. Not to mention greedy as hell."

"My mom passed away not long ago, and I finally sold her house. She left me with a nice nest egg, a really nice nest egg. I did have an adequate job. I saved a lot of money over the years," she said with a shrug of one shoulder.

He nodded and stepped toward her. "I guess we need to celebrate then?" He bobbed his eyebrows.

Savannah covered her mouth to contain the laugh that slipped out, and Emmit smiled. She made a fake attempt to dodge him. He played along and caught her, kissed her. She smiled beneath his lips. All Emmit cared about right then was she was staying.

"I don't know that I've ever seen you so happy," Emmit said, stepping back to take in the joy on her face.

"I *am* happy. I can't even begin to tell you how happy."

"You're staying then?" He was almost positive. But almost is a long detour.

"I'm staying," she whispered. "How do you feel about that?"

"I could get used to it, I suppose," he said, but his heart was racing.

"Could you?" Savannah asked, biting her lower lip.

"I think so. But right now, we have to find whoever's after us. Tomorrow, we're going to move the girls into Sadie's house. Seems it's full of passageways and hidden rooms. According to Sadie, the late Mr. Madison had a bad case of paranoia."

Savannah didn't say anything, just frowned, then glanced at her watch.

Emmit didn't want her to leave yet. "How about I buy you supper?"

"In my own restaurant?" she teased.

"Certainly, give the gossips something else to talk about for a while. Besides, if we're out having supper like we have no care in the world, it'll solidify our story that the girls are in Florida." Emmit grabbed his keys and went to shut off the lights.

"I see your point. All right, Evan did say to take as long as I wanted." Savannah smiled. "Lead the way, Mr. McKay."

Chapter Twenty-Eight

The girls sat in a small circle on the floor as Evan paced. He kept muttering to himself, reminding Charlie of someone who was about to have a nervous breakdown. She couldn't tell what he was saying exactly, something about "finding out" and weaving "tangled webs" or something.

"You think he's losing it?" Charlie asked. She shivered. "You know, like that movie. The one where the family goes to stay at the hotel, and the dad goes crazy. And the boy uses that creepy voice?"

"You mean the movie Daddy told you not to watch?" Alexandra asked.

Charlie rolled her eyes. Alexandra knew she'd watched it anyway. "Yeah, like that one?"

"Naw, Charlie, I don't think he's lost it. Just worried about Van, I reckon," Casey said. She leaned in and whispered, "But he is acting a mite suspicious, and it's making me uneasy."

"Van'll be back soon, so it won't matter," Fletcher said in a low voice, then scooted closer inside the circle. "I's think we's need to talk about names for the baby."

"I think so too," Charlie agreed. Casey and Alexandra rolled their eyes but made their suggestions anyway. They all jumped when Evan did.

"Girls, grab your bags and get in the closet!" he whispered harshly, looking out the window. "Damn, it might be too late…now!"

"Uncle Evan, I's don't like closets. Please, please, don't make me go in there," Fletcher begged, sucking in air.

"I'm sorry, sweetheart. There isn't any choice." He kissed the top of her head, then opened the closet door and shoved them all inside with their sleeping bags. One hand holding the knob, Evan leaned down and whispered, "No one move. No one make a sound. And don't leave this closet. Understood?" He glanced over his shoulder when there was knock on the door. "I love you, girls," he said and shut them in.

The closet was dark, and with four of them in there, it was tight. Fletcher sat in Casey's lap, while Alexandra sat in Charlie's. They barely breathed. The front door opened, but the voices were muffled by the closet walls.

"So you figured it out?"

"It made sense after I thought about it."

"I'm surprised it took you so long. Like recognizes like, doesn't it?"

"What are you talking about?"

"I'm not the only one with secrets, isn't that right? Oh, you thought no one knew."

In the closet, the sisters grabbed hands. A laugh vibrated through the door. It was a chilling sound, like the one in the movie Charlie had been talking about.

"How the fuck do you know?"

"With my connections, I know everybody's secrets in this damn town. Where are they? And the woman. I warned her, didn't I? Everyone knows they're staying here; you can't keep a secret like that for long in Blue Creek."

"They ain't here now."

"Where are they?"

"You really think I'm gonna tell you?…What the hell is that for?"

"Insurance."

Outside the closet, there were sounds of struggling, glass shattering, and then a solid thud. Feet shuffled around the room; then the door slammed, and someone ran down the steps. The girls didn't move a muscle until after an engine started and a vehicle pulled away.

"We have to get out there!" Casey insisted, shaking. Her sisters nodded, and slowly Alexandra twisted the knob.

The apartment was a mess. Some of the furniture had been overturned. One of the lamps lay in pieces. The only light left came from the kitchen. Quietly, they piled out of the closet, taking in their surroundings.

"Oh God, no!" Charlie whispered, looking down at the floor.

"Blood's already seeping into the carpet," Alexandra said, pointing to the dark spreading stain.

"Holy shit!" Casey choked out. She looked up at the ceiling, while Fletcher ran over to the body.

Evan lay on the ground awash in red. He had slashes across his chest, and his arms were a mess. But most of the blood gushed from a long opening at his throat. His eyelashes fluttered.

"He's still alive!" Fletcher hollered. "I's checked his pulse like the doctors checked mine in the hospital. He's gots one, and he's breathing but…but barely."

Casey swallowed and took a seat with her sisters around Evan's body.

"There's no phone up here," Alexandra said as she

took off her cardigan and quickly covered Evan's throat.

"Casey, you and Charlie go get help."

Casey didn't budge, she could only stare at the dying body of the uncle she loved so much.

Alexandra shoved her with her foot. "Go get some damn help, Casey!"

Casey glared at Alexandra for two seconds, then jumped up and grabbed Charlie's hand. She ran for all she was worth, and Charlie was right behind her. They ran down the steps of the apartment to the garage. Charlie stumbled but righted herself.

Casey searched around for the phone and found it. She picked it up, but there was no tone. "Whoever tried to kill Uncle Evan must have cut the phone lines, that or Ward didn't pay his damn bill." Casey slammed down the receiver. "We need to get to a phone." She knew where they were, and Ida's was closest. Pops wouldn't be at the store this late. "Ida's," she said and grabbed Charlie's hand again, running faster than she'd ever run before.

"We're never going make it in time, Casey," Charlie cried out.

"We have to try. Alex and Fletcher are doing their part. We have to do ours." Where the hell was everyone? "You'd think people would be out and about," she muttered, tugging her sister's hand. The lights were on at Ida's, and they ran for it.

****

Savannah glanced at her watch.

"It's about that time, isn't it?" Emmit asked, smiling at her.

"The girls will be getting anxious," she said, rising.

If she had thought she loved him before, she was even more in love with him now. He had a wicked sense of humor that matched her own. This was one of the few times when they'd had a long discussion where neither of them stormed out at the end. That thought made her grin.

"Savannah…I—"

"You two need to leave," Ida hissed after she'd hurried to the table.

Savannah frowned. "Ida, what's wrong?" The older woman was as white as a sheet.

"Word's broke," she whispered. "Everyone knows the girls aren't in Florida."

Savannah sucked in a sharp breath and covered her mouth with her hand as Emmit stood up quickly. They had to get to the girls.

"Does anyone know where they are?" Emmit asked, pulling money out of his wallet. Ida put her hands on his, stopping him.

"Talk is they're hiding out in Ward Jessup's garage," Ida said, then glancing over her shoulder, she gasped and clutched her chest.

Savannah whirled around when Casey and Charlie came running to a stop. Emmit jumped in front of her and knelt down.

"Girls, where are your sisters?"

Casey gasped. "Call the police and hurry." Savannah went for the phone, but Ida beat her to it as the few other people in the diner stood up to see what was happening.

"Your sisters?" Emmit asked again, looking from one girl to the other.

"They're with Uncle Evan," Charlie said, shaking

her head. Casey knocked her in the shoulder.

"They're fine, Pops," Casey said. "It's Uncle Evan."

"What's wrong with Evan?" Savannah asked, her heart sinking.

"Someone came to the apartment, and Uncle Evan shoved us in the closet. It was whoever shot Fletcher; I know it was 'cause we could hear them talking," Charlie explained, her voice shaking.

"Did you recognize the voice?" Emmit asked, standing now.

"It was muffled. We could only make out some of it," Charlie said.

"We opened the door after we heard a vehicle pull away, and Uncle Evan was on the floor." Casey choked.

"I don't think we'll make it in time. His throat was cut, and he'd been s-stabbed p-pretty bad," Charlie finished.

"Alex and Fletcher stayed with him. We tried the phone at the shop, but it didn't work."

"The police and ambulance are on their way," Ida hollered from where she stood with the phone in her hand.

Savannah only thought about it for a moment, then took off her heels and ran toward the door. She stopped, holding her shoes in her hand and looked back. "Are you coming or what?" Emmit looked at her for a split second and started after her.

Savannah knew he told the girls to stay with Ida, but when they started running down the street, the girls were right behind them.

****

After her sisters had run out, Alexandra turned to

Fletcher, her hands still on Evan's throat. "Fletcher, you hold something to his chest. When you were shot, Daddy said to put pressure on the wound, so that's what we'll do."

Fletcher nodded. Her arm was still in a sling, and she swore a blue streak when she slipped out of it to take off one of her shirts to cover Evan's chest. "You's don't try to talk, Uncle Evan. Casey and Charlie went to get help."

When Fletcher's eyes met her own, Alexandra mouthed, *He's not going to make it.* Fletcher gulped. Alexandra stared into her uncle's eyes, and taking one hand off the cardigan she held at his neck, she wiped away his tears. "Shhh, it'll be all right."

Evan was moving his arm as if it weighed a ton; he slowly pulled out a letter with his bloody fingers, then held it out to her. His eyes were begging Alexandra to take it. And then, Evan Jessup was forever released from his pain. His hand dropped on Alexandra's lap. Swallowing, she stared at the letter in her uncle's lifeless hand. It was addressed to their father.

"Maybe it tells who's did this," Fletcher whispered, closing Evan's eyes.

Alexandra nodded. She slowly retrieved the envelope from Evan's fingers. She kissed his hand and placed it beside his body.

Alexandra's own bloody hand trembled as she took the letter from the envelope. She read the letter, her eyes darting across the page. "Oh, my God," she whispered and covered her mouth with one hand.

"What's it say, Alex? Does it say who's did this? Damn it, Alexandra, tell me."

"No, it doesn't say anything about that," Alexandra

breathed.

"What does it say then?" Fletcher asked; then with a hiss of pain, she snatched the letter before Alexandra could stop her. "Holy shit," Fletcher whispered and stared at her uncle's dead body. "Alex, you's know what this means?"

The world is crashing down, Alexandra thought for a moment, then snapped out of her daze to grab the letter back from Fletcher. She shoved it back in the envelope and folded it until it fit in the palm of her blood-stained hands. She grabbed Fletcher's good shoulder, her eyes a fathomless blue.

"We tell no one...ever." Fletcher shook her head. "Do you understand what this means, Fletcher? This could destroy us," she said, holding up the envelope.

"I's don't think so, Alex."

"That's right, you're not thinking. Let me make this clear; it would kill Daddy. Got it? I don't know if anyone would ever forgive Uncle Evan." Alexandra bit her lip. "We can never tell anyone." She was adamant. Alexandra knew she was right. Knew it! Fletcher was still shaking her head. Damn her honest hide. "Damn it, Fletcher, we don't have time for your crap."

"We's can't keep it forever, Alex," she whispered.

Alexandra thought fast. "Fine, we'll tell everyone in...in ten years, okay?"

"Alex, I's don't know...this is too big," Fletcher whispered.

"He died to protect us. Doesn't that mean anything to you?"

Fletcher gulped and nodded. But then she shook her head. Alexandra didn't think, and for the first time in her life, she used an open palm across her sister's face. "You listen to me. We aren't telling anyone a thing about this letter. Do. You. Understand?"

"We's won't tell anyone…for ten years," Fletcher agreed, covering her cheek with her hand. Alexandra gave her the folded letter.

"Do what you do best, Fletcher, and hide the damn thing. Make sure no one finds it until it's time." Fletcher nodded and stuck the letter in the bottom of her shoe. Alexandra bent down to her uncle and kissed his forehead. "Your secret is safe with us," she told him, then glanced at Fletcher, and Alexandra only then realized what she had done.

"Oh, my God, Fletcher, I'm so sorry." She crawled over to Fletcher, who threw her good arm around her.

"S'okay. I's was impressed," she said into Alexandra's hair.

Alexandra kissed her sister's forehead. "Do you forgive me?" Fletcher nodded and hugged her again.

"I's won't tell, Alex. I's promise," she whispered just as the door swung open and their father stormed in.

Chapter Twenty-Nine

Sheriff Hart was yelling as he ran up the stairs behind them, but Savannah ignored him. She pushed Emmit out of the way to get to the girls.

"He didn't make it," Alexandra said, letting go of Fletcher to stand up. She bent down and helped her sister to her feet. "I'm sorry, Daddy." She whimpered as tears began to fall down her cheeks. Emmit rushed to pick her up, while Savannah took hold of Fletcher.

"We's tried to keep the blood in, but it won't stop," Fletcher told her.

"Oh, baby. I know you did everything you could, both of you," Savannah said and caught Emmit's eyes over the child's head.

"You girls did the best you could," Emmit started, then switched children with Savannah. "And your sisters did the best they could by getting help."

"Holy God," Sheriff Hart whispered.

Savannah turned to where he was looking. She hadn't seen Evan yet. When she did, she almost dropped Alexandra. She set the girl down roughly and ran to the bathroom.

Savannah threw up everything in her stomach. Someone rubbed her back, and she glanced over her shoulder. Charlie was running her small hand up and down Savannah's spine.

"It's okay, Savannah. I wanted to do that too,"

Charlie admitted with a small smile. Savannah nodded.

"You okay?" Emmit asked from the doorway.

"She'll be fine. Casey, get Savannah a glass of water," Charlie called out. Emmit nodded and went back to the other room.

"Here you go," Casey said, offering Savannah the glass. Savannah snatched it and guzzled, keeping her eyes closed. When she opened them, all four McKay girls were with her.

"How are you guys doing? Honestly?"

"We want to go home," Casey said, and the others nodded.

"Sounds like a plan. Let's get out of here." Savannah got up slowly and led them out of the bathroom. "Emmit, I'm taking the girls home." He nodded, understanding she was taking them to their own home.

"You're not serious," Sheriff Hart said, stopping Savannah.

"I need to take the children home," Savannah insisted, her voice thick with tears.

"You can't go there," the sheriff hissed.

"No, Jasper, it's fine. I had a security system put in," Emmit said. His gaze followed the deputies and EMTs as they moved around Evan.

Savannah bit her lip. How could she forget this wasn't over? Her throat threatened to close up on her. She tried to swallow the fear...and sorrow. She was brought out of her thoughts when Charlie stepped lightly on her foot. She looked at the girl, who widened her eyes and inclined her head toward the two men, who were arguing about where they should go.

Savannah cleared her throat loud enough to stop

the bickering. "Sheriff, what if your deputies do a complete search of the house first, just to make sure it's safe? Then we will have the security system armed, and we'll be fine."

"All right. Ms. Walker, you and the girls come with me. I'll search the house myself, take the girls' statements, and then come back here," the sheriff said and took Savannah's hand. She went with him, glad he was leading her and the children away from blood and death.

****

It was almost two in the morning when Emmit arrived home. Savannah hurried to disarm the alarm and met him at the door. He looked as tired as she felt. He shut the door behind him and walked into her arms.

"I can't believe he's gone," he whispered into her neck.

"I know." It was surreal. They had been together earlier, laughing and joking with the girls. She let what-ifs roll around in her head until she made herself stop. They couldn't change what was.

"Are the girls sleeping?" Emmit asked as he stepped back and ran his fingers through his hair.

"Yes, for a while now. It took an hour to scrub down Fletcher and Alexandra." She shivered remembering the darkened water. She hadn't wanted to leave even a trace of blood, so she'd insisted they wash three times.

"Charlie and Casey took baths too. Then we sat around discussing happier things. Like Sadie's new title of Granny Vaughn, and what I'll do with Ida's once I take over." They had talked about baby names for both girls and boys. "We spoke about what happened tonight

251

and cried together," she told him.

"Thank you for that, Savannah," he said with a half smile.

"I needed it as much as they did," she said, taking a seat across from him once he'd sat down at the kitchen table.

"I've been thinking about the day I met Evan. We were about five. It was the first day of school, and I was sitting under a tree eating my lunch when this big kid came over and sat next to me. I couldn't believe this kid was talking to me. Me, Emmit McKay, just a scrap of a thing." He laughed and shook his head.

"It was Evan?" Savannah asked, smiling as she imagined it.

"Yeah. We sat there talking when this other kid, smaller than I was, jumped up in the tree above us. He was being chased by the bigger kids."

"Kyle, of course," Savannah said with a laugh.

Emmit nodded, and his lips quirked. "Yep. I told Evan he had to do something to help. Evan asked what I expected him to do; he was only five. Once I convinced him that he was bigger than the others, he huffed and he puffed until the kids ran away. Kyle came down and thanked us, and we've been friends ever since."

"Thank you for sharing that with me, Emmit," Savannah said, reaching across the table to take his hand. "He was a good friend."

Emmit nodded and rubbed his red eyes. "Did I ever tell you Evan found the orphanage where I adopted Casey, Alexandra, and Fletcher?"

Savannah shook her head.

"It's true. Evan does—or did—a lot of charity work, and when Gracie and I decided to start a family, he gave me the name of an orphanage he'd delivered donations to, and I found the girls. He and Kyle even came with us the day we picked them up." Emmit shook his head. "And he found Charlie too."

"You're kidding." Savannah smiled. Evan had such a good heart.

"No, he stumbled on a bake sale when he'd gone out of town to pick up parts. The proceeds went to the local orphanage. He told me that very night on the phone the little orphan who took his money also took his heart."

Savannah couldn't help a teary laugh. "Charlie."

Emmit smiled. "Who else? I knew after speaking with some of the staff at the orphanage that Charlie belonged with us. And the rest is history."

Savannah waited while Emmit took a moment to compose himself. He rubbed his hands over his face. "The hardest thing I've had to do in my life was go with Jasper to find Ward and tell him. Jasper said he'd do the talking, but I insisted it come from me."

Savannah swallowed. "What did Ward say?"

"He just stared at me for a while, then sat down on the floor and cried." Emmit covered his mouth with his hand and swallowed. "In all my life, I've never seen Ward Jessup cry. It's always been just the two of them. Evan's mom died when he was born." Emmit met Savannah's eyes. "He's dead because of me."

"He's dead because he was protecting the nieces he loved, Emmit. He died to save them. We can't demean what he did. Neither of us," she told him, tears falling down her cheeks. "Whoever did this, Emmit, Evan knew. The girls told me."

"I know. And I'll get the son of a bitch if it's the

253

last thing I do." He got up and started for his room. "Will you stay with me tonight? Just to sleep, Savannah? I…" He didn't finish.

Savannah grabbed his hand and led the way. They went to sleep and woke in each other's arms.

Chapter Thirty

The following days were somber ones for the people of Blue Creek. Evan's funeral was held at the end of the week, once the police released his body. Everyone was there. The McKays, the Vaughns, the Maes, and even the Thomas family showed up. Mildred Lawrence held Ward Jessup's hand through the entire service. Savannah stood with Emmit and the girls. Kyle stood next to Charlie. He had shown up at Emmit's the afternoon after Evan was killed.

"Tell me it's not true, Emmit. Please," he'd said as if hoping there was some mistake. He crumpled on the porch with silent tears tracing his face when he wasn't given a reprieve. He had sat with Emmit for hours talking about the adventures the three had had together.

Now Kyle stood next to Charlie holding the child's hand and wearing his tears like a badge of honor. Emmit, too, had tears in his eyes, as did every man, woman, and child. There was no doubt that Evan Jessup would be missed.

Emmit knew Jasper Hart was standing in back watching the crowd. He had spoken with the sheriff earlier. They had agreed a murderer was among them, but neither of them had a clue who it could be.

"In all my years as sheriff, there's never been a homicide in Blue Creek. Now, we're faced with the murder of a good man and the treachery of another,"

Jasper had said, shaking his head. "I'll never forget how we found him—hardest thing I've ever witnessed was seeing Evan's ravaged body."

Emmit couldn't argue with that. He knew the image would be ingrained in his memory forever. His friend since boyhood lying on the floor in a puddle of his own blood. Two of his daughters sitting there holding each other. They had been covered, from the tips of their fingers to their elbows, in Evan's blood. It was smeared on their faces, and they hadn't even known. Like Jasper, he wouldn't ever forget...he couldn't.

****

Ida invited everyone to the diner after the funeral. People were whispering and telling stories about Evan. Ward Jessup, Evan's father, sat alone at a small booth in the back. His thinning black hair, which was streaked with gray, was combed instead of covered by his usual hat. His coveralls were replaced by a simple black suit, white shirt, and faded black tie. His eyes, so much like Evan's, were pools of loss that would break anyone's heart. The conversations in the diner turned to whispers as the four McKay children went to sit with the father of the deceased. Ward let out a shaky breath as he scooted over to make room for the girls to sit.

"Ward, we just wanted to say that we loved Uncle Evan very much," Charlie told him as she sniffled.

"He loved you girls very much too. Always talking about his girls, he was." Ward glanced at them. "Evan loved his nieces."

"We tried to help him, but we couldn't." Alexandra hung her head.

"We's sorry we's couldn't save him, but he went

fast. I's don't think he was in pain for long," Fletcher said, a tear slipping down her cheek.

"My boy died fast," Ward whispered. "Jasper told me, 'course, but if feels more honest coming from you children." He jumped when Casey put her hand in his.

"He saved our lives, you know. Did they tell you that?" Casey asked, squeezing his hand. "He saved us. We won't ever forget that our uncle was a hero. Ever."

"I guess I didn't think of that," Ward said, and though tears filled his eyes, he smiled. "Evan Jessup, the hero. He would have eaten that up with a spoon, he would. Thank you." The girls nodded and one by one kissed his wrinkled cheek, then left him to his thoughts.

****

After news had spread of Evan's death, they hadn't been able to relocate to Sadie's house right away. They had discussed it and decided to wait until after Evan's funeral. So that evening, the McKays packed up some of their things and moved into Sadie's home. The girls spent hours with Granny Vaughn and the Judge learning the secrets of the house.

There were five hidden rooms: two in the attic, one in the master bedroom, another under the back staircase, and finally one inside the pantry. The passageways were built between the walls and almost every closet had a secret panel which allowed access to them. This connected all of the hidden rooms, allowing people to move from place to place and floor to floor unseen.

A ladder led from the hidden room in the pantry directly to the one in the master bedroom. From there, you could take another ladder to one of the rooms in the attic. The room under the stairs led directly to the attic, allowing someone to make a quick exit if they needed to. Mr. Madison had planned thoroughly, because there was a lighting system inside the passageways, making it easy to navigate.

Savannah and Emmit had taken the time to learn the different routes. Now they all sat at the kitchen table working on escape plans; if necessary, they would know what paths to take.

"Do you really think it will come to this?" Savannah asked.

"I want to be prepared just in case," Emmit told her. "Let's go over it again."

Savannah sat back in her seat as Emmit pointed out paths on the map. He'd told her that they had to take this seriously. In the beginning, he'd said, he was convinced the killer only wanted him and would leave everyone else alone. But after all that had happened, Emmit no longer believed that. Evan had somehow uncovered the truth and been killed because he was a loose end. Why hadn't Evan told them as soon as he found out? That was one thing no one could understand.

"We've got it down, Pops," Casey said loudly, bringing Savannah back from her thoughts.

"That's what I like to hear. Team players, these four," J. T. said, then rose and took Sadie's hand. "We best be on our way. If you need us, just call the house."

"And you had better call too," Sadie said, following her husband out after giving hugs to the group.

The girls went upstairs to get ready for bed. "I'll be up in about ten minutes," Savannah told them.

"Ten minutes?" Emmit asked, raising one black brow.

"I need to grab a few things from the apartment, and I want to get them now before I forget." She headed for the door.

"I'll go; what do you need?"

"A couple of my *Murder, She Wrote* tapes and my mother's afghan. It's in the chest at the end of the bed." Emmit was laughing as he headed for the side door. "Go ahead and laugh," Savannah shouted down at him and began walking upstairs. "Fletcher and I happen to like *Murder, She Wrote*."

She peeked into the first bedroom where the girls were in bed together. It was king-sized; they hadn't slept separately since Evan's murder. She spied them whispering from the doorway. "What are you four plotting now?"

They looked at her with sly smiles.

"We weren't plotting," Charlie said, then burst out laughing. She fell onto her back when Casey shoved her.

"No? Then what were you doing?" Savannah sat down at the foot of the bed.

"We were talking about how fat you're gonna get," Casey said, then snickered.

"Shh." Savannah gave them a dirty look after she looked over her shoulder. "Thanks a lot."

"We all agreed you'll still be beautiful," Alexandra said.

"That makes it okay then," Savannah said in her prissiest voice, making them giggle.

"We's also agreed that we's gonna have to tell Pops soon 'cause you's gonna gets too big for him not to notice," Fletcher told her as she puffed out her cheeks.

Savannah groaned. "I know. Now go to bed, you little heathens." She chuckled as she got up and turned out the light.

Back downstairs, Savannah poured herself a cup of decaffeinated coffee. She waited another five minutes and went searching for Emmit. He was taking a long time, and she was getting worried.

She found him at the apartment in her bedroom. She looked down at the small green notebook he held in his hand. She swallowed and met his steely gaze. Oh no.

"Where did you get this?" he asked calmly, standing. He towered over her, using his size to intimidate her. She bit her lip to stop the trembling. "I'd like an answer now, Savannah."

"I'm sorry, Emmit," she whispered and turned to leave.

He grabbed her arm and spun her around shoving the book under her nose. "Where in the fuck did you get this?"

"I told you once, Emmit McKay, words like 'fuck' do not scare me." Words like betrayal did. And his eyes were accusing. She shifted her spine and yanked on her arm. His grip tightened. "Let go of my arm, Emmit." She twisted in his grasp. "You're hurting me."

He loosened his grip but didn't let her go. "Answer the damn question, Savannah!"

"No," she said, and she kicked at him; he let go of her arm. She raced out the door and down the steps.

Savannah hurried to the main house, ignoring Emmit as he called her name. She locked her bedroom door and leaned against the wall staring at the knob. How could she have been so stupid? She knew where that appalling book was, but she hadn't thought about it. Her room was downstairs right under where the girls were sleeping, and she glanced at the ceiling when Emmit started banging on the door.

"Savannah, you need to open this door." He banged harder.

"Leave me alone, you baboon."

"Savannah, if you don't open this goddamn door, I'm gonna break it down."

She thought she heard him say, "Fine," and before she could react, he did just what he threatened. He kicked the door right off its hinges. It landed with a crash. Savannah jumped to the side and crossed her arms over her sweatshirt.

"Oh, big bad man knocks door down," she taunted, backing up until the back of her knees hit the mattress.

"Tell me where you found this," Emmit shouted, holding up the book.

"No! Leave me the hell alone!" she shouted just as loud.

"Savannah, you've obviously read it. What did you think? Did you enjoy it?" he sneered.

"You bastard," she whispered.

"Leave her alone, Pops; I found it," Casey confessed, stepping into the room.

Emmit sucked in a breath and grew pale.

"That's not exactly true. I's, ah, kinda stole it," Fletcher said, stepping around Casey.

Savannah and Emmit said, "What?" in unison.

"I was the one who asked her to look for it in the first place. I knew Gracie always wrote in it," Alexandra said, coming into the room to join the others.

"I never met the horrid woman, but I support my

sisters' efforts wholeheartedly," Charlie told him.

Emmit sat down on the bed next to where Savannah stood; he rested his arms on his knees and his face in his hands.

"We's read every damn word," Fletcher spat out with her eyes narrowed.

"Fletcher," Casey hissed.

"Gracie Vaughn wasn't a mother to me. I's hated her, and she hated me and everyone else. She was an evil whore," Fletcher said, then slapped a hand over her mouth.

Emmit's throat worked, and Savannah figured he was trying to find the right words to respond with. She went over to stand in front of the girls. "Fletcher, I know all about Grace, but, honey, those are harsh words."

"They are true, though." Everyone looked at Alexandra, who shrugged one shoulder. "I'm sorry Fletcher and I didn't tell you, Casey, because we thought it would be the last straw and you'd do something terrible."

"What are you talking about?" Emmit asked.

"We…uh…I don't know how to say this…" Alexandra bit her lip and stared at the ceiling for a minute.

"What she's trying to tell yah is we's heard Gracie doing the nasty with other men." Fletcher patted Alexandra's shoulder. "You's can't make that pretty no matter how hard you's try."

"I knew she cheated." Casey nodded. "But you're right; if I'd known you heard it, I would have killed her," she said, punching a fist into her opposite palm.

"I'm always right about these things," Alexandra

said, nudging Fletcher, who nodded.

"Men? As in more than one?" Emmit asked.

Fletcher rocked back on her heels. "Yep. More'n one and more'n one time," she said.

"Who was it? Who were they?" Emmit demanded, slapping the journal against his thigh.

Emmit's chest rose and fell as he sucked in air, and there was a fine sheen to his brow. His shoulders heaved, and then he ran over to the small trash can and retched. Savannah was torn between going to him and staying where she was. She felt queasy herself. Emmit wiped his mouth and asked the girls again, but they only stared at him.

"Why won't anyone answer me?"

"Once was with Marylou's father," Alexandra said.

Savannah gagged. "Ian Thomas?"

"Gross," Charlie said, her gaze darting across the room, then she turned red. "Sorry."

"It's okay, sweetheart," Savannah told her because she was thinking the same thing.

"And the other one?"

"Just tell him, honey," Savannah urged Alexandra when tears filled the child's eyes. Alexandra couldn't get the words past her throat. Savannah glanced at Fletcher, who had tears running down her cheeks as well.

"I's...it w-was Uncle E-e-van," Fletcher told the room. Savannah sucked in a breath, and Emmit threw up again.

"You lying piece of shit!" Casey accused and slapped Fletcher across the face.

"Casey, stop it," Savannah demanded, grabbing the older girl's hand before it could make contact with

Alexandra's face.

"Go ahead, Casey, I dare you!" Alexandra's eyes flashed with anger. The fight went out of Casey, so Savannah let her go, and Alexandra said, "You don't have to believe us. We don't really care one way or the other. Do we, Fletcher?" Alexandra turned to go, taking Fletcher's hand; she stopped when their father spoke.

"Was there anyone else?"

Defeat swept across Emmit's face before he could hide it. Savannah's heart ached for him. He had just learned that not only his wife but also his best friend had betrayed him. Tears prickled her eyes when he met her gaze, then looked away.

"I don't need your pity, Savannah," Emmit whispered. Savannah shook her head and was about to tell him he was wrong when he asked, "Was there anyone else I should know about?"

"We didn't see all of them."

"All of them," Emmit scoffed.

"Well, there could have been more, but we only saw Evan and Marylou's father in the house," Alexandra said.

"Where did all this happen?" Savannah asked before Alexandra went into further detail.

"When we lived in our house in town. Fletcher and I were supposed to be taking naps. Casey was at school, and you were at the store, Dad." Alexandra took a breath. "We were hiding in the pantry when we heard Grace and Uncle Evan arguing. He said she slept with everyone, and he was disgusted he had fallen for her lies. He told her it would never happen again, and he was going to tell you."

"She died a week later, so he musta let the dead

lie," Fletcher said, rubbing her nose.

"Anything else you'd like to share?"

"Emmit, that's enough," Savannah pleaded. She couldn't listen to this.

"Van, he's needin' to know the truth!" Fletcher said, pointing a finger at her father.

Alexandra straightened. "Like I said, we heard a lot of things. But there were times once or twice a week when she would actually lock us in our room and turn the stereo up."

"At least it won't the closet," Fletcher whispered. Savannah rubbed the child's back.

"We were locked in our room the day before she died," Alexandra said with a lift of her shoulder.

"He must be the one," Emmit mumbled, and Savannah's eyes clashed with his, but he looked away.

"Girls, I think this is enough for one night," Savannah told them.

She waited until the girls were out of the room to speak. "I'm so sorry you had to find out about Grace this way, Emmit. We all know how much you loved her." The laugh Emmit produced sent a chill over her skin.

"Loved her? Loved her? God forgive me"—he shook his head—"I hated that woman to the very depth of my soul."

"What?" Savannah screeched, not believing her ears. All four girls came rushing back into the room. Savannah stared at him while he rubbed his hands over his pale face.

"You heard me. I despised her."

Savannah sat down on the bed while her feet were still under her.

"You knew she hated us, and you didn't do nothing?" Casey asked, her face red and fists clenched.

"At first I…I didn't see it because I didn't want to. When I figured it out, I started sending you girls to stay with Sadie more often," he said. "Then I wanted to adopt Charlie, and I needed Gracie to do it." He looked ill. "At least, I thought I did."

"You stayed with her to get me?" Charlie whispered.

Emmit reached out and took Charlie's hand. He brought it to his lips and kissed her fingers. "Don't give it a second thought," he said. Charlie nodded, and with tears in her brown eyes, she stepped back to stand next to Casey. He looked at his daughters. "I'm sorry you girls didn't think you could tell me the truth about what was happening. I promise I would have done something about it—protected you from it. I'm sorrier than I can say. You never should have been exposed to this…to her…"

"I can understand why you hated her, Emmit, but something tells me there's more to this," Savannah said. He didn't love Grace. He wasn't in denial or pining away for the hateful woman.

"What? None of you have figured it out yet?" Emmit asked, lifting his hands and then letting them drop. "*She* was the one who wanted me shot. She tried to kill me," he announced, standing up as Savannah and the girls gasped.

"She hired that Mr. X person?" Savannah asked, then covered her mouth and looked at the girls.

"Don't worry, Van, ain't nothing we's didn't already know," Fletcher said, nodding.

"Pops wasn't whispering when he was talking to

Sheriff Hart," Casey said, and Savannah almost laughed.

"Figures." Emmit sighed. "To answer your question, Savannah, yes, Gracie hired Mr. X. Then someone else joined in on her plan. I'm guessing it's the man she turned the stereo up for."

Savannah was stunned. "You knew this whole time, and you didn't say a word?"

"I told Evan." He shook his head and sat back down on the bed. "It's not like you were sharing information, Savannah," he reminded her, holding up the small book. "The moment I saw this, I knew what it was; never in my darkest thoughts could I have imagined the vileness on these pages. Where did you find this, Savannah? Did someone one give it to you? Casey?"

"No, I gave it to Granny Vaughn, and she gave it to Savannah."

"Sadie knew too, huh?" Emmit sighed. "That means J. T. knows. I didn't want that. He probably thinks Gracie's sickness was his fault." Emmit hung his head. "Why didn't you come to me? Do you think I'm completely blind?" he asked and met Savannah's eyes.

"I think this is enough for one night, don't you? We can talk more about this in the morning. It's time to go to bed," Savannah said as she looked away from Emmit and toward the girls. They were all staring at their father.

"I love you," Emmit said to the girls in a soft voice. "Nothing will ever change that. No secret, no lie, and no Gracie. Now go to bed."

Relief was plain on their faces, and Savannah sighed. She followed them to their room, glancing over her shoulder when Emmit set the splintered door against the wall.

Chapter Thirty-One

A noise woke Emmit in the middle of the night, and he got out of bed to investigate. He found Savannah in the kitchen sipping on a glass of water and staring out the window. She was wearing a flannel gown, and her long hair was haloed in the moonlight. Emmit stepped up behind her and wrapped his arms around her waist, then lifted a hand to shift her hair to one side of her neck, giving him access to the other. He kissed her, and she shivered.

Emmit turned her around to face him; there were tears in her eyes. "What are these for?"

"For you, me, the girls, Evan, even J. T.," she said with a weak smile.

"Savannah, don't cry for me, baby," he whispered, leaning down to kiss the tears from her cheeks. "You don't ever need to cry for me." He rested his forehead on hers.

"Who will, if not me?" She laid her head on his chest and wrapped her arms around his waist.

Emmit loved the feel of her.

"How could you stand it? Knowing what kind of person she was." She looked up at him with those beautiful eyes.

"It wasn't like that at first." He let her go and hopped up on the counter. "When the Judge moved here, we were sixteen." He shrugged. "People in Blue

Creek had never met anyone like Gracie Vaughn. She looked like an angel, and everyone wanted to be around her. Except me; all I'd thought about was getting out of this damn place." He shook his head. "Everyone knew I wanted out; it wasn't a secret, and Gracie had wanted to get away from her controlling father. We bonded on that first, and later we fell in love."

"But you *did* love her?" Savannah asked as she took a seat at the kitchen table.

"When I was seventeen?" He rubbed his shoulder. "Yeah, I thought so."

"You married her," Savannah said, frowning.

"What can I say, I was twenty-two and had just gotten a bachelor's in administrative justice. The weekend of graduation, the school held a convention, and there were contests. One was marksmanship." Emmit shrugged. "I'd been winning competitions since I was seven, so I signed up. There was a man from the Bureau there, and he saw me win, said he'd never seen skill like mine. And I was thinking he'd never been to Blue Creek." Emmit shook his head staring off into memories.

"The guy offered me an opportunity to join the FBI, and I jumped at the chance. Gracie was there with me, and I asked her to marry me that night. A few months after our wedding, she got sick. I put in for a transfer, we moved back here, and I drove the hour-and-a-half commute every day. It's funny, my whole life I'd wanted out of Blue Creek, but when Gracie got sick, I didn't even hesitate coming back."

Savannah shrugged one shoulder. "It's your home."

"It is. And, despite what I thought when I was

younger, I knew I wouldn't want to raise my children anywhere else. Then Gracie told me we couldn't have kids, and I said we'd adopt a dozen. But work was demanding, and I was rarely home; I was relieved when she told me we could wait to start our family." He laughed at the irony.

"Then you got shot, quit your job, and adopted the girls," Savannah summed up for him.

He nodded. "Somewhere in between all of that, I realized I didn't love Gracie and maybe I never had. I did make a vow to her though, and I intended to keep it. I figured I could make myself love her, but things didn't add up. She would say one thing when I knew the other was true. The girls were different around her. I suspected she was having an affair. I didn't know how many or who with." He got down from the counter to pace, running his fingers through his hair. "I didn't know about Evan." He stopped in front of Savannah. "She probably seduced him. She could seduce anybody." His laugh was humorless. "Once Gracie got her claws in something, she never let go."

Savannah didn't say a word.

Emmit sighed, then sat in the chair across from her. "I'd already been thinking about leaving her, when Evan met Charlie. Gracie was less than thrilled at the prospect of another child, and her façade began to slip. For a while, I stayed with her to insure I got Charlie, which makes me almost as bad as Gracie. But then I couldn't take it anymore and asked for a divorce."

Savannah sat up straighter and stared at him, her eyes wide. Emmit had never told anyone about asking for a divorce. Let them believe what they wanted, he hadn't cared. But now he needed Savannah to understand the truth, and he wanted the weight of it off his shoulders.

"She went berserk. She threw our wedding album at my head and said she should have had me killed when she had the chance. I asked her to explain, and she laughed at me. At that point, I told her I never wanted to see her again. She slapped me and took my keys. She never made it to where she was going." He looked up at Savannah. "The last thing she said to me bugged me, but I forgot about it, figured she just came up with the worst thing she could think of to hurt me. She said it was wonderful sleeping with my worst enemy. She lashed out whenever she got mad, and she was enraged that night. I only made the connection when I got the letter from Mr. X."

"Okay," Savannah said, "and now we know one of the men Gracie was sleeping with wanted you dead...and still does. But who?" Savannah rose and walked back to the sink. "It's almost like she's still playing some sick game from the grave."

Emmit nodded. "Hard not to agree with that."

Savannah turned, leaned against the sink, and looked at him. "I can't believe you've lived with this all these years and never said anything. That woman was ill, even more so than I thought."

Emmit went to her and rubbed his hands up her arms feeling the small goose bumps. "Savannah..." He kissed her neck and hugged her to him. He loved the way she felt against him—perfect. Her body fit his, and just thinking about that awakened a need within him.

She lifted her head and looked into his eyes. "I feel so foolish. We were all trying to protect your memory of Grace. But you knew...of course. How could you not?" She shook her head. "It wasn't that we were lying to you, Emmit. I think in our own way all of us wanted to spare you."

Emmit smiled and kissed her nose.

Savannah straightened and took a deep breath. "There's something else I haven't told you yet."

He raised one brow.

"I love you, Emmit McKay," she whispered and kissed his lips.

"Savannah, I..." His heart stopped for a second, then sped up when she covered his lips with a finger.

"You don't have to say anything. Just make love to me, Emmit. Just love me tonight."

After he led her to his room, that's exactly what he did.

Chapter Thirty-Two

The next morning Casey, Fletcher, and Charlie were all sitting up in the king-size bed when Alexandra came in humming. She hopped onto the bed and started jumping up and down, her feet landing on her sisters.

"Damn it, Alex, will you stop?" Casey said, grabbing Alexandra's leg and yanking her down onto the mattress.

"Why you's so happy, Alex?" Fletcher asked.

"You've been acting awfully funny lately, *Alex,*" Charlie said with narrowed eyes, then she began massaging Alexandra's scalp.

"What in the world are you doing?" Alexandra asked, pulling away from Charlie's hands.

"Checking for lumps."

"She's one big lump, Charlie, or had you forgotten?" Casey said, pushing up her glasses.

"Why would you's be checking for lumps?" Fletcher took Alexandra's hand and played with her sister's fingers.

"I think she may have hit her head," Charlie said, studying Alexandra from side to side.

"I didn't hit my head." Alexandra shrugged one shoulder. "I'm just happy."

"How's come?" Fletcher wanted to know.

"Well, I went to see Savannah, and she wasn't in her room."

"That isn't good." Casey jumped off the bed. "How can you think that's good?"

"Will you let me finish?" She rolled her eyes. "I would have been worried, but then I checked on Daddy, and his door was locked."

"And?" Charlie encouraged, circling her hand.

"*And*...when has Daddy ever locked his door? Plus, Savannah's Jeep's still here. Sooo, they're in his room...together." Her sisters looked at her for another minute and started giggling.

"This is wonderful. Happy ending, here we come!" Charlie cheered, then blushed when their father cleared his throat from the doorway.

"How long you been standing there?" Casey asked, narrowing her eyes.

"Long enough to be thankful I locked my door this morning," he said and glanced up to the ceiling, shaking his head. He took a breath. "About last night—"

"We're real sorry about keeping all that from you," Casey said.

"It was the best option at the time," Alexandra told him. Fletcher squeezed her hand. "We hadn't wanted to tell you the other thing though."

"About Uncle Evan. See, we's figured everyone makes mistakes, and he was planning to tell yah." Fletcher shrugged.

"I can understand that. Let's close the door on last night. No need to bring it up again. We all know the truth now, and rehashing it will just be upsetting. But if you want or need to talk about the way all of this has made you feel—"

"We're good, Dad," Alexandra said and her sisters

agreed.

"Besides, you'd probably puke again anyway," Casey said, smirking.

"There is that," he mumbled. He squirmed when they started giggling.

"Where's Savannah?" Charlie asked.

"She's taking a shower." He closed the bedroom door and sat down on the bed. "That's what I want to talk to you girls about…"

****

Savannah was sitting in the closed-in patio enjoying the unseasonably warm day when Sadie came in. She smiled at Sadie and patted the cushion next to her so that the other woman would sit.

"You look a mite pleased with yourself, dear child. Want to tell me why?"

"I'm just happy." She shook her head. "Emmit knew, Sadie. He always knew what Grace was."

"What?" Sadie's jaw dropped. "How? Did you ask him about it?"

"No, I asked him to get something from my room." She pointed toward the apartment. "I forgot I left the book there. Emmit found it, then threw a fit when I wouldn't tell him who had given it to me." She regarded Sadie with a small smile. "He, uh, broke one of the bedroom doors down. Took it right off the hinges. He thought I was going to use the journal for some sinister purpose, I suppose." Savannah shivered. Like that was something she would do.

"Don't worry about the door. I'm sure he'll fix it." Sadie patted Savannah's hand and tried to hide her smile.

"There's more, Sadie." Savannah gave Sadie the

rundown of last night's events, feeling responsible for the anguish her friend couldn't hide.

"God in heaven." Sadie closed her eyes to expel the tears. "Did they actually see her? Did they know these men? No, wait don't tell me; I don't want to know."

"I do."

"J. T.!" Savannah winced. "How long have you been standing there?"

"Long enough." J. T. sighed.

Sadie jumped up and went to her husband. "Oh, darling, why torture yourself? It's been over for years. It doesn't matter."

"It does to me, Sadie. I loved my daughter, Savannah. She was my whole world," he said, sitting down on the loveseat opposite Savannah when Sadie did. "But I saw a selfishness—a sickness—in her when she was a young girl. I…I thought she'd grow out of it. And until Sadie showed me that journal, I believed she had. Maybe if I'd gotten her some help…" He shook his head.

"Oh, darling," Sadie whispered, covering her mouth with her hand.

"Don't fret, my dear," he told Sadie, then looked at Savannah. "I want to know, Savannah."

"I don't know that it's my place."

"Please, Savannah, rip off the Band-Aid." He sat straighter as if trying to prepare himself for the blow.

"I'll tell you what you want to know," Emmit said from the doorway. He sighed and took the seat next to her. Savannah gave him a small smile, and he put his arm around her shoulders. "Before I start, I want to say the girls and I decided this subject is no longer open for discussion. After today, I'll expect you both to respect that."

Shadows played across J. T.'s wrinkled face. Then both he and Sadie nodded.

"Agreed," Sadie said, taking her husband's hand.

Emmit's throat worked.

Oh, goodness, Savannah thought, I hope he doesn't throw up again. She rubbed his thigh to reassure him.

"I guess I'll start then."

"I'm surprised you didn't think it was me, before all this came out," J. T. said once Emmit finished recounting the ugly truth.

"I thought about it," Emmit admitted. "Then I dismissed it. I've considered all of Blue Creek as suspect, and now even knowing what I do…" He trailed off, massaging his temples.

"I think we're going to say hello to the girls and be on our way," Sadie said, standing up and tugging on her husband's hand. "Too much excitement for one day."

"That was awful," Emmit said after they left.

Savannah kissed his cheek. She laughed when he pulled her into his lap and kissed her thoroughly. Once he let go of her lips, he held her. Savannah sighed and thought about what he'd said. "The truth is always hard when it's been buried for so long," she told him. Savannah turned a bit so she was looking into his blue-gray eyes. "I meant what I said last night, Emmit." He raised a brow, and she rolled her eyes with a smile. "About loving you…I do love you."

His eyes closed, and he sighed. "Savannah…"

She was worried about what he was going to say, when the girls bustled into the room.

"Is it done?" Charlie asked, eyes wide.

"Did you do it yet, Pops?" Casey asked, her gaze darting between Savannah and Emmit.

"I's don't think he's done it yet," Fletcher said, shifting from foot to foot.

"Obviously!" Alexandra rolled her eyes.

"Would you give me a chance?" Emmit groused.

"Did Sadie and the Judge leave?" Savannah asked, untangling herself from Emmit's lap. She stood and smoothed her hair. A blush crept up her neck.

"Not yet, Van," Fletcher said, not meeting Savannah's eyes. She grabbed Alexandra's hand, who grabbed Charlie's, who then took Casey's hand, and they started forward.

"Seems there's something going on here," Sadie said to J. T. as they came back out on the patio. "Better we stand back out of the way," she said softly, and he agreed with a nod. Savannah's brow furrowed at everyone's odd behavior.

"Now's a good time," Charlie said, and her sisters nodded.

"A good time for what?" Savannah wanted to know. Everyone was staring at her. She sighed dramatically, making the girls smile.

"Right now?" Emmit choked.

"Yep. We're all here, so you may as well," Casey said.

"Fine. Savannah, would you please sit down?"

She laughed at Emmit's pained expression but sat anyway. He was swallowing hard as he got down on one knee. She stopped breathing.

"Savannah," Emmit began, and Sadie gasped. He reached into his back pocket, then cleared his throat. "Would you marry me?" He extended his hand; nestled between his thumb and index finger was a ring.

Savannah gasped as she studied what he held. The diamond was princess cut and set in platinum. She could say with the utmost certainty that she had never seen anything more beautiful.

"Do you want to marry the man or not? It's not a hard question," Alexandra said in her haughtiest tone of voice. "A simple yes would do fine."

"We do need a mother, you know. I could use a break." Charlie grinned and winked at Savannah.

"We all agreed we want you as our ma. It was unanimous," Casey said, cleaning her glasses.

"You's wanna be our mama, right?" Fletcher squirmed.

Savannah looked over to where the Judge was whispering into Sadie's ear, and Sadie was smiling and nodding with tears in her eyes. She looked at the girls again. They were staring at her, waiting for her to respond.

"If the peanut gallery is finished, I'd like to hear an answer," Emmit said, and Savannah gazed into his eyes. He caressed her cheek after the first two tears fell. "Savannah, what'll it be?"

"I'll marry you, Emmit," she whispered. He hadn't said he loved her, but to Savannah that hardly mattered in her present state of euphoria.

Emmit stood up so fast, the next thing she knew she was standing too, and his mouth was on hers. He kissed her hard at first, then more gently as she pulled away and flexed her fingers.

"I'd like my ring now, please." She beamed when he slipped it on her finger. It was a perfect fit. She blushed at the applause from Sadie and the Judge.

"Hot damn, she said yes!" Casey said, blinking behind her glasses.

"Did you expect her to say no?" Charlie asked grinning.

"Who wouldn't say yes?" Alexandra feigned confusion, then smiled.

"I have no idea," Savannah said, laughing. She looked at Emmit and kissed him again. "Thank you."

"You've got it wrong, darling; thank *you* for being willing to take a chance on me, on us." He hugged her. "You can't change your mind," he said, then smiled sheepishly when she rolled her eyes at him.

"Congratulations," J. T. said as he came over to shake Emmit's hand while Sadie hugged Savannah, then traded places with Charlie.

"I'm so happy," Sadie said as she hugged Emmit and dabbed her eyes.

Fletcher tugged on the hem of Savannah's sweater; Savannah let go of Charlie to lean down. Fletcher's blue-green eyes were shimmering with tears.

"You's gonna be my mama now, Van," she whispered in Savannah's ear after she'd wrapped her good arm around Savannah's neck.

"It looks that way, and you're going to be my daughter now," she whispered back.

"Are you's gonna tell him now?" Fletcher asked, her lips pressed against Savannah's ear.

"Tonight," Savannah replied, then turned when Casey tapped her on the shoulder.

"I guess this means you're my ma." Casey sighed, then looked everywhere but at Savannah. "Do you think you'd want...I mean, would you want to...adopt us, too?"

"Oh yes, Casey," Savannah said, lifting Casey's chin so they were looking eye to eye. "I would love nothing more…if that's what everyone wants." She let go of Casey to look at all the girls with tears in her eyes and her heart in her throat.

"Oh, it is!" Charlie told Savannah.

"It most definitely is," Alexandra confirmed as Fletcher's head bobbed.

Chapter Thirty-Three

Emmit had just seen J. T. and Sadie off and was making his way inside, when the sheriff's vehicle pulled in around back. Emmit had promised the older couple he would call with any news. He closed the front door and headed to where Jasper was talking to Savannah in the kitchen.

"Good evening, Sheriff, what may I ask is the reason for your late visit? Or do I want to know?"

"As I've said before, Savannah, please call me Jasper. And it's nothing bad this time, I promise."

"Jasper," Emmit said as he came into the kitchen. He walked over and stood directly behind Savannah, rubbing her arms and waiting for the news.

"Just came by to return this," Jasper said. He pulled out Fletcher's locket and handed it to Savannah. "Figured she'd like it back, and I'm done with it."

"Thank you, Jasper, I'll give it to her in the morning," Savannah said, then paused. "Actually, I think I'll take it back to the jeweler and see if he can change the inscription."

"What does it say now?" Emmit asked.

"Wouldn't you love to know? And, Jasper, if you say anything, I'll sic my girls on you." She winked and left the room.

"Her girls, is it? Ain't that interesting," Jasper said, raising a brow at Emmit.

"May as well be the first outside the family to know, Jasper. Savannah's agreed to marry me."

"She's real good," Jasper said, rocking back on his heels. "Never even suspected it."

"What didn't you suspect?" Savannah asked, coming back into the room.

"That you was plumb crazy. Marrying McKay." He shook his head. "Should've known after you bought Ida's place. Only a loon would do that."

Savannah laughed.

"Is that all, Jasper?"

"That's all, McKay. Congratulations, Savannah, even if you are crazy." Jasper chuckled all the way out the door.

****

"Do you think I'm crazy too, Mr. McKay?" Savannah asked a while later after she'd tucked the girls in. She gathered their coffee cups from the kitchen table and set them in the sink, then turned waiting for a response. "Well, do you?" she asked again with a hint of a smile.

"Absolutely," he said and laughed, dodging when she swatted at him. "But, hey, I'm right there with you. I…Savannah, I…"

"Doesn't this make the perfect picture!"

Emmit swung around toward the voice. Savannah stepped around him to see who it was.

"What are you doing sneaking around? You scared the shit out of me," Emmit said with a chuckle, then looked at what was in the man's hand.

"Good," the gunman said, aiming at Savannah and pulling the trigger.

****

"Was that what I think it was?" Charlie asked, jumping up to grab the phone.

"Holy shit, someone's shooting. Battle stations, everybody!" Casey shouted, rushing toward the passageway in the bedroom closet. Charlie ran after them.

"The phone is dead. I'm getting really pissed off," she said and closed the hidden door behind her. They made their way through the walls and climbed down the ladder that led into the room inside the pantry. They stopped when the shouting grew louder.

"I'm gonna get the guns from the study. You guys stay here," Casey whispered.

"I'm coming with you," Alexandra said, not getting an argument.

****

"There. Now we're even."

"What the fuck are you talking about? Why are you doing this?" Emmit glanced down at Savannah and swallowed. Blood was seeping from her arm, and she'd hit her head, but she was very much alive. Thank God.

Kyle Ruthie leered at Emmit. "Why? *Why?* Let's see, oh yes, you stole Gracie from me. How about we start there?"

Emmit could only stare at this man who was supposed to have been his friend. When Kyle had pulled out his weapon, Emmit had been stunned, and Savannah had been hurt because of that. "I didn't steal her from anybody!"

Kyle's laugh was guttural, and Emmit cringed. "No, of course you didn't. Emmit McKay has never done anything wrong in his life. That's the biggest lie of all. She was a beautiful person until you twisted her,"

Kyle said, using his hands to demonstrate. "I wasn't good enough for her, oh no. But Emmit McKay, he was the one no one could have. And that, my old friend, made you priceless to her."

"Why are you doing this?" Emmit asked again, aware of the other man's agitated movements as Kyle circled around him. "Why now after all these years?"

"First, I was happy having Gracie behind your back. I'd outsmarted the brilliant Emmit McKay." Kyle winked at Emmit. "I've always been smarter than you. Always better, but no one could see that. Then Gracie hired that incompetent hit man, so you would quit work and be home to take care of her." Kyle tsked. "She had cancer, and you were hardly around. I didn't mind because I was the one who looked after her then. But when she hired that imbecile, I thought, hey, why not get rid of him? It was so damn close too. A few inches to the left and all my problems would have been over."

Kyle moved closer to Emmit, who had been backing up toward the counter. Emmit glanced around searching for something he could use as a weapon.

"Stand still, Emmit. I have a lot to get off my chest."

Emmit froze.

Kyle pulled out a chair and using the barrel of his gun motioned for Emmit to sit. When he did, Kyle pulled out a roll of wire and cutters. "You always told me to be prepared. Thank you for the advice, Emmit, because I always am." He held the barrel of the gun against the back of Emmit's head while he secured the wire with one hand.

"I practiced this move with my father when I broke my arm. You remember that, Emmit? Of course, it was fence posts then. But, hey, use the skills you got!" Kyle grinned and stood once Emmit was immobile.

Kylie huffed. Emmit was looking at Savannah. "Focus, Emmit," he jeered, then proceeded to bind Savannah, whose head rolled to the side. Kyle cupped her cheek. "More's the pity, sweetheart," he whispered, then stood. "Now, where was I?" He tapped the barrel of the gun to his temple, while smiling at Emmit.

"Ah, yes. You survived, but it turned out all right because you wanted to adopt those stupid brats. Gracie hated kids. I knew if I helped you get them, she'd leave you, and I'd finally have her all to myself. But Gracie surprised me and stayed anyway. I never understood her reasoning," Kyle said, gesturing wildly with the gun. "Didn't matter; I still had her once or twice a week. Fucked her in your bed. God, she was the best lay. But you knew that. She got off on doing it in your room while the girls were right next door. Those were the days."

Bile rose in Emmit's throat. "I asked her for a divorce the night she died," he spat.

Kyle smiled sadly. "I figured you would after she confessed what she'd done. Besides, she was hardly able to keep her contempt for the girls to herself by then." Kyle shook his head. "As much as I relish your confusion, I have to say you're disappointing me, Emmit. I can't believe you didn't figure any of this out. But then, I was careful. Gracie called me that night before she left the house and divulged what had happened. She neglected, however, to tell me about you wanting a divorce. Shame on her! But, honestly, by then it was a moot point. I'd already cut the brake line on the car."

"You were still trying to kill me, but you killed her instead," Emmit said with disgust.

"At that point your death was no longer pertinent…think about it, Emmit; you always drove your SUV, never your car. Gracie always took the car joyriding. Never told anybody, of course." Kyle frowned. "My Gracie so loved her games."

"You murdered her. I thought you loved her."

"I did, but she slept with Evan. I see you knew about him. That bitch seduced him. Next to secrets, she loved her petty revenge. I couldn't live with that. Evan, poor, poor Evan came to me and confessed. Broke down like a baby."

"You killed Evan. You sat on my porch and cried over him. You murdered him."

"Of course I did. The big ape figured out my role in all of this." Kyle smirked. "He never could leave well enough alone. Evan wasn't so perfect, you know. Oh, wait, you don't know because you didn't figure out his secret either. I guess I'm not surprised considering what I've been getting away with all these years."

"The break-in three years ago?" Emmit asked, but he knew the answer. "The vandalism, the threatening notes, and taunting phone calls were all you."

Kyle tapped the barrel of the gun to his nose and pointed at Emmit. "Bingo! The vandalism was my way of sticking it to the man, so to speak, and to keep you on edge. The phone calls would have been more fun if the girls had actually told you about it—shame on them!"

"You shot my daughter." Emmit was twisting his hands almost loose. He had held his wrists slightly apart while Kyle tied them. The wire was cutting into his flesh, but he ignored it. "What set you off again?"

"Always the same question, Emmit. You are quite tedious, my friend." Kyle got up and went to a drawer pulling out a roll of duct tape. "You gotta love Sadie; she never changes where she keeps things." He walked over to Emmit, holding the gun to Emmit's ear while he pulled off a piece of duct tape and ripped it with his teeth. He slapped it across Emmit's mouth, then grinned and slapped him again.

"Stop it!" Savannah screamed, tears running down her cheeks.

Kyle moved to where Savannah was leaning against the cabinets. "Welcome back!" he said, then sighed. "You're beautiful, Savannah; it *is* a shame. If you'd have just stayed with *me*, none of this would have happened. But no, you had to have McKay. Everyone always has to have McKay," he growled, then pointed to Savannah. "The blood spilt is on your hands."

"There is no blood on my hands, you sick bastard. You're a murderer!" she spat. He laughed and grabbed the duct tape again to shut her up. She squirmed and shook her head back and forth, but that didn't deter him from securing the tape. He grabbed her hair and pulled hard, bringing it to his nose to inhale deeply.

"I am going to savor having you, Savannah." He grinned at Emmit. "Why do you care if I accidentally shot one of the girls? They aren't worth much; they're just delinquents. I tried to spare you the fourth. You remember how hard it was to get Charlie? I was playing both sides." Kyle laughed. "Now, should I kill you first, Emmit? Or should I let you watch me take your woman here on the floor? Decisions, decisions. What do you think?"

****

"I think you need to drop your weapon, Uncle Kyle," Casey said, pointing her rifle at him. She was behind her dad, who jerked when she spoke. She and Alexandra had found the guns Granny Vaughn always had in a case in the study. They'd gone back to Fletcher and Charlie, so they were all armed with guns except Fletcher, who had the hunting knife. Then they'd split up. Alexandra and Charlie had gone outside. Charlie would come around back, and they would signal Alexandra. Casey had come from the room under the stairs, while Fletcher was waiting in the pantry for her signal.

"And I think you should listen to my sister," Charlie said, coming in from the porch.

"Isn't this nice! One big happy family. Really, Emmit? Guns?" Kyle shook his head. "I disapprove of this behavior," he said and made a grab for Charlie, snatching her by the hair and pulling her to him. He smiled when Emmit shouted through his duct tape. Kyle took the revolver from Charlie and put it in the sink. "Now, my dear, I suggest you put down *your* rifle. Girls shouldn't play with guns." Casey lowered her weapon and put it in the sink as Kyle requested.

"You okay?" Casey asked Savannah as she took a seat next to her.

Savannah nodded, rolling her eyes.

"I'm sorry, Ma," Casey whispered. Savannah shook her head, breathing hard through her nostrils.

"Now, where are the other two? Come out, come out, wherever you are," Kyle taunted and spun around. "I'm getting terribly bored. I can make you talk." He backhanded Charlie, making Emmit jerk in his chair and Savannah cry out as Charlie hit the floor with a grunt. "Take her over there," Kyle instructed Casey, who dragged Charlie over to where Savannah was.

"That wasn't very nice, Kyle," Charlie told him, wiping the blood from her lip.

"Like I care. Now, be a good girl and tie up your sister." He handed her the wire. He sat back down, pointing his gun at them and talking to Emmit. "You know, old friend, if you had just let me have Savannah, none of this would have happened. You really are a greedy bastard. I wouldn't do that if I were you, Emmit," he said when Emmit shifted.

****

Emmit had to do something; Kyle was insane. Without a doubt, he would kill all of them. He closed his eyes briefly, only to see Kyle tying Charlie up when he opened them. He put duct tape over her mouth as well.

"Finally, something shut you up. Now, where was I?" Kyle tapped the barrel of the gun to his bottom lip, then lowered it. "Ah, yes. I think I'll start with Savannah, and you can all watch. Yes, that's a wonderful idea. Stand up, my darling," he said to Savannah.

"I's don't think you's wanna be hurting my mama," Fletcher said, coming out of the pantry. A glimmer of metal rested against her good arm; Emmit glanced at Kyle, who spun around to face Fletcher.

"Your mama, huh?" Kyle laughed.

"Yep, she's made me a promise to be a big sister. Got my baby sister in her tummy, and if you's hurt her, I's be a mite pissed off."

Emmit's head swung around to Savannah. She looked at him, her blue eyes bright with tears, and nodded. A baby? They were going to have a baby. She could have picked a better time to tell him. He struggled all the more, and he was almost free.

"Goddamn it," Kyle snarled and stomped around the kitchen. "Unacceptable, Savannah. Un-fucking-acceptable." He turned back to face Fletcher and raised his gun.

It all happened at once and in slow motion. Fletcher dropped her knife to grip the handle, then threw it just as Emmit freed himself and the bay window shattered. Kyle got off a shot as the knife plunged deep into his chest; he fell to the floor as the bullet from his gun slammed Fletcher against the wall. There was a hole in his forehead. Sirens wailed, and Savannah screamed against the duct tape.

Chapter Thirty-Four

Emmit stepped over the body of his childhood friend to get to his daughter just as Alexandra ran inside, rifle in one hand, hem of her nightgown in the other.

"I got the son of a bitch," Alexandra shouted. Emmit stared at Alexandra for a second and shook his head. She swallowed as she took in the state of the room.

"Alexandra, untie Savannah and your sisters please," Emmit instructed while he checked Fletcher's pulse. She was white as a sheet and her eyes were closed, but she was breathing. God, he could not do this again. He pulled off his shirt and tried to keep the pressure on.

Savannah was trying to stand up, while Alexandra cut her loose. Finally free, she hugged Alexandra hard, then ripped the tape off her mouth and dashed over to Emmit.

Alexandra took the tape off Casey's mouth and freed her.

"Took you long enough," Casey chided but hugged Alexandra anyway.

"Well, excuse me for having to run all the way to the apartment to call for back-up. You ungrateful witch," she said with a smile. She turned to Charlie. "Oh, Charlie, your poor lip."

"Took one for the team, didn't I?" Charlie said with a wobble in her voice after Alexandra removed the tape. They all turned to where Emmit and Savannah huddled around Fletcher.

"Where was she hit?" Savannah asked Emmit, touching Fletcher's cheek. "My poor baby."

"Blood's coming from her shoulder." He continued applying pressure to the wound.

Fletcher opened one eye. "Dagnabbit, why's I's the one always gets shot?" she asked between labored breaths. "I's only been out of that stupid sling for one day!" She looked at Savannah, who was slobbering all over her. "Mama, don't cry. I's had to break my promise to buy some time. 'Sides, you's was gonna tell Pops tonight anyway."

Emmit dropped on his butt when he remembered. "Savannah, we're going to have a baby?" She nodded, and he clutched her face, kissing her hard, one hand still holding his shirt to Fletcher's shoulder. Savannah kissed him back, throwing her arms around him, then gasped.

"Oh, darling. I'm sorry…your arm."

"Jeez, Pops, it's only a scratch. Ma's tough," Casey said with a grin.

"Yeah, Emmit, it's just a scratch," Savannah said, winking at him.

"I love you, Savannah." He kissed her again, tenderly, and she smiled under his lips.

"Could you's maybe do that later. I's bleeding here," Fletcher reminded them with her head resting against the wall. They broke apart looking sheepish just as Jasper stormed in with medics.

"You people don't know the meaning of ordinary

lives, do you? And, Alexandra, next time you call the police, don't curse at them, all right? It only flusters 'em." Jasper looked down to the body on the floor. "Holy Mary, Mother of God. That's Kyle Ruthie." He took a step back. "Who killed him?"

"I's think I's did," Fletcher admitted.

"Wrong, I killed him," Alexandra argued. "Gunshot to the head." She snapped her fingers. "He didn't have a chance."

Jasper gaped.

"Knife to the heart," Fletcher retorted, ignoring Emmit's glare. "And I's gots him first." She smiled up at Savannah, then passed out as the EMTs came through the door. No one spoke while they loaded Fletcher up. Emmit helped Savannah to her feet.

"I'll go with Fletcher," Savannah said. "You talk to Jasper, and I'll meet you at the hospital." She rose up on tiptoe to kiss him after he nodded, then followed the paramedics out.

They moved out of the kitchen to give the crime techs and coroner room to work.

"All right, speak up. Tell me what happened," Jasper said, taking notes as Emmit recounted the entire story. Jasper shook his head. "You need to get those wrists checked out, McKay," Jasper said, then he turned to Alexandra. "You, the prissy one, explain yourself."

"Again? We've gone over this twice already."

"Well, I want to hear it again, missy!"

Alexandra rolled her blue eyes. "I ran back to the main house after calling the police from the apartment. I climbed up on the tree by the porch banister and held my aim until I got a good shot. I was doing my part in this. Casey and Charlie would go in, and if they got in trouble, then I was to wait for Fletcher to come out and distract him," she said, glaring at her big sister for the umpteenth time. "Then, if they weren't able to stop him, I was supposed to take him down. Which I did! Perfectly, I might add. It was all self-defense, really."

"I agree, absolutely. That's how it's going in the report," he said. "But what I want to know is why you? That's what I don't get."

Emmit looked up at the ceiling.

"She's the best damn marksman in town," Casey said and patted her sister on the back. "Course, you wouldn't know it looking at her." Alexandra sighed. "Shoot, Alexandra's won tons of awards for marksmanship."

"Really?" Jasper said. "I had no idea."

Alexandra shrugged one shoulder. "What can I say? I've always loved ribbons."

"Are we done here, Jasper?" Emmit asked. "I'd like to go see my youngest daughter now."

"Sure, sure," Jasper mumbled, still staring at Alexandra.

Chapter Thirty-Five

Savannah flipped the switch so the neon sign let everyone in Blue Creek know McKay's was open for business. The grand opening six months ago had been a huge success. It had been so busy, she'd hired Ida Mae on as a waitress. The older woman helped Savannah learn the ropes. Evan had been right; this was more to her liking.

People were still talking about Kyle Ruthie, and Savannah suspected they always would. It had taken months, but it was finally over. The case was closed; there were no more questions to answer, and no more threats.

Savannah was now Mrs. Emmit McKay. She and Emmit had gotten married four months ago. It had been a beautiful ceremony. Anyone and everyone in Blue Creek had attended, except the Thomases, who hadn't been invited. Emmit's parents had come up from Florida, and Savannah had fallen in love with them.

Emmit had asked Ward Jessup to stand in Evan's place. Savannah knew Emmit still mourned his best friend. And though that had made the wedding hard for Emmit, he'd told Savannah he would do whatever it took to be with her.

The Judge had given her away, and Sadie had been her matron of honor. Charlie and Alexandra had been flower girls and Casey a bridesmaid. Savannah laughed in the empty diner. Fletcher, of course, had thrown a fit; she flatly refused to wear a dress. She'd gone as far as threatening to hide in the woods until it was over. Savannah wouldn't have given in if Emmit hadn't told her Fletcher would do it and they wouldn't find her for weeks. So they'd compromised.

Fletcher had worn a little suit and been the ring barrier. The suit had been peach to match the bridesmaid dresses; hence, the compromise. Savannah's daughters, now *legally* hers, had been beautiful. And Emmit, well, she had always thought of him as handsome, but in a tux and polished up, he was drop-dead gorgeous. She was definitely a lucky woman.

Savannah turned when the bell, compliments of Charlie, rang. She smiled when her daughters hustled in. It was summer, and they helped out around both Emmit's store and the diner.

"Morning, Ma," Casey greeted, walking around the counter to get some juice. She was thirteen now, and her body was developing—much to Emmit's dismay.

They had all had birthdays within the last few months. They had thrown huge parties. Marge Pruitt, who ran the movie theater, had let them rent it out for Charlie's birthday, and Trixy had let Alexandra have her party in the beauty parlor. Casey and Fletcher were happy to have their parties at home with a weekend of camping to boot.

"Good morning, Casey," she said, then greeted her other daughters. They had driven over with their father this morning.

"What are we cooking for the special today?" Charlie asked. They had gone to Trixy last week, and Charlie had gotten her hair cut. She was sick of long curls, but her hair was still long enough for a ponytail, which now bobbed along with her eyebrows.

"Whatever you want, sweetheart. You're more creative in the kitchen than I am." Thank you, God, Savannah thought and not for the first time. Charlie smiled and headed into the kitchen. Savannah did have a professional cook. His name was Tiny, and he had been with Ida for years. Ida said he was her secret weapon. Savannah figured, why fix it if it isn't broken?

"I was thinking we should invite Granny Vaughn over for supper before she and Granddaddy leave," Alexandra suggested. Savannah had worried about Alexandra with all the death she had witnessed, but the girl was amazingly resilient. She'd bounced back after a few months, though she still had nightmares once in a while. Now she was prissier than ever, which annoyed Savannah's husband to no end.

"I think that's a wonderful idea, Alexandra!" And she did. The older couple was moving to Florida. Emmit's parents had persuaded Sadie and J. T. Florida was the best place to retire. After many late nights of discussion, they had decided to take a chance. Of course, they would only stay six months out of the year; Granny Vaughn couldn't bear to be apart from her grandbabies for too long.

"How you's feeling today, Mama?" Fletcher asked, as she did every day. Her little tyrant was up to her same old tricks. When Savannah had quit being a principal, she hadn't expected to go back. But she'd had to at least twice a month—to collect Fletcher. Now Emmit tensed up every time Mildred called, but he'd relax when Savannah said she'd take care of it. She reminded him that he'd married a principal. He just laughed and reminded her she was retired.

"I feel fine, Fletcher." Savannah rolled her eyes when Fletcher narrowed hers. "I promise." Savannah rested her hand on her belly. She was eight months along and as big as a house. She had trouble walking because she couldn't see her feet.

"Are you bugging your mother?" Emmit asked as he walked in. Savannah blushed at his stare. Emmit had told her several times she was stunning pregnant, which, considering how she felt about her own appearance, was wonderful. They didn't know if it was a boy or girl yet, and they wanted it to be a surprise.

"They aren't bothering me," she assured her husband, pulling on his ears so he would lean down and kiss her.

"They're at it again," Casey sniffed, then hid her smile behind her glass of juice.

"Again? Did they ever stop?" Charlie asked with a laugh.

"Will you two get over it, already?" Alexandra hissed but watched her parents as well.

"I's vote we let them do what they want. It ain't like she can get pregnant," Fletcher told her sisters, then winced.

"I heard that, Fletcher," Emmit said and let go of Savannah to go after the girls, who all started running around the diner in mock horror. Savannah turned when the sheriff walked in shaking his head.

"You claiming that bunch of heathens over there, Savannah?" he asked, gesturing to Emmit and the girls.

Savannah grinned. "I most certainly am, Jasper." I most certainly am.

Epilogue

"Whatcha doing, Casey?" eight-year-old Jebb McKay asked his big sister.

"None of your business, bullfrog," Casey said, smiling over her shoulder. She knew he hated it when she called him that. His name was Jebbediah, which was close enough to Jeremiah for the nickname to work. What her parents had been thinking, she'd never know. She was twenty and home for spring break. They all were home for the break. The McKay girls went to college together. They'd even graduated from high school together. It had made Casey antsy when Fletcher had released to the world the fact she was a freaking egghead.

Her little sister, the genius. Who would have thought? Casey smiled. It pissed Alexandra off to no end. Alexandra and Charlie hadn't had any trouble skipping a few grades either. Casey was just glad she was the oldest and hadn't had to apply herself as much as her sisters had. She looked at her little brother, who was huffing his annoyance. He looked like Pops, with the same black hair and stubborn jaw. He had gotten Ma's eyes, though, and her temper. A temper Casey had sparked many times. The kid was going to be a giant.

"Okay, bullfrog. You can help me if you want to."

Jebb hopped to attention. "What's we looking for?"

"Somewhere in this pigsty, there used to be a

wonderful attic…before you came along. I put a picture of the Judge and Granny Vaughn up here, and I want to find it." It was her favorite photo of her grandparents, and she wanted to keep a little piece of them with her. The Judge had died of a heart attack two years ago, and Granny Vaughn had passed a year after that. It had devastated all of them. But Casey and her sisters had agreed they were in heaven together.

"It's here somewhere," Casey said. "I know it is." She was digging around under Jebb's toys. "You search in all the corners, okay?"

Jebb nodded.

Casey looked behind the stereo and spotted the picture. It took her a few minutes, but she got it. "I found it, twerp." She looked around to find him digging into the floor inside the closet. "What in the hell are you doing?" She went over to look around him and poked herself in the eye. She hadn't worn glasses in three years, but it was a habit to push them up, even when they weren't there.

"I's found something. Someone cut a hole in the floor. Got it," he said, putting his pocket knife back in his pocket. He lifted up the board and reached into the blackness. "There's something in here. I can almost reach it." He strained, then grinned, and pulled out a folded envelope. "What's that brown stuff, Casey?"

She didn't answer him. She knew it was blood. Old blood. "Go get the sisters, Jebb. Just the sisters, okay? Not Ma and Pops." He nodded and ran down the steps.

Casey unfolded the envelope and took out the letter. Her hands were shaking as she regarded the small fingerprints. The fingers had been covered with blood the last time this was out in the open. She read the letter, not believing her eyes. She looked up when her sisters came charging up the steps with Jebb right behind them.

"What in the world is going on, Casey?" Charlie asked, her brown eyes worried. "What's that?" she asked, stepping closer.

"Ask them," she said, pointing to where both Alexandra and Fletcher had stopped. She let Charlie read the letter, and her sister gasped.

"You two knew about this, didn't you?" Casey's shouting made Jebb hide behind Charlie. "Didn't you!"

"Yes," Alexandra answered calmly.

"And you, Fletch?"

"I was the one who put it in the floor," Fletcher admitted.

"Oh, guys, how could you keep this from us?" Charlie asked, her eyes filling.

Casey snatched the letter from her sister's hand. She pointed at Jebb. "You don't tell anyone, not a fucking soul, about finding this. Got that?"

Jebb nodded, his lower lip wobbling.

Casey walked over to her sisters. Sisters? That was a joke. Casey pulled her hand back and slapped Fletcher because her betrayal was the worst. "You both can take this note to hell with you when you go," she growled and dropped the letter at their feet.

Casey ran to the steps, her eyes flooding. She had only cried three times in her memory and this made four. A fitting number in this case. She swore to herself she'd never cry again. She stopped to look at the people in the room. "As of this moment, I only have one sister. You two are as dead to me as the writer of that letter." And with that, Casey ran out and never looked back.

W. L. Brooks

A word about the author...

W. L. Brooks likes to write like she reads—with a bit of mystery, romance, suspense, and, to keep it interesting, the occasional dash of the paranormal.

Living in western North Carolina, she is currently working on her next novel. Check out her website at www.wlbrooks.com or on Facebook @authorwlbrooks.

Thank you for purchasing
this publication of The Wild Rose Press, Inc.

If you enjoyed the story, we would appreciate your
letting others know by leaving a review.

For other wonderful stories,
please visit our on-line bookstore at
www.thewildrosepress.com.

For questions or more information
contact us at
info@thewildrosepress.com.

The Wild Rose Press, Inc.
www.thewildrosepress.com

Stay current with The Wild Rose Press, Inc.

Like us on Facebook

https://www.facebook.com/TheWildRosePress

And Follow us on Twitter
https://twitter.com/WildRosePress

Made in the USA
Middletown, DE
14 September 2017